EVERYMAN,

I WILL GO WITH THEE,

AND BE THY GUIDE,

IN THY MOST NEED

TO GO BY THY SIDE

GOLF
STORIES

EDITED BY CHARLES McGRATH

EVERYMAN'S POCKET CLASSICS
Alfred A. Knopf New York London Toronto

THIS IS A BORZOI BOOK
PUBLISHED BY ALFRED A. KNOPF

This selection by Charles McGrath first published in
Everyman's Library, 2011
Copyright © 2011 by Everyman's Library
A list of acknowledgments to copyright owners appears at the back
of this volume.

US website: www.randomhouse.com/everymans

ISBN: 978-0-307-59689-5 (US)
978-1-84159-609-9 (UK)

A CIP catalogue reference for this book is available from the
British Library

Library of Congress Cataloging-in-Publication Data
Golf stories / edited by Charles McGrath.
p. cm.— (Everyman's pocket classics)
ISBN 978-0-307-59689-5 (hardcover: alk. paper) 1. Golf stories,
American. 2. Golf stories, English. I. McGrath, Charles.
PS648.G64G58 2011   2010054259
810.8'0357—dc22

Typography by Peter B. Willberg

Typeset in the UK by AccComputing, North Barrow, Somerset

Printed and bound in Germany by GGP Media GmbH, Pössneck

GOLF
STORIES

Contents

FOREWORD

GEORGE PLIMPTON used to invoke what he called the small-ball theory of sportswriting – the idea that the quality of the literature about a game is inversely proportional to the size of the ball it employs. This notion was always a little sketchy. Where are the great ping-pong writers, the classic works on marbles? And yet when it comes to fiction about sports there may be some truth here, for the golf ball, whether dimpled, feathery or guttie, has probably inspired more good short stories than any of the larger round things. A great majority of these stories are humorous, which seems a little counter-intuitive at first, because golf when you play it – or when I play, anyway – is not particularly funny at all. Tragic is more like it.

The other form that golf fiction seems to gravitate towards is mystery, and that seems more appropriate. To most of us the game is a puzzle we will never solve, and it's also not un-common for a golfer to think a murderous thought or two. What recommends both genres – comedy and mystery – is that they offer resolution and impose a shapeliness and orderliness on a game that often seems so random and arbit-rary and in which punishments are often cruelly out of whack with the mistake that incurs them.

Golf fiction, in other words, is escape-reading in the best sense. It lifts us from the rigors, uncertainty, and injustice of golf as it is actually played and unfolds for us another, more satisfying and lighthearted world in which everything makes sense in the end. In that respect golf fiction is a lot like the stories we tell ourselves, playing a round over again in our heads on the way home, or each other, lingering in the club house over a cold one. Golf itself is a narrative of sorts. We set off and journey outward, full of hope and purpose; we're tested, we suffer, we experience a few momentary glimpses of bliss; and then we turn and head for home, our progress grimly charted by those numbers inexorably mounting on the card. Then, in the retelling, we make it all sound a little better, a little cheerier. That 90 you shot could easily have been an 80; for all practical purposes it *was*, in fact. Golf stories are the imaginative equivalent of nudging the ball to improve your lie. They give you a little lift.

In putting together this anthology I've tried to give some sense of the range and variety of golf fiction over the years, and the stories are arranged in roughly chronological order to suggest how golf, or writing about it, has evolved. A lot of the selections were self-evident. That there would be a story by P. G. Wodehouse, for example, was a no-brainer. The chore, if you can call it that, was deciding which one, and I spent many happy hours reading and rereading Wodehouse's dozens of golf stories before throwing up my hands and deciding that it almost didn't matter. They are all pretty wonderful, practically interchangeable

That John Updike's story "Farrell's Caddy" would be here was also a foregone conclusion. To my mind it's the best golf story ever: funny, surprising, beautifully written, and sneak-ily insightful about the relationship that sometimes develops between a player and his caddy. This is one of those golf stories that rise from escape-reading to genuine greatness. Another is F. Scott Fitzgerald's "Winter Dreams," which you could argue is barely a golf story at all. For me, the story, which was written before *The Great Gatsby*, merits inclusion for the interesting way it uses golf not as a setting or a plot device but as a symbol or emblem of class, wealth, and longing – all the great Fitzgerald preoccupations. It's also the deepest exploration I know of a persistent little sub-theme that pops up often in golf fiction, especially in Wodehouse: the mysterious link between golf and the distant, unattainable female.

Without something by Rick Reilly and Dan Jenkins a book like this would hardly be complete, and how could I leave out the great golf chapter – a story in itself – from Ian Fleming's *Goldfinger*? Nor should it be a surprise that so many stories here are from the Twenties and Thirties, the Golden Age not just of golf fiction but of sports fiction in general.

Along the way, though, I also made some surprising discoveries. I knew, for example, that Bernard Darwin, the great English golf chronicler, had written some golf fiction, but I never imagined that his disciple, Herbert Warren Wind, for so many years *The New Yorker*'s golf writer, had done so as well. And who knew that A. W. Tillinghast, the golf architect who created masterpieces like Winged Foot, Baltusrol, and Bethpage Black, wrote golf fiction? I certainly didn't. Tillinghast's stories are not, in truth, nearly as good as his golf courses, but that he wrote them at all is testament to his energy and enterprise. During this same period he also tried to build an indoor miniature golf course in New York that would be a front for a speakeasy.

Careful readers of a more literary bent may notice some curious lines of influence and relationship here. Rex Lardner, whose *Out of the Bunker and Into the Trees*, both a parody of golf writing and an inspired addition to it, deserves to be far better known, was Ring Lardner's nephew. Ring Lardner, represented here by one of his lesser-known efforts,

"Mr. Frisbie," is more famous for his baseball stories, especially the novel *You Know Me Al*, of which Herbert Warren Wind's Harry Sprague story is a transparent imitation. Or maybe translation is a better word. Wind took Lardner's conceit – a series of letters written by a clueless, swollen-headed and semi-literate athlete – and switched it over from baseball to golf with equally foolproof results. Similarly, James Kaplan's story "The Mower" – an anti-golf story, really – was clearly inspired by Updike's classic short story "A & P." And my own contribution, "Sneaking On," about a guy trying to play his way across town from one golf course to another, is a fairly shameless rip-off of John Cheever's great story "The Swimmer." Good golfers know that you can always borrow a trick or two from the pros, and writing golf fiction is no different.

Finally, a number of the stories here were written early enough that they use the old-fashioned names for golf clubs, so here's a conversion table:

Brassie = No. 2 wood
Spoon = No. 3 wood
Cleek = 2-iron
Mid-mashie = 3-iron
Mashie = 5-iron
Spade mashie = 6-iron
Mashie niblick = 7-iron
Niblick = 9-iron
Baffing spoon = wedge.

Charles McGrath

P. G. WODEHOUSE

THE SALVATION OF GEORGE MACKINTOSH

THE YOUNG MAN came into the clubhouse. There was a frown on his usually cheerful face, and he ordered a ginger-ale in the sort of voice which an ancient Greek would have used when asking the executioner to bring on the hemlock.

Sunk in the recesses of his favourite settee the Oldest Member had watched him with silent sympathy.

'How did you get on?' he inquired.

'He beat me.'

The Oldest Member nodded his venerable head.

'You have had a trying time, if I am not mistaken. I feared as much when I saw you go out with Pobsley. How many a young man have I seen go out with Herbert Pobsley exulting in his youth, and crawl back at eventide looking like a toad under the harrow! He talked?'

'All the time, confound it! Put me right off my stroke.'

The Oldest Member sighed.

'The talking golfer is undeniably the most pronounced pest of our complex modern civilization,' he said, 'and the most difficult to deal with. It is a melancholy thought that the noblest of games should have produced such a scourge. I have frequently marked Herbert Pobsley in action. As the crackling of thorns under a pot. . . . He is almost as bad as poor George Mackintosh in his worst period. Did I ever tell you about George Mackintosh?'

'I don't think so.'

'His,' said the Sage, 'is the only case of golfing garrulity

I have ever known where a permanent cure was effected. If you would care to hear about it—?'

George Mackintosh (said the Oldest Member), when I first knew him, was one of the most admirable young fellows I have ever met. A handsome, well-set-up man, with no vices except a tendency to use the mashie for shots which should have been made with the light iron. And as for his positive virtues, they were too numerous to mention. He never swayed his body, moved his head, or pressed. He was always ready to utter a tactful grunt when his opponent foozled. And when he himself achieved a glaring fluke, his self-reproachful click of the tongue was music to his adversary's bruised soul. But of all his virtues the one that most endeared him to me and to all thinking men was the fact that, from the start of a round to the finish, he never spoke a word except when absolutely compelled to do so by the exigencies of the game. And it was this man who subsequently, for a black period which lives in the memory of all his contemporaries, was known as Gabby George and became a shade less popular than the germ of Spanish Influenza. Truly, *corruptio optimi pessima!*

One of the things that sadden a man as he grows older and reviews his life is the reflection that his most devastating deeds were generally the ones which he did with the best motives. The thought is disheartening. I can honestly say that, when George Mackintosh came to me and told me his troubles, my sole desire was to ameliorate his lot. That I might be starting on the downward path a man whom I liked and respected never once occurred to me.

One night after dinner when George Mackintosh came in, I could see at once that there was something on his mind, but what this could be I was at a loss to imagine, for I had been playing with him myself all the afternoon, and he had done an eighty-one and a seventy-nine. And, as I had not left the links till dusk was beginning to fall, it was practically impossible that he could have gone out again and done badly. The idea of financial trouble seemed equally out of the question. George had a good job with the old-established legal firm of Peabody, Peabody, Peabody, Peabody, Cootes, Toots, and Peabody. The third alternative, that he might be in love, I rejected at once. In all the time I had known him I had never seen a sign that George Mackintosh gave a thought to the opposite sex.

Yet this, bizarre as it seemed, was the true solution. Scarcely had he seated himself and lit a cigar when he blurted out his confession.

'What would you do in a case like this?' he said.

'Like what?'

'Well—' He choked, and a rich blush permeated his surface. 'Well, it seems a silly thing to say and all that, but I'm in love with Miss Tennant, you know!'

'You are in love with Celia Tennant?'

'Of course I am. I've got eyes, haven't I? Who else is there that any sane man could possibly be in love with? That,' he went on, moodily, 'is the whole trouble. There's a field of about twenty-nine, and I should think my place in the betting is about thirty-three to one.'

'I cannot agree with you there,' I said. 'You have every advantage, it appears to me. You are young, amiable, good-looking, comfortably off, scratch—'

'But I can't talk, confound it!' he burst out. 'And how is a man to get anywhere at this sort of game without talking?'

'You are talking perfectly fluently now.'

'Yes, to you. But put me in front of Celia Tennant, and I simply make a sort of gurgling noise like a sheep with the

17

botts. It kills my chances stone dead. You know these other men. I can give Claude Mainwaring a third and beat him. I can give Eustace Brinkley a stroke a hole and simply trample on his corpse. But when it comes to talking to a girl, I'm not in their class.'

'You must not be diffident.'

'But I *am* diffident. What's the good of saying I mustn't be diffident when I'm the man who wrote the words and music, when Diffidence is my middle name and my telegraphic address? I can't help being diffident.'

'Surely you could overcome it?'

'But how? It was in the hope that you might be able to suggest something that I came round tonight.'

And this was where I did the fatal thing. It happened that, just before I took up 'Braid on the Push-Shot', I had been dipping into the current number of a magazine, and one of the advertisements, I chanced to remember, might have been framed with a special eye to George's unfortunate case. It was that one, which I have no doubt you have seen, which treats of 'How to Become a Convincing Talker'. I picked up this magazine now and handed it to George.

He studied it for a few minutes in thoughtful silence. He looked at the picture of the Man who had taken the course being fawned upon by lovely women, while the man who had let this opportunity slip stood outside the group gazing with a wistful envy.

'They never do that to me,' said George.

'Do what, my boy?'

'Cluster round, clinging cooingly.'

'I gather from the letterpress that they will if you write for the booklet.'

'You think there is really something in it?'

'I see no reason why eloquence should not be taught by

18

mail. One seems to be able to acquire every other desirable quality in that manner nowadays.'

'I might try it. After all, it's not expensive. There's no doubt about it,' he murmured, returning to his perusal, 'that fellow does look popular. Of course, the evening dress may have something to do with it.'

'Not at all. The other man, you will notice, is also wearing evening dress, and yet he is merely among those on the out-skirts. It is simply a question of writing for the booklet.'

'Sent post free.'

'Sent, as you say, post free.'

'I've a good mind to try it.'

'I see no reason why you should not.'

'I will, by Duncan!' He tore the page out of the magazine and put it in his pocket. 'I'll tell you what I'll do. I'll give this thing a trial for a week or two, and at the end of that time I'll go to the boss and see how he reacts when I ask for a rise of salary. If he crawls, it'll show there's something in this. If he flings me out, it will prove the thing's no good.'

We left it at that, and I am bound to say – owing, no doubt, to my not having written for the booklet of the Memory Training Course advertised on the adjoining page of the magazine – the matter slipped from my mind. When, therefore, a few weeks later, I received a telegram from young Mackintosh which ran:

WORKED LIKE MAGIC

I confess I was intensely puzzled. It was only a quarter of an hour before George himself arrived that I solved the problem of its meaning.

'So the boss crawled?' I said, as he came in.

He gave a light, confident laugh. I had not seen him, as

I say, for some time, and I was struck by the alteration in his appearance. In what exactly this alteration consisted I could not at first have said; but gradually it began to impress itself on me that his eye was brighter, his jaw squarer, his carriage a trifle more upright than it had been. But it was his eye that struck me most forcibly. The George Mackintosh I had known had had a pleasing gaze, but, though frank and agreeable, it had never been more dynamic than a fried egg. This new George had an eye that was a combination of a gimlet and a searchlight. Coleridge's Ancient Mariner, I imagine, must have been somewhat similarly equipped. The Ancient Mariner stopped a wedding guest on his way to a wedding; George Mackintosh gave me the impression that he could have stopped the Cornish Riviera express on its way to Penzance. Self-confidence – aye, and more than self-confidence – a sort of sinful, overbearing swank seemed to exude from his very pores.

'Crawled?' he said. 'Well, he didn't actually lick my boots, because I saw him coming and side-stepped; but he did everything short of that. I hadn't been talking an hour when—'

'An hour!' I gasped. 'Did you talk for an hour?'

'Certainly. You wouldn't have had me be abrupt, would you? I went into his private office and found him alone. I think at first he would have been just as well pleased if I had retired. In fact, he said as much. But I soon adjusted that outlook. I took a seat and a cigarette, and then I started to sketch out for him the history of my connection with the firm. He began to wilt before the end of the first ten minutes. At the quarter of an hour mark he was looking at me like a lost dog that's just found its owner. By the half-hour he was making little bleating noises and massaging my coat-sleeve. And when, after perhaps an hour and a half, I came to my peroration and suggested a rise, he choked back a sob, gave me double what I had asked, and invited me to dine at his club next Tuesday. I'm a little sorry now I cut the thing so short. A few minutes more, and I fancy he would have given me his sock-suspenders and made over his life-insurance in my favour.'

'Well,' I said, as soon as I could speak, for I was finding my young friend a trifle overpowering, 'this is most satisfactory.'

'So-so,' said George. 'Not un-so-so. A man wants an addition to his income when he is going to get married.'

'Ah!' I said. 'That, of course, will be the real test.'

'What do you mean?'

'Why, when you propose to Celia Tennant. You remember you were saying when we spoke of this before—'

'Oh, that!' said George, carelessly. 'I've arranged all that.'

'What!'

'Oh, yes. On my way up from the station. I looked in on Celia about an hour ago, and it's all settled.'

'Amazing!'

'Well, I don't know. I just put the thing to her, and she seemed to see it.'

'I congratulate you. So now, like Alexander, you have no more worlds to conquer.'

'Well, I don't know so much about that,' said George. 'The way it looks to me is that I'm just starting. This eloquence is a thing that rather grows on one. You didn't hear about my after-dinner speech at the anniversary banquet of the firm, I suppose? My dear fellow, a riot! A positive stampede. Had 'em laughing and then crying and then laughing again and then crying once more till six of 'em had to be led out and the rest down with hiccoughs. Napkins waving . . . three tables broken . . . waiters in hysterics. I tell you, I played on them as on a stringed instrument. . . .'

'Can you play on a stringed instrument?'

'As it happens, no. But as I would have played on a stringed instrument if I could play on a stringed instrument. Wonderful sense of power it gives you. I mean to go in pretty largely for that sort of thing in future.'

'You must not let it interfere with your golf.'

He gave a laugh which turned my blood cold.

'Golf!' he said. 'After all, what is golf? Just pushing a small ball into a hole. A child could do it. Indeed, children have done it with great success. I see an infant of fourteen has just won some sort of championship. Could that stripling convulse a roomful of banqueters? I think not! To sway your fellow-men with a word, to hold them with a gesture . . . that is the real salt of life. I don't suppose I shall play much more golf now. I'm making arrangements for a lecturing-tour, and I'm booked up for fifteen lunches already.'

Those were his words. A man who had once done the lake-hole in one. A man whom the committee were grooming for the amateur championship. I am no weakling, but I confess they sent a chill shiver down my spine.

George Mackintosh did not, I am glad to say, carry out his mad project to the letter. He did not altogether sever himself from golf. He was still to be seen occasionally on the links. But now – and I know of nothing more tragic that can befall a man – he found himself gradually shunned, he who in the days of his sanity had been besieged with more offers of games than he could manage to accept. Men simply would not stand his incessant flow of talk. One by one they dropped off, until the only person he could find to go round with him was old Major Moseby, whose hearing completely petered out as long ago as the year '98. And, of course, Celia Tennant would play with him occasionally; but it seemed to me that even she, greatly as no doubt she loved him, was beginning to crack under the strain.

So surely had I read the pallor of her face and the wild look of dumb agony in her eyes that I was not surprised when, as I sat one morning in my garden reading Ray on Taking Turf, my man announced her name. I had been half expecting her to come to me for advice and consolation, for I had known her ever since she was a child. It was I who had given her her first driver and taught her infant lips to lisp 'Fore!' It is not easy to lisp the word 'Fore!' but I had taught her to do it, and this constituted a bond between us which had been strengthened rather than weakened by the passage of time.

She sat down on the grass beside my chair, and looked up at my face in silent pain. We had known each other so long that I know that it was not my face that pained her, but rather some unspoken *malaise* of the soul. I waited for her to speak, and suddenly she burst out impetuously as though she could hold back her sorrow no longer.

'Oh, I can't stand it! I can't stand it!'

'You mean . . . ?' I said, though I knew only too well.

'This horrible obsession of poor George's,' she cried passionately. 'I don't think he has stopped talking once since we have been engaged.'

'He *is* chatty,' I agreed. 'Has he told you the story about the Irishman?'

'Half a dozen times. And the one about the Swede oftener than that. But I would not mind an occasional anecdote. Women have to learn to bear anecdotes from the men they love. It is the curse of Eve. It is his incessant easy flow of chatter on all topics that is undermining even my devotion.'

'But surely, when he proposed to you, he must have given you an inkling of the truth. He only hinted at it when he spoke to me, but I gather that he was eloquent.'

'When he proposed,' said Celia dreamily, 'he was wonderful. He spoke for twenty minutes without stopping. He said I was the essence of his every hope, the tree on which the fruit of his life grew; his Present, his Future, his Past ... oh, and all that sort of thing. If he would only confine his conversation now to remarks of a similar nature, I could listen to him all day long. But he doesn't. He talks politics and statistics and philosophy and ... oh, and everything. He makes my head ache.'

'And your heart also, I fear,' I said gravely.

'I love him!' she replied simply. 'In spite of everything, I love him dearly. But what to do? What to do? I have an awful fear that when we are getting married instead of answering "I will," he will go into the pulpit and deliver an address on Marriage Ceremonies of All Ages. The world to him is a vast lecture-platform. He looks on life as one long after-dinner, with himself as the principal speaker of the evening. It is breaking my heart. I see him shunned by his former friends. Shunned! They run a mile when they see him coming. The mere sound of his voice outside the clubhouse is enough to send brave men diving for safety beneath the sofas. Can you wonder that I am in despair? What have I to live for?'

'There is always golf.'

'Yes, there is always golf,' she whispered bravely.

'Come and have a round this afternoon.'

'I had promised to go for a walk ...' She shuddered, then pulled herself together. '... for a walk with George.'

I hesitated for a moment.

'Bring him along,' I said, and patted her hand. 'It may be that together we shall find an opportunity of reasoning with him.'

She shook her head.

'You can't reason with George. He never stops talking long enough to give you time.'

'Nevertheless, there is no harm in trying. I have an idea that this malady of his is not permanent and incurable. The very violence with which the germ of loquacity has attacked him gives me hope. You must remember that before this seizure he was rather a noticeably silent man. Sometimes I think that it is just Nature's way of restoring the average, and that soon the fever may burn itself out. Or it may be that a sudden shock ... At any rate, have courage.'

'I will try to be brave.'

'Capital! At half-past two on the first tee, then.'

'You will have to give me a stroke on the third, ninth, twelfth, fifteenth, sixteenth and eighteenth,' she said, with a quaver in her voice. 'My golf has fallen off rather lately.'

I patted her hand again.

'I understand,' I said gently. 'I understand.'

The steady drone of a baritone voice as I alighted from my car and approached the first tee told me that George had not forgotten the tryst. He was sitting on the stone seat under the chestnut-tree, speaking a few well-chosen words on the Labour Movement.

'To what conclusion, then, do we come?' he was saying. 'We come to the foregone and inevitable conclusion that ...'

'Good afternoon, George,' I said.

He nodded briefly, but without verbal salutation. He seemed to regard my remark as he would have regarded the unmannerly heckling of some one at the back of the hall. He proceeded evenly with his speech, and was still talking when Celia addressed her ball and drove off. Her drive, coinciding with a sharp rhetorical question from George, wavered in mid-air, and the ball trickled off into the rough half-way down the hill. I can see the poor girl's tortured face even now. But she breathed no word of reproach. Such is the miracle of women's love.

'Where you went wrong there,' said George, breaking off his remarks on Labour, 'was that you have not studied the dynamics of golf sufficiently. You did not pivot properly. You allowed your left heel to point down the course when you were at the top of your swing. This makes for instability and loss of distance. The fundamental law of the dynamics of golf is that the left foot shall be solidly on the ground at the moment of impact. If you allow your heel to point down the course, it is almost impossible to bring it back in time to make the foot a solid fulcrum.'

I drove, and managed to clear the rough and reach the fairway. But it was not one of my best drives. George Mackintosh, I confess, had unnerved me. The feeling he gave me resembled the self-conscious panic which I used to experience in my childhood when informed that there was One Awful Eye that watched my every movement and saw my every act. It was only the fact that poor Celia appeared even more affected by his espionage that enabled me to win the first hole in seven.

On the way to the second tee George discoursed on the beauties of Nature, pointing out at considerable length how exquisitely the silver glitter of the lake harmonized with the vivid emerald turf near the hole and the duller green of the rough beyond it. As Celia teed up her ball, he directed her attention to the golden glory of the sand-pit to the left of the flag. It was not the spirit in which to approach the lake-hole, and I was not surprised when the unfortunate girl's ball fell with a sickening plop half-way across the water.

'Where you went wrong there,' said George, 'was that you made the stroke a sudden heave instead of a smooth, snappy flick of the wrists. Pressing is always bad, but with the mashie—'

'I think I will give you this hole,' said Celia to me, for my shot had cleared the water and was lying on the edge of the green. 'I wish I hadn't used a new ball.'

'The price of golf-balls,' said George, as we started to round the lake, 'is a matter to which economists should give some attention. I am credibly informed that rubber at the present time is exceptionally cheap. Yet we see no decrease in the price of golf-balls, which, as I need scarcely inform you, are rubber-cored. Why should this be so? You will say that the wages of skilled labour have gone up. True. But—'

'One moment, George, while I drive,' I said. For we had now arrived at the third tee.

'A curious thing, concentration,' said George, 'and why certain phenomena should prevent us from focusing our attention— This brings me to the vexed question of sleep. Why is it that we are able to sleep through some vast convulsion of Nature when a dripping tap is enough to keep us awake? I am told that there were people who slumbered peacefully through the San Francisco earthquake, merely stirring drowsily from time to time to tell an imaginary person to leave it on the mat. Yet these same people—'

Celia's drive bounded into the deep ravine which yawns some fifty yards from the tee. A low moan escaped her.

'Where you went wrong there—' said George.

'I know,' said Celia. 'I lifted my head.'

I had never heard her speak so abruptly before. Her manner, in a girl less noticeably pretty, might almost have been called snappish. George, however, did not appear to have noticed anything amiss. He filled his pipe and followed her into the ravine.

'Remarkable,' he said, 'how fundamental a principle of

golf is this keeping the head still. You will hear professionals tell their pupils to keep their eye on the ball. Keeping the eye on the ball is only a secondary matter. What they really mean is that the head should be kept rigid, as otherwise it is impossible to—'

His voice died away. I had sliced my drive into the woods on the right, and after playing another had gone off to try to find my ball, leaving Celia and George in the ravine behind me. My last glimpse of them showed me that her ball had fallen into a stone-studded cavity in the side of the hill, and she was drawing her niblick from her bag as I passed out of sight. George's voice, blurred by distance to a monotonous murmur, followed me until I was out of earshot.

I was just about to give up the hunt for my ball in despair, when I heard Celia's voice calling to me from the edge of the undergrowth. There was a sharp note in it which startled me.

I came out, trailing a portion of some unknown shrub which had twined itself about my ankle.

'Yes?' I said, picking twigs out of my hair.

'I want your advice,' said Celia.

'Certainly. What is the trouble? By the way,' I said, looking round, 'where is your *fiancé*?'

'I have no *fiancé*,' she said, in a dull, hard voice.

'You have broken off the engagement?'

'Not exactly. And yet – well, I suppose it amounts to that.'

'I don't quite understand.'

'Well, the fact is,' said Celia, in a burst of girlish frankness, 'I rather think I've killed George.'

'Killed him, eh?'

It was a solution that had not occurred to me, but now that it was presented for my inspection I could see its merits. In these days of national effort, when we are all working

28

together to try to make our beloved land fit for heroes to live in, it was astonishing that nobody before had thought of a simple, obvious thing like killing George Mackintosh. George Mackintosh was undoubtedly better dead, but it had taken a woman's intuition to see it.

'I killed him with my niblick,' said Celia.

I nodded. If the thing was to be done at all, it was unquestionably a niblick shot.

'I had just made my eleventh attempt to get out of that ravine,' the girl went on, 'with George talking all the time about the recent excavations in Egypt, when suddenly – you know what it is when something seems to snap—'

'I had the experience with my shoe-lace only this morning.'

'Yes, it was like that. Sharp – sudden – happening all in a moment. I suppose I must have said something, for George stopped talking about Egypt and said that he was reminded by a remark of the last speaker's of a certain Irishman—'

I pressed her hand.

'Don't go on if it hurts you,' I said, gently.

'Well, there is very little more to tell. He bent his head to light his pipe, and well – the temptation was too much for me. That's all.'

'You were quite right.'

'You really think so?'

'I certainly do. A rather similar action, under far less provocation, once made Jael the wife of Heber the most popular woman in Israel.'

'I wish I could think so too,' she murmured. 'At the moment, you know, I was conscious of nothing but an awful elation. But – but – oh, he was such a darling before he got this dreadful affliction. I can't help thinking of G-George as he used to be.'

She burst into a torrent of sobs.

'Would you care for me to view the remains?' I said.

'Perhaps it would be as well.'

She led me silently into the ravine. George Mackintosh was lying on his back where he had fallen.

'There!' said Celia.

And, as she spoke, George Mackintosh gave a kind of snorting groan and sat up. Celia uttered a sharp shriek and sank on her knees before him. George blinked once or twice and looked about him dazedly.

'Save the women and children!' he cried. 'I can swim.'

'Oh, George!' said Celia.

'Feeling a little better?' I asked.

'A little. How many people were hurt?'

'Hurt?'

'When the express ran into us.' He cast another glance around him. 'Why, how did I get here?'

'You were here all the time,' I said.

'Do you mean after the roof fell in or before?'

Celia was crying quietly down the back of his neck.

'Oh, George!' she said, again.

He groped out feebly for her hand and patted it.

'Brave little woman!' he said. 'Brave little woman! She stuck by me all through. Tell me – I am strong enough to bear it – what caused the explosion?'

It seemed to me a case where much unpleasant explanation might be avoided by the exercise of a little tact.

'Well, some say one thing and some another,' I said. 'Whether it was a spark from a cigarette—'

Celia interrupted me. The woman in her made her revolt against this well-intentioned subterfuge.

'I hit you, George!'

'Hit me?' he repeated, curiously. 'What with? The Eiffel Tower?'

'With my niblick.'

'You hit me with your niblick? But why?'

She hesitated. Then she faced him bravely.

'Because you wouldn't stop talking.'

He gaped.

'Me!' he said. '*I* wouldn't stop talking! But I hardly talk at all. I'm noted for it.'

Celia's eyes met mine in agonized inquiry. But I saw what had happened. The blow, the sudden shock, had operated on George's brain-cells in such a way as to effect a complete cure. I have not the technical knowledge to be able to explain it, but the facts were plain.

'Lately, my dear fellow,' I assured him, 'you have dropped into the habit of talking rather a good deal. Ever since we started out this afternoon you have kept up an incessant flow of conversation!'

'Me! On the links! It isn't possible.'

'It is only too true, I fear. And that is why this brave girl hit you with her niblick. You started to tell her a funny story just as she was making her eleventh shot to get her ball out of this ravine, and she took what she considered the necessary steps.'

'Can you ever forgive me, George?' cried Celia.

George Mackintosh stared at me. Then a crimson blush mantled his face.

'So I did! It's all beginning to come back to me. Oh, heavens!'

'*Can* you forgive me, George?' cried Celia again.

He took her hand in his.

'Forgive you?' he muttered. 'Can *you* forgive *me*? Me –

a tee-talker, a green-gabbler, a prattler on the links, the lowest form of life known to science! I am unclean, unclean!'

'It's only a little mud, dearest,' said Celia, looking at the sleeve of his coat. 'It will brush off when it's dry.'

'How can you link your lot with a man who talks when people are making their shots?'

'You will never do it again.'

'But I have done it. And you stuck to me all through! Oh, Celia!'

'I loved you, George!'

The man seemed to swell with a sudden emotion. His eye lit up, and he thrust one hand into the breast of his coat while he raised the other in a sweeping gesture. For an instant he appeared on the verge of a flood of eloquence. And then, as if he had been made sharply aware of what it was that he intended to do, he suddenly sagged. The gleam died out of his eyes. He lowered his hand.

'Well, I must say that was rather decent of you,' he said.

A lame speech, but one that brought an infinite joy to both his hearers. For it showed that George Mackintosh was cured beyond possibility of relapse.

'Yes, I must say you are rather a corker,' he added.

'George!' cried Celia.

I said nothing, but I clasped his hand; and then, taking my clubs, I retired. When I looked round she was still in his arms. I left them there, alone together in the great silence.

And so (concluded the Oldest Member) you see that a cure is possible, though it needs a woman's gentle hand to bring it about. And how few women are capable of doing what Celia Tennant did. Apart from the difficulty of summoning up the necessary resolution, an act like hers requires a straight eye and a pair of strong and supple wrists. It seems to me that for the ordinary talking golfer there is no hope. And the race seems to be getting more numerous every day. Yet the finest golfers are always the least loquacious. It is related of the illustrious Sandy McHoots that when, on the occasion of his winning the British Open Championship, he was interviewed by reporters from the leading daily papers as to his views on Tariff Reform, Bimetallism, the Trial by Jury System, and the Modern Craze for Dancing, all they could extract from him was the single word 'Mphm!' Having uttered which, he shouldered his bag and went home to tea. A great man. I wish there were more like him.

A. W. TILLINGHAST

ONE EVERY
MINUTE

FRED OGDEN KNEW in his heart that he was a dub, but yet in this same heart there lurked hope. 'It takes five years for a man to learn golf,' someone once had said in his hearing, and this statement was his bright lodestar that ever twinkled through the rifts in the clouds of his despair. Ogden still had a margin of two years to test it.

Once in a great while he was asked to make up a four, and if the knowledge that he was the only man around at the time caused him in a measure to question the warmth of the invitation, it bothered him not at all. And he reveled over the course with the same intoxication of joy as a cat rolling in a newly-found bed of cat-nip. On several occasions Andrew Graves, the scratch man, actually asked him to play with him (Ogden never quite understood why) and from that moment he worshipped at the champion's shrine, hanging on every word that fell from his lips like a hungry dog fawning for scraps flung from the rich man's table. Now and then he would screw up sufficient courage to ask Graves a question concerning his stance or grip, but his confusion immediately would overwhelm him to such a degree that the advice fell on buzzing and unhearing ears. MacPherson, the pro, had labored with his game, but without avail – Ogden still remained a little fidgety dub after three years of patient, fruit-less effort. But he was consumed with the thirst for that knowledge that he knew must come to him and drag him from his Slough of Despond – a golfer.

The sun was low and the course deserted as Ogden, alone with his driver, was patiently slicing ball after ball from the shadows of the fourth teeing ground.

'Did you ever try standing on one foot?' At the sound of a voice Ogden whirled around and faced a man who had stepped forward from among the pines. 'I beg your pardon, sir, I fear I startled you,' the stranger continued, 'but I have been observing your efforts for some time, and I thought that possibly you might welcome a suggestion – may I say, from one who knows?'

Ogden noted that the other was well dressed and polished in his manner, and he smiled sheepishly at the reference to his solitary practice as he replied: 'My dear sir, I can assure you that any suggestion that may remedy my many faults will be most welcome – my name is Ogden.'

They shook hands cordially. 'And mine,' volunteered the stranger, 'is Benton. You may have heard of me,' he added modestly. But as Ogden did not reply he said with a tone of condescension, 'I take it, Mr Ogden, that you have not been long at golf,' and the accused admitted with embarrassment that he had not.

'That explains it then,' Benton exclaimed. 'I once was a member of Cobble Valley, but I've been away now for a long time.' There was a touch of sadness in the man's voice, and he was silent for a moment; then he said impulsively: 'I would like to help you, if you will let me!'

Tears sprung unbidden to the eyes of the duffer. Here was a man who wanted to help him, actually wanted to. Ogden scarcely could credit it, but his face brightened with a smile, and he almost shouted, 'Let you? Why, my dear sir, if you can cure my slice I will be your debtor for life!'

'Never fear, I can do it,' said Benton, 'but possibly my methods may seem a trifle unorthodox.'

'You may depend on me to follow your directions to the letter, sir.'

'Well, then – first of all you must have confidence; supreme confidence in yourself, and confidence in me. Let me endeavor to instill the latter. While my name seems to be unknown to you, this may be attributed to your inexperience; yet fifteen years ago the name of Benton was known in every part of the world of golf. My theories were unique, but effective, and although ignorant men scoffed at first, afterwards they gladly embraced them.

'Then I went away from here, and when I defeated Harry Vardon, over his own course, golfers were aghast. Though I say this to you, pray do not think for a moment that ego prompts it. No, no! I want only for you to know that I am a past master of golf, and capable of showing you how to play the game as it should be played. Why, my dear Mr Ogden, in that memorable match with Vardon there was not a single department of the game in which I did not excel; from teeing ground to cup, – Benton was supreme!'

Ogden licked his lips with a dry tongue and his emotion threatened to master him. 'Tell me about it,' he said huskily.

'Not now, my friend, not now,' Benton replied modestly. 'It is of yourself and your golf that we shall talk – let us to work! I noticed that you are left-handed. Unfortunate, very unfortunate! Southpaws usually are chronic slicers.'

'When I hit the ball at all, I do slice,' Ogden sorrowfully admitted.

'Don't let it worry you for a moment,' Benton quickly responded: 'it is not incurable when you know how.' Ogden brightened perceptibly and drew a deep breath.

'When I interrupted your practice, you may remember that I suggested that you stand on one foot. That was no jest, I assure you! It is of vital importance, but great care should be used in selecting the foot. Ordinarily it would be the right one, but in your case – the left. Your other foot must be extended straight out in front of you on a level with the waist. Just try the position, Mr Ogden – Ah! That's it! Fine! Thank you!

'Now take your driver – No! – never mind the balls yet; – time enough for them afterwards. One must look before one leaps you know. – Now face me, with your entire weight on the left, raising your other, so. That's it! – Now take the club in your right hand only, and grasp the lobe of your left ear with the hand that is free.'

Ogden did so without a murmur and awaited further orders. He got them after a moment, during which time his instructor surveyed the position with critical eyes and puckered brow, first with his head on one side, then on the other. 'Not bad, not bad at all,' he finally murmured approvingly. Ogden was glad for he felt uncomfortable and he harbored the suspicion that he must look like a ballet girl.

'Throw the body back just a trifle, not too much,' Benton admonished. 'That's fine! Now look intently at a spot on the ground about two inches in advance of the toe, – and take your driver with the right hand until the back of it touches the left ear. No! the back of your hand, Mr Ogden – not the driver! Try it again – That's better! – Now again! Right! Once more! – Good! Again! – Very good! – Now we are ready for the stroke itself. – Keeping your eye on the spot on the ground, try to strike it with the club head as vigorously as possible and permit the club head to go on through as far as it may. No, no! Not with both hands – Take the position you've been trying and let the club go through hard!'

The club went through hard, so hard, indeed, that it nearly fractured Ogden's right ankle, which, poised in the air, had in some way interfered with the happy finish of the club head. Ogden felt that it was wrong, and Benton did not leave him long in doubt: 'There, that's why you slice!' he exclaimed. 'But I know the reason! – It's mental! Ah! Yes, my dear Ogden, mentality is golf's prime factor. – Now we must get to the root of the evil. – Assume the original position, but only take the club back, – do not go through with the stroke. Each time, after going back, gently replace it on the ground. At first whisper, "I will not slice," repeating the words louder with every time back. Try it! That's it – I will not slice! Right! I will not slice! Right! I will not slice! Good! – Go on!'

By the time Ogden had followed instructions closely twenty times, his face was red to bursting and he was shouting 'I will not slice,' so lustily that Benton begged him to desist.

'How did I do it?' he asked.

'Fine!' admitted Benton, who was seated on the bench, puffing away on a large black cigar. 'You really did it very well, and I may add that you possess a particularly good voice. You brought out that last "slice" very agreeably! But now you may try a shot with a ball teed up. Your slice is cured!'

Ogden looked at him in amazement – 'So you mean to say that I can't slice now?'

'Your slice is cured!' reiterated Benton with conviction.

With trembling fingers Ogden fashioned his tee with sand from the nearby box, and took the position, which was changed a half dozen times before Benton was entirely satisfied. Ogden was getting impatient, for the sun had set and night was settling down.

'Now remember the "I will not slice," Mr Ogden; you must address the ball with those words, ten times before hitting it.' Once more the leg was pointed straight out, but now

Benton permitted his pupil to put both hands on the club, but only after many changes of grips. Once more in his ostrich-like pose Ogden began his whispered 'I will not slice,' repeating it with added emphasis with each address, until his voice boomed far into the twilight – and then he struck. But as he struck his foot slipped, yet not until he had felt his club land squarely on the ball.

Falling, he raised himself from the ground and gazed after his drive – and then he buried his face in his hands and cried for joy. He had seen the best ball he ever had hit and it actually was pulling over for the right edge of the fairway.

At last he arose and gazed with awe at Benton, who, with his black cigar in the corner of his smiling mouth, was regarding his pupil complacently.

Ogden walked over to him and feverishly whispered as though to keep his words secret from the pines, 'Benton! Tell me truly, I saw it right, didn't I? It didn't slice, did it?' Benton flicked the ashes from his cigar –

'I knew it wouldn't! Didn't I tell you that your slice was cured?'

Ogden grasped his hand and wrung it effusively. 'You don't know what you've done for me, Mr Benton, – I'll never forget it!'

The one-time slicer peered out over the darkening course. 'If it wasn't so dark I would pull another one,' he suddenly announced; – 'but the moon will be up soon and I'll wait.'

He looked at his new friend timidly and then, as his courage gathered, he blurted out – 'Won't you tell me all about your match with Vardon?'

'Which one?' calmly replied Benton.

'Why *the* match, – the time you beat him.'

Benton looked at his questioner with pitying eyes, –

'I have always beaten him,' he said with dignity.

Ogden's eyes grew big with wonder as the blood leaped through his veins. Here was he, dub of dubs, actually talking to the master-mind of golf and the master of all golfers. He attempted to speak, but his tongue was paralyzed. With an effort he at last found his voice.

'What was the worst licking you ever gave him?'

'Ten and eight,' was the terse reply. 'I got around in 67 that time, – out in 34; back in 33, – and it was a beast of a day, too, – raining and blowing a gale.'

Just as Benton got to the turn in his description of the match, both men jumped to their feet, for the sudden snapping of a twig in the pine walk had startled them. Then a voice close at hand, – 'Here he is, doctor, I thought we might find him here.'

Two shadows from the pines assumed human proportions. As they stepped close Ogden noted that one was a tall, dignified-looking man with a white beard; the other wore a blue uniform and a visored cap, on which Ogden descried this word, – 'Attendant.'

'Now, Benton, you go along with David and take a nice walk.'

'All right, Doc,' quietly spoke the erstwhile instructor, 'I must admit that I am a trifle hungry, but I would have liked to have had sufficient time to show Mr Ogden my corkscrew mashie shot.' And as they turned and walked through the pines Ogden heard him say, 'By the way, David, how is Napoleon this evening? He was not feeling any too well when I left.'

The tall gentleman had remained standing by Ogden's side. 'I am Dr Lorimer and Benton has been a patient at my sanitarium for a number of years, but he slipped away this afternoon. I trust, sir, that he has not annoyed you in any way. But I think that this is unlikely, as he is quite harmless.

After a futile search David suggested that we might find him here, for it was at this very spot he lost his reason. I am not a golfer myself, but I have been told that our unfortunate friend, after taking lessons from every professional coach that he could find, and an exhaustive study of many books of instruction, at last succeeded in driving a ball from this spot, and when he found that he had driven something over one hundred yards the sudden joyful shock bereft him of his reason.'

'But did he never play Vardon?' timorously inquired Ogden.

'Oh, yes; he plays them all. If I remember rightly, every Tuesday is his Vardon match day. Good-night sir! My car is waiting and I must get him back.'

Ogden stood for some moments looking vacantly through the pines, but finally he turned and sighed deeply, looking out over the moon-lit course. Evidently his thoughts were not comforting, for he shook his head dolefully. He thought of his little hour of enchantment; of the rude awakening, and then of his fellow club members who undoubtedly would be congregated in the tap room on his return. Should he tell them? He pondered over this last thought for a moment, and then decided, 'No, I guess not.' But in the midst of his melancholy reverie, suddenly there came back to him the delicious thrill of that one ball which he had hit and he permitted his eyes to rove out over the fairway to the big hickory on the right, which marked the end of that drive. And then he started to pace off the distance. At the one hundred and eighty-seventh step he stopped, for his ball was at his feet, and as he looked back toward the distant teeing ground in the shadow of the pines, he muttered; – 'Well, he wasn't such a rotten teacher at that!'

HOLWORTHY HALL

THE LAST ROUND

OVERNIGHT, AN INSOLENT wind had dashed down in a guerrilla raid from the north, plundered the unsuspecting country as it might, and fled, frost-laden, from the sturdy counter-attack of the October sun; so that by noon the atmosphere was calm again, and unharassed: But as marauding parties, even when repulsed, leave signs of things accomplished, and plain warnings of more raids to come, so had the first of this year's gales left in the air an ultimatum, half portent, and half reminiscence; and, in the meantime, set the world a-tingle with strong light and stronger color, and the fresh stimulant of its own rare ether. The sky was none of your blued-steel firmaments, belligerent and cold; it was immaculately blue, immeasurably distant, but nowise chill, and prophetic, rather than intimidating. The sun, ever so slightly fagged from its defensive sortie, was in supreme command, yet not despotic in its domination. The temperature was that of a perverted June. And so by axiom, all sound-minded men who were unhampered by the stress of trade were out-of-doors; and those whose wisdom was impeccable were playing golf; and from this latter class a happy muster of privileged enthusiasts were taking profit from their membership at Templeton.

On the veranda of the clubhouse, three men were sitting to overlook the private driveway, and the turn-around. There was an elderly man in conventionally striking checks and wool; there was a middle-aged man in knickerbockers and Norfolk four years worn; there was a slender youth in creamy flannels. Characteristically, as they sat and watched, they smoked, – the boy a cigarette, the shabby man a pipe, the senior of the group a plump cigar. Smoking at ease, they also smoked in reticence; now and then they craned in unison at a motor gliding along the avenue of trees; occasionally they ennobled experts on the adjoining thirteenth green by rising from their chairs to estimate the difficulty of a putt, and to evolve the odds against success. At the minimum, they had maintained this lethargy for a quarter hour; they seemed as callous to the opportunity for golf, as insensible to the superb links at hand, as though they were so many uninstructed aliens, ignorant of the history of Scotland, immune to the insidious temptations bred at Templeton.

At length, the boy in flannels tossed away his cigarette, and spoke at random.

'Well,' he remarked lugubriously, 'it's about time, isn't it?

The man in shabby knickers nodded patiently.

'It's late,' he said, with an accent so delicate, so all but imperceptible, that few would have supposed his grandfather had gone about in kilts.

'Oh, not very,' commented the elderly gentleman. 'He had to get his massage, you know.'

The flanneled youth scratched a match on his heel, and lighted another cigarette, taking excessive care with all mechanics of the act.

'Feels like a funeral, doesn't it?' he shuddered. 'Br-r-r-r!'

'That depends on your discreemination,' conceded the pipe-smoker, who had registered on the handicap list as Peters, D. A. . . . 7. 'How about you, Kingsland?'

Kingsland contemplated the wrapper of his cigar, and smiled grimly. Grimness was typical of him; impertinent members referred to him as 'the old war-horse.'

48

'To tell the truth,' he said, 'I'm not relishing the prospect of this afternoon very much, and I don't imagine you are, either. But we've got to make it as pleasant for Norton as we can. Put yourselves in his place. . . .'

The youth, who was popularly called Bunker because his surname was Hazzard, had depths in his eyes as he gazed out over the landscape. He was a rhapsodist, afraid of detection.

'I wonder,' he mused. 'What d'you suppose *he's* thinking?'

'If you're that inqueesitive,' said Peters abruptly, 'go be a convict.'

Hazzard sniffed. 'That's hardly a parallel.' Nevertheless, he slumped into his chair and considered it.

'It isn't too remote,' said Kingsland, fondling his tie. 'Billy Norton loves golf the way some people love life. He's been at it for twenty-two years – picked it up when it was a joke, and everybody wore red coats and thought thirty-five cents was an outrageous price for Silvertowns. Why, Billy Norton was a topnotcher when rubber-cored balls came in; he was winning sectional tournaments when young Hazzard there was going to bed in daylight. He's a student and an arbiter and a savant and an encyclopedia. I've seen him swinging on a jute mat in his garage in February, and I've seen sixteen mashies in his house at one time. It took him a calendar year to pick the one he could trust. And—'

'Any duffer could do that,' growled Peters, resting on his elbows. 'But Billy Norton's the most inveterate enemy bogy ever had. He hasn't won as many competitions as some people, but for reliabeelity—'

'The thing about him that gets *me*,' said Hazzard, 'is his disposition. My Lord! When he beats you, he makes you feel he was doing his best to win, but he's so darned sorry it had to be *you* he beat – and if you'd been on your game you'd have slaughtered him. And of course I haven't known him very long, but no matter what happened, I never heard him make a single excuse—'

'That's plausible – because he never made one,' said Kingsland, conveying reproof. 'He told me at least ten years ago that the most valuable lesson he ever learned was that nobody but himself was interested in Billy Norton's game. . . . *How* he'll miss it!'

Peters coughed gruffly.

'Are his doctors too meteeculous, Kingsland?'

'Hardly. There were three of 'em in consultation. You see, he was standing up in the vestibule when the crash came, and he was thrown squarely against the brake-wheel—'

'Oh, those commuters are fools,' said Hazzard bitterly. 'They start to pile out when the train's half a mile from Grand Central. I thought Norton had more sense. But one bump shouldn't have put him out of business – he must have had a bad heart anyway.'

'He did,' agreed Kingsland. 'But it wouldn't have stopped his golf unless he'd had that terrific fall. . . . The doctors know what they're doing.'

'And after twenty years,' said Peters reflectively, 'they tell him that this is the last round he can ever play. It'll be grievous hard for Billy.'

There was a moment devoted, by each of the three, to altruistic revery. Alike, they were inordinately fond of the game, but not with Norton's sovereign and enduring passion. They were performers of equal distinction, but none of them could approximate, on the season's average, within two strokes of Norton. Besides that, Hazzard was the local tennis champion, and Peters a fancy skater and a famous swimmer, and Kingsland notably adroit with firearms. Norton was a golfer and always a golfer, and exclusively a golfer. Divorce him from the links, and his biography thenceforward must inevitably be a record of blank despondency, with never a chance to prove again that once he, too, had earned his pinnacle. His friends knew this, and they were sorely burdened by the certainty.

'I heard,' said Hazzard, subdued, 'that before he could persuade 'em to let him play this one round he had to have daily treatments for six weeks. And he had to beg like a pirate at that!'

'I hope to Heaven he can score,' said Kingsland, shaking his head. 'It's a wonderful day. The greens ought to be fast as lightning.'

Peters shrugged his shoulders.

'After resting since the middle of July? He'll be lucky to break 90. I suggest we have the tee-plates moved up to the limit.'

'Billy wouldn't approve of that,' doubted Kingsland, 'but if he doesn't break 80, he'll break his heart, and that's gospel. ... He wants to finish with a good round. ... Don't you forget, we've got to keep him cheered up. That's what we're here for.' He peered fixedly down the avenue of trees, and got to his feet. 'There's Billy's car now! Come on over and meet him, everybody!'

Leisurely they crossed the veranda toward the motor entrance. Kingsland and Peters were admirably composed, but Hazzard, whose temperament made him a marvelous medal but an erratic match player, was unutterably downcast. Somehow he had managed to incorporate himself into Norton's shoes, and into Norton's psychology, and his sympathies were rapidly getting the better of him when Peters, cannily alert, put out a brawny hand and gripped his unflexed biceps in a clutch which brought agony to Hazzard's face, and in a flash dispelled his vapors.

'Ouch! What in thunder's the matter with you ... !'

'Smile, Bunker!' said Peters, indicating the slowing motor. 'This is Billy Norton's exodus from golf. Make it cheerful. Smile, damn you, – smile!' His own jaw tightened, and then his lips curved artificially. 'You, *Billy*!' cried Peters with solemn boisterousness, as he went ahead.

At forty-five, Norton was a man of no remarkable physique; indeed, he would have passed unnoticed for his bulk in almost any gathering of athletes. A closer scrutiny, however, would show that muscularly he was compact and well-equipped; he was slim-waisted, but his torso illustrated the precise symmetry, with relationship to the rest of him, which trainers look for in the football squads. His hands were small, and his fingers tapering, but his wrists were bundles of tempered and twisted wire. His eyes were large, and humorous, and steady; his complexion was a tribute to his manners and customs; his entire countenance was indicative of frankness and generosity, and a certain ingrained idealism; and yet there were lines about his expressive mouth, and a solid bit of sculpturing in the region of his chin, which betrayed no lack of the attributes which men call fighting qualities. Today these lines were cut more prominently than usual; and there was a constant contraction and expansion of Norton's pupils. A series of infinitesimal furrows had crept upon his forehead, and his nostrils appeared to be abnormally sensitive. On the veranda and in the locker-room, he had laughed easily and chatted without restraint; but from the instant he stepped out upon the sod, preoccupation had seized and silenced him. At the first tee, he had paused in introspective woe; presently he looked up, and flinched at the broadside of triple commiseration.

'Come, come!' said Norton, assuming a tone of raillery. 'What is this, – a wake?'

'Er ... I'm sorry, Billy,' said Kingsland in haste. 'All the good caddies had gone out. We've got four infants. Do you mind?'

Norton inspected the undersized specimen of vitality which was in charge of his clubs. The caddy was ridiculously small, impossibly dirty, but electrically alert and eager; and Norton's approbation was spontaneous. The caddy's physiognomy relieved him, too, of some of his depression.

'Not a bit,' he denied. 'But what I was going to say was that I asked you three to play with me because you're the best golfing friends I ever had. So I hope you'll understand me. ... Please don't let's bet on the match ... just for once.'

'Quite so, quite so,' assented Peters. 'And shall we play foursomes or independently?'

'Why, unless you ... why don't we go independently? No teams, and no gambling. I'd rather appreciate it. Would it spoil your game?'

'No, indeed,' said Kingsland with great heartiness. 'We'll learn how much we're really good for.... You take the honor, Billy.'

Accordingly, Norton requisitioned a pinch of sand from the tee-box.

'A lot of people joke me about it,' he said, 'but for years and years I've kept a golf diary.... Altogether, I've played nearly three thousand rounds of golf. That's a lot, isn't it? I've played Templeton over four hundred times. And it's ... it's a trifle disconcerting to look off down this hill ... and realize that if I made a bad start now I can't come back tomorrow, and ...' He stopped, and when he resumed, his tone was deprecatory. 'I hate to hold you fellows up, but I've simply got to take a couple of practice swings.'

'Go ahead,' said Hazzard, squinting at the ground. 'Nobody behind us.' He was staggered to discern that even in so great extremities, Norton disdained an alibi.

Kingsland and Peters, side by side, were regarding Norton with evident concern. There was no use whatsoever in belittling his recent shock and illness; his quondam smoothness and adroit coordination of impulses had deserted him, and his form was ominously atypical. Even in his preliminary motions he revealed the injunctions laid upon him by his nostalgia; and Kingsland and Peters, simultaneously aware of what mishap the afternoon might bring to Billy Norton, were no less conscious of the dream he cherished, and the struggle he was making to reestablish what self-reliance he had lost. Witnessing his faultiness, they sickened with the apprehension of pure logic.

'That'll do,' said Norton, and addressed his ball.

Blindfold, any of the trio could have sensed from the sound of contact that Norton had topped his first drive. There was no precision in his swing; there was no audacity; worst of all, there was no trace of that indescribable contempt for the ball, of its antecedents and consequents, which is an integral and a vital factor in any shot. Hazzard, who hadn't lifted his head until the echo of the impact, almost groaned. The others, unable to predict whether Norton would be more wounded by condolences, or disheartened by the lack of them, murmured incoherently. Norton stepped back from the plates, and swished his driver at a leaf of sorrel.

'Good medicine,' he said calmly, 'for an inflamed conceit. I pressed.'

Nevertheless, as he later strolled down the fairway on the trail of his inefficiency, he couldn't refrain from picturing to himself the prodigious swipes he had sometime made from that initial tee. He was glad that Peters and Kingsland had got off so well – and eventually they would get off even better; he regretted that Hazzard had hooked his tremendous liner into the rough – but there remained to Hazzard a calendar full of days on which to redeem himself. It was only Billy Norton whose franchise was running out, and couldn't be renewed. He smiled paternally at his caddy, and possessed himself of a beloved iron.

'Oh, well,' he said aloud, 'there's one good thing about it – we'll never make another bad start as long as we live!'

The caddy grinned, disclosing wide gaps in upper and lower teeth.

'Nope,' he conceded amicably. 'We topped it, didn't we?'

'We'll make it up on this one,' promised Norton.

'Huh! Betcha!' The caddy was supercilious toward failure.

Norton, warmed by the stubborn loyalty, played the iron. He had completed a cursory audit of his bodily resources; he was convinced that if he relentlessly cleansed his mind of its inhibitions, he should mechanically revert to form. He was in no corporeal pain; he was merely sluggish, and soft. And because, out of his plenteous store of golf psychology, he knew how best to grapple for the elusive item of confidence, he played the iron with all his strength; and to his ineffable satisfaction, the recovery would have done credit to Edward Ray. The trajectory was low, and the momentum great; the ball, dipping to earth after a sheer carry of two hundred yards, sped straight as a plumbline through twin traps, and scurried on in search of shorter grass to rest in.

'Huh! Betcha!' cackled the caddy, appropriating an interest in the laurels.

Peters and Kingsland were also in the neighborhood of the green, and Hazzard, who had been nervously treading turf, and kneading it with the sole of his brassey, beamed to the utmost, and shafted his second shot without resentment. And soon thereafter, the three friends halted motionless in a little knot, and focused upon the bowed back of Billy Norton with such profound intensity that two week-end guests at Templeton, who beheld the tableau from the nearby seventh, spoke cynically of the evils of heavy gambling, which makes men importune the fates to bring confusion to a vigorous opponent. The week-end guests, however, didn't observe that when the careful player pitched within a club's-length of the cup, his three companions applauded energetically; nor did they overhear a caddy whispering loudly to his fellows: 'Betcha little kernick we sink it!'

In the proper order, Norton sank it solidly, and as the ball rattled against the shining zinc, he was for the moment transported with delight which couldn't be concealed. The infection burned in his veins; the sweetness of redemption soothed his soul; he was mad to hasten to the second tee, to do this thing again, again, and ceaselessly; and then, summarily minded of his status in the universe of golf, he hesitated, and his smile faded, and the lines crept out once more upon his forehead. Let the pendulum of the years wag on; let golfers come and golfers go, and stroke by stroke the incalculable sum of all the strokes increase; but insofar as the first of the eighteen holes at Templeton was included in that division of his ephemeral experience, he had achieved the ultimate. And fighter as he had always been, fighter as still he was, Norton knew that his wrists were trembling, and that the shame of senility had come upon him.

The sincere compliments of his friends rang crude to Norton; he was sentient of the forced gaiety in their tones. A wave of mortification drenched him; he wished that he hadn't ventured so absurd a farewell to sportsmanship. And then, involuntarily, he smiled. He was thinking of his cyclonic feat with the iron and of the placid assurance of the freckled caddy.

'I believe,' said Norton, 'it's still my honor.'

There was a pronounced improvement in the timing of his subsequent swing. His normal rhythm had come home to him, and he was conciliated and emboldened by the surety of one par hole already on his card. And yet, although he battled doggedly against the concept, he was unable to free himself as soon as he had executed the shot, from the premonition that after this, each effort was certain to hurt him – to hurt him physically, locally, acutely, so that he couldn't continue to play; so that he couldn't consummate the round. The instructions of his physicians were piling themselves into a tumbled heap in his brain; he could recall verbatim how the medicos had argued with him when he first pleaded for the boon of this anti-climax to his career, and how they had implied that the effects of it might convert him to the belief that even physicians sometimes know what they're talking about. To be sure, he had driven lustily and without discomfort; thus far, he had been visited by not the faintest symptom of distress; nevertheless, he was intermittently worried by what he interpreted as an intuition, and his uneasiness was so patent that Kingsland rallied instantly to his support.

'If we speed up a little,' said Kingsland casually, 'we ought to be able to get in twenty-seven holes. That'll please you, won't it? The extra nine is velvet.'

Norton gestured to signify the negative.

'No – a round of golf is eighteen holes. I'd rather concentrate.'

'*That's* discreemination!' said Peters. 'I'm counting on you to hang up an eighty-five, Billy.'

'*Eighty-five!*' spluttered Norton. 'Why, if I can't do a seventy-nine or better I ought to resign! Eighty-five! Class B stuff!'

Hazzard edged over to him, and got his attention.

'Say,' he said, half-apologetically. 'You've got such wonderful direction, Mr Norton – if you just keep on the line and don't bother about distance you can break eighty *easy*. . . . I noticed you're hitting awfully hard.'

Norton was grateful for the misplaced kindness.

'There may be something in that, Bunker, but I want to be in the seventies. I've got to be radical.'

'Here's an example on this shot,' entreated Hazzard. 'You've got a good lie; don't try to make the plateau; play safe. You're sure of your five if you do.'

Norton wavered.

'No,' he declared finally. 'This dog-leg isn't an accident; it's engineering. We're supposed to shoot for the pin. I like to go for the hole. If I flub, I *deserve* the punishment. If I don't . . . well, any novice can play short.'

'It's a deeficult carry,' frowned Peters. 'I'd use the wood.'

Norton deliberately chose his favorite iron.

'Boys,' he said, delaying, 'you're all talking and acting as though I'm a doddering old cripple. . . . If I'd thought you'd let me get on your nerves like that, I'd have gone around alone – I honestly would! You forget it! I'm not squealing. Let's play golf!' And with the paralysis of fear exerting its baneful influence upon his poise, he topped dismally into the luxuriant weeds of remorse.

At that juncture, nothing more salutary could have befallen him. His will, grown flaccid during his weary confinement, had hitherto balked him and he had allowed himself to succumb to his own pathology, but automatically, when he saw the ball disappearing among the weeds, his reason, trained to eliminate the non-essentials, busied itself with the sole problem of extrication. His spirits rose prodigiously; and Norton himself didn't realize that he was fundamentally happier not because he had man-handled a shot, but because he had stopped thinking about everything but golf. He had utterly dissociated himself from his ailments and his gnawing afflictions; the topic of mashie-niblicks held a monopoly upon his rational faculties. As he followed his buoyant caddy through the lush vegetation, he whistled a melancholy strain which was melancholy only because Norton's atrocious whistling was chronic; it had no reference to the state of his infelicity.

'There!' said Kingsland obliquely to Peters. 'If he keeps up chirruping like that, he'll shoot golf!'

And Norton was keeping it up most dolefully, in spite of the fact that his stance was uneven, and that in order to get down to the ball, he must necessarily carve through a thick buffer of rank vegetation. He was absorbed in the building up of a working theory, and his whistling increased in volume as he pondered.

'Betcha!' announced his caddy, intolerant of the pinch. Norton chuckled, and having settled with himself the type of endeavor most suited to the lie, and to the complications of the rough, procrastinated no longer. He bent his knees a little so as to retain all possible weight on the ground, and to provide sufficient resistance to counteract a potential loss of balance; he gripped the mashie-niblick more firmly; he went for the ball with the conclusive ounce of his vigor and intrepidity. The blade tore through the slippery weeds; the ball rose sharply, cleared the intervening herbage, and fell so closely to its predetermined location that Norton could hardly have bettered his strategy if, instead of using the mashie-niblick, he had simply walked on for half a furlong and placed the ball where he wanted it.

'Great work!' shouted Peters, waving his congratulations.
'Bully!' said Hazzard, breathing deeply.

'Right on your game, Billy,' acknowledged Kingsland. 'But you'll have to go some for your par five.'

'I told you so,' muttered the earthy caddy.

But Norton knew that second green too well. It was an undulating green, close-clipped and perilously fast; it was hard to reach and hold, even with back-spin; and yonder there was a tract of rock and gorse, inimical to scoring and to temper. He was content to run up modestly with a jigger, and to take his allotted two putts, and a six, rather than apply for the lesser figure, and perhaps be called to judgment for an over-approach. And the consciousness that he was only one over par for two holes, and not yet beaten by his deficiencies, tended to inspire him.

The third was a matter of two hundred yards, and the quartet assailed it with renewed vivacity. It was a perfect specimen of a one-shot hole; its green was totally surrounded by sand and kneehigh scrub; and in front, a serrated ridge of stubble estopped the players from any but high and accurately directed drives. Invariably it had baffled Norton; it was his bugaboo; he disliked the distance, and habitually overplayed, or, if he gaged the yardage to a nicety, rolled to a crescent trap which was the southern boundary of the green. He was inconceivably anxious now to sever his acquaintance with this hole on his own terms. He was so anxious that in his zeal to escape the fateful crescent, he put an arching shot squarely in the center of the opposite pit.

'There!' he said, explosively. 'Thank Heaven it's done with! This ratty little hole has kept me awake more nights. . . . Never again!'

'A brave hypocrisy, man!' said Peters to Kingsland.

And, for a verity, Norton had prevaricated in gross. His malfeasance was a source of anguish which not for thousands would he have consented to express. Here was a sin of

60

commission for which he never could atone by practise, or by postnate virtue. He might indeed retrieve the squandered stroke by superlative genius on some other hole, but this, the third, had ensnared him according to its wont, and so must read the docket. But he chipped out cleverly, and gained an acceptable four; and none of his comrades guessed the blackness of his vast self-condemnation.

Out of the precious eighteen holes vouchsafed to him, three were already in the past, and thirteen strokes were entered on the books. Norton, whose technical horizon was commonly defined by the very next shot, and nothing ulterior, found himself involved in simple mathematics – thirteen from seventy-nine leaves sixty-six. Sixty-six strokes for fifteen holes remained to him; in former days the allowance would have offered speculative possibilities. But Norton, subconsciously induced by Hazzard's pleading, was vacillating between recklessness and caution; he was obsessed by the knowledge that since he himself had set his own objective, a degeneration from it would permanently disqualify him in his own esteem. Should it be rashness, or conservatism? At the outset, he was inclined to yield to Hazzard.

'And yet . . .' said Norton, unwittingly aloud.

'What's that?' asked Kingsland.

Norton started, and smiled feebly.

'I was just thinking about an old golf verse,' he said. 'It's like this –

> 'If the pleasure in golf lies in hitting the ball,
> And in seven a hole you do,
> Then I, who have played fourteen in all
> Have had twice as much fun as you!'

'Good stuff,' said Kingsland appreciatively.

Norton shook himself, and stated profanely to his *alter ego* that there must be no repetition of this mental cowardice. It wasn't fair to himself, and it wasn't fair to his friends. He had no right to cover them with the pall of his own gloom. He ought to plot his campaign for himself, and adhere to it. He plotted it forthwith; and he adhered to it so steadfastly that his application to the game was quite incompatible with social intercourse. The next six holes he played as in a trance.

Now because his friends recognized – to the extent that it is possible for one man to fathom the emotions of another – the importance to Norton of this personally inflicted ordeal; and because they coincided perfectly in a diagnosis of his wishes, they unanimously, from the moment of Norton's severance or oral communication, held their peace. They argued that he had withdrawn by choice into the solitude of his own reflections, and that tact required of them the courtesy of silence. From tee to green, and from green to tee they accompanied him; they were monosyllabic among themselves; they perceived that Norton was living in a world apart, and that in meeting and surmounting obstacles, or being blessed with and receiving luck, he was playing solely by instinct, dazedly, subjectively. He was so overwhelmed by the cruel rule which was to govern his golfless future that realities no longer impressed themselves upon him. Hypnotized by his very tenacity of purpose, he went six holes without awakening to etiquette, or to dynamics or to topography.

Still plunged in his fit of abstraction, he had holed a long putt on the ninth, and straightened himself to stare with stolid eyes at a prospect of maple trees and a reach of terraced lawn, when Kingsland touched his arm, and spoke to him. Norton jumped.

'What? What's that?' he stammered.

'You turned in forty,' repeated Kingsland. 'Nice work.'

'*Turned? I* – why – what was that you said?'

'In forty,' reiterated Kingsland.

Norton, stupefied, fell back a pace or two.

'Good God!' he faltered, rubbing his forehead. 'Have *we* ... *we can't have played nine holes!* I didn't ... realize that!'

No one laughed. On the contrary, Hazzard, blinking rapidly, also took up the study of that panorama of maples, and apostrophized them in the curtest of sentences. Kingsland and Peters both coughed uneasily, and interchanged glances of smarting helplessness. They had comprehended Norton's intellectual aloofness, but they were stunned by the revelation that he had dreamed and conjured himself around in a medal forty, while supinely obeying reflexes, and gathering neither pain nor pleasure from the strange performance. And now that Norton was summoned to the material world again, he was in an agony of embarrassment; his friends no less.

In the meantime, the warmth was slowly receding from the sun, and a fretful wind was whipping across the plains. Kingsland shivered.

'Let's get started,' he exhorted bruskly. 'It's blowing up colder. Billy, if you don't look out, you'll lose your amateur standing! Just out of the hospital, and forty strokes to here!'

Norton smiled at him without mirth.

'Old man,' he demurred, 'you know I'm not complaining ... but you certainly did upset me. I ... I feel as though a word's been lopped off my vocabulary. ...'

'What word's that, Billy?'

' "Turn," ' said Norton. 'In the sense *you* meant it.' He bit his lip and flushed; then, stiffening, he walked in a direct line to Kingsland, and faced him sternly. 'Look here,' he said. 'If I pull any more stuff like that from now on – *brain* me!

I'm making a damned fool and a baby out of myself! I haven't the grit of any oyster! All of you – I beg your pardon.'

'Nonsense!' said Peters. 'And keep your head down!'

'We're with you, Billy,' said Kingsland.

'Same here,' added Hazzard, incapable of sustained speech.

'No – I do beg your pardon,' insisted Norton. 'I won't pretend this isn't a hard day for me, but I don't need to be a wet-blanket *all* the time. From here on we'll have some fun out of it. My honor?'

'Right,' said Peters. 'Well earned.'

As Norton prepared to drive, Hazzard sidled toward Kingsland, and accosted him in an undertone.

'I thought,' he said, with traces of sarcasm, 'your idea was for us to keep him cheered up!'

'Well, it was!'

'And a sweet mess we've made of it, haven't we?'

'A misunderstanding, Bunker – nothing more.'

'Granted – but why don't we *do* something?'

'We will. Go ahead and be facetious. He's getting a grip on himself. . . . *Nice one*, Billy!'

Norton was admittedly proud of that drive. It was the best he had yet obtained, and eventually it proved to be the best of the four, outstripping Hazzard's mighty slash by a clear twenty yards. And as soon as the party quitted the tee, it was evident that Norton was forcing himself to joviality in order to quiet his conscience, and propitiate his friends. He chattered volubly; laughed when there was little to laugh at; and conducted himself generally in a way to discount his primary ethics of a golf match. If his taciturn period had brought sorrow to the three who partnered him, this interlude of superficial glee brought with it a measure of discomfort which was irresistibly demoralizing. Hazzard's equilibrium was the first to lapse; he missed his second shot most execrably, took five to reach the harbor of the green, and went from bad to worse on the tantalizing eleventh. Kingsland capitulated on the twelfth, and picked up shame-lessly when he was playing seven. Peters, steadiest of the trio, blew up at the tricky thirteenth, putting four successive spoon shots out of bounds. And through this cataclysm of bathos, regardless of the poor examples set for him, Norton went indefatigably forward, talking in little bursts of almost hysterical intensity, laughing with metallic dissimulation at things not humorous, and playing without a flaw. Negligent on the tee, he was appallingly true to the direction flag; through the fairway he was insouciant to the point of apathy; he putted without apparent discretion, and still the putts went down. For five holes he continued this wild rev-elry of shattered nerves; on the fifteenth he sliced to a patch of woodland, and, declining assistance, pursued his caddy in search of the hiding ball.

'Whew!' said Kingsland, when Norton was out of range. 'Isn't it *terrible*?'

'Awful – awful!' Hazzard was agitated as with the palsy.

'The man's raving with it,' said Peters compassionately. 'Once I saw the psychopathic ward on Sunday morning. . . .'

Within the copse, Norton and the caddy were hunting diligently for the missing ball. By this time, the wind had doubled in velocity; Norton, removing his cap, took it with gratitude, for despite the lowered temperature, his head was moist with perspiration. And as he tramped through the crackling underbush, he was unexpectedly visited by an exquisite thrill of desolation; a despairing wrench at his heart-strings which left him palpitant and numb. He could remember how often he had cursed inwardly at such contin-gencies as this; how he had appraised the loss of a ball as an unforgivable misdemeanor, chargeable first to himself, who had driven it off the course, and secondly to the boy who labored in vain to find it. Now he was sensing the innate sweetness of ill fortune as well as godsend; he was convinced, at the end, that golf is even greater than its own philosophy. Norton wondered what would have become of his character if he had taken other disasters as stormily as he was taking his discharge from golf. He wondered how, if his reactions today were congenital, he should accept more serious burdens – such as the discharge from mortality. He stood stock-still, and applied the searchlight of reason to his inbeing.

'I – I guess it's a lost ball,' ventured the caddy, surrendering to the obvious.

'Didn't you mark it?'

'No, sir – didn't *see* it.'

Norton transfixed that caddy, and the boy wilted. 'That's very unusual. Most boys say they marked it. Why didn't you?'

The caddy dug his toes into the soft loam. 'Didn't *see* it.'

'I know – but most boys say they did, anyway, when they lose a ball. They don't want to be scolded, so they say they marked it. Why didn't you say so?'

The caddy reddened under the grime, and posed heron-like on one foot.

'Dunno,' he answered.

'I do,' said Norton kindly. 'You're all right, caddy! I'm not going to scold you.'

The boy eyed him shrewdly, and condescended to disclose the basis of his rectitude.

'I'm a – Scout.'

'Oh! What's that got to do with it?'

'Scouts is . . . truthful. That's a . . . a law.'

Norton caught his breath.

'Come on back; I'll have to play another ball. So you're a Scout, are you? What made you join?'

The boy, trotting swiftly to keep pace with Norton, was ludicrous in his amalgamation of sheepishness and unction.

'Ma did.'

'Oh! She did, did she? What for?'

'Said it'd make me brave.'

'Weren't you before?'

'Naw,' confessed the Scout, blushing.

'Wouldn't you fight?'

'*Sure*, but—'

'But what?'

'When I got licked, I . . . I bawled.'

Norton, emerging to the fairway, signaled to his friends, and tossed a ball to the turf.

'Sonny,' he said, 'I ought to join your troop myself! Let's have the heavy mid-iron!'

The two-stroke penalty gave him a seven for the long hole; he required two fours and a three for his coveted seventy-nine. And, to the astonishment and relief of his associates, he played the first two of those holes in a mood comparable only to Norton's golfing moods at their highest. Artificiality had gone from him; he was boyishly intent upon his score, but he radiated a new placidity and a dignified resignation which did much to restore the sinking spirits of his loyal mates. The lines receded from his mouth, his eyes betokened retrospective fancies, not of grief; he was the Norton of old, a trifle repressed, but the merest trifle; and the repression was amiable, and complaisant. In particular, his attitude toward his caddy was rather extraordinarily benign; and Hazzard was all the more amazed, because the stupidity of that dirt-encrusted gamin had cost Norton two unnecessary strokes.

Norton got his four, another four, and had the eighteenth left to play, par three for seventy-nine. This terminal hole was two hundred and ten yards, a bothersome carry over the most treacherous of pits – a great crevasse of fine and shifting sand – and it had outposts of lesser pits to guard it. At the rear, there was a shelving bank inclining to a weed-infested pond; to the left, the roadway; and to the right, impenetrable swamps. The wind, which had grown to threatening proportions, swept at right-angles across the line of play, constructively lengthening the distance. Norton wavered, and exhaled stupendously.

'This is the only favor I've asked,' he said. 'I do want a three . . . let me drive last. Does anybody mind?'

He was manifestly composed, and his will was indomitable, but no amount of dogma could controvert the fact that he had come to the final hole of the final round. Chance and the wind combined to make it a severer test than he had expected. That hole had become the very apotheosis of golf; it was the ultimate examination of his prowess. And Norton, lingering there under gray skies, a man with fifty thousand holes already scored, and one to play, was shaken not so much by the drama of the hole as by the dramatic value of his own thoughts; he wasn't pitying himself as much as he was allowing the justification he had to be pitied. It was, he thought, a smashing, spectacular sort of climax – the scudding clouds, the wind, the frowning pits, the pond – and par three needed for the seventy-nine craved.

Kingsland blundered in sparing the cleek, and Norton leaned far forward to analyze the flight. For a hundred yards the ball engaged to journey far and sure, but of a sudden it was checked, it submitted weakly, it dropped in docile impotence to the hugest pit, twenty degrees off its bearings, and short by a hundred feet.

'More to the left,' said Norton half-aloud. 'And a full swing.'

Peters glowered, and tried the spoon. He was a slugger, Peters, and in playing prepensely to the left, he hit hard from a medium tee; but the ball had not yet reached its fullest height when Norton could predict its landing.

'That's short, too!' he muttered. Indeed, it also buried itself in granular sand.

Hazzard, relying on the brassey, essayed to snatch advantage from the wind, but he used a tee so low that the ball, taking no impertinence from the weather, landed fairly on the green, bounded once and twice, and splashed in the waters of the further pond. It was Norton's shot.

As he advanced to drive, he was attacked by a convulsive twitching of the muscles which brought him near to apoplexy. The entire purport of his undertaking was centered on this paramount eighteenth hole; he had seen three well-hit drives fall into trouble; he had seen what unparagoned execution was demanded of a man who would hole his putt for a model three. And Norton longed for that card of seventy-nine; he had adjured himself that if, in his sore predicament, he could break eighty for this pregnant round, he would be content. To break eighty was to triumph over mind and body; it would salve his coming disability, and give oblivion a cud to chew on. And to a man of his mature attainments, a dreadful gulf lies between seventy-nine and eighty; it is a difference which no layman can find transparent; but to a golfer it represents a variation tenfold greater than its arithmetic. It seemed to him that never since he was born had he yearned for anything as now he yearned for that all but insuperable par.

Beyond the pit, and verging to the confines of the green, there was an arid quarter acre of pebbly soil. Ladies and timorous men of 18-handicap played conspicuously for it, and used a niblick for the second shot, and not infrequently arrived at the tin in four. Norton, if unadventurous, could get an eighty; he would have wagered every penny of his resources that he could do no worse. If he used wood, and overdrove, like Hazzard, he could foresee no better fortune than five for an eighty-one. If he were bold, but fraternized with Peters and Kingsland in the sand, he might conceivably take five, or six, or seven, since the pit was craftily constructed, both in shape and substance. So that Norton's talent was on trial, and his acumen as well; he must elect his policy, and take a certain four, or chance his three, and run the risk of strokes unlimited in number. And as he balanced one alternative against the other, the dead weight of the crisis fell upon and harrowed him. He was in a ghastly quandary; the intrinsic value of that eighteen hole as a criterion of golf was trivial in comparison with its emphasis as a meridian. It was the culmination of fifty thousand holes.

Norton glanced at his caddy, who was disputing vigorously but inaudibly with his chums.

'Better play safe, Billy,' said Kingsland.

'Aw, I betcha!' shrilled Norton's caddy, stung to resonance.

'Boy!' snapped Peters ominously.

'He ain't no quitter! A nickel he gets a three!'

'*Caddy!*' roared Kingsland.

'Brassey,' said Norton. 'Give me the brassey.'

A chorus of protests rose in opposition.

'Billy – don't! Play it safe!'

'You'll have to sky it – and listen to that wind!'

'Play short, Billy – use common-sense! Take your eighty! That's good enough!'

'Brassey,' said Norton, pluckily. 'If it's the last hole I'll ever play, I'm going to play it right.'

His voice contained the least imaginable tremor; but his heart was pounding precariously, and for the first time this afternoon, he was physically racked – so wrung with torment that, as he took his stance, he doubted if he could even swing the club. Lights danced before his eyes, and roaring echoes filled his ears; he had no stomach, and his arms and wrists and shoulders quaked in synchronism with his knees. The wind was tugging strongly at his coat; he felt powerless to withstand it by any effort of his own. The green was so very, very distant.... Norton gulped, and dried his palms on his handkerchief.

What he wanted was a three, no more, no less. A four would satisfy him no better than a seven, or a seventeen. He had published his intention to break eighty, and until he had played his seventy-ninth stroke without holding out, he would still direct his inexorable perseverance to that one resolve. But struggle as he would, Norton couldn't separate himself from the tragedy which was crushing him with every clock-tick. The desperate catastrophe of the thing was what unmanned him; after this eighteenth hole he was through with golf, expatriated, superannuated. He was to be torn incontinently from his passion; he was condemned to be at best a listener, and a raconteur. He, the general who had harkened to the applause of a multitude, was reduced to the ranks; he was swaying on the last tee, he had teed the last ball, he was facing the last hole. A choking sob caught in his throat, and lead was in his breast. He was strangled, suffocated; and, concurrently, nauseated by the tumult within himself.

'This is the ... the finish,' he whispered.

He drew an imaginary line to the left of the green, and gave the wind the benefit of another point; he teed perilously high. Then judgment failed him, and his motor impulses assumed authority. He addressed the ball; confirmed his direction; smiled with a curiously repulsive grimace; and swung; and as his body completed the follow-through, he dropped the club because his hands were no longer able to hold it. He had reached the uttermost limit of his endurance.

The ball, against a background of lofty trees, was flying geometrically to the line. It was billeted for the road, and out of bounds, unless a miracle intervened, and Hazzard, white-lipped, raised his hand in quite involuntary supplication.

'She's coming around!' yelled Peters, snatching at Kingsland's elbow.

'You're *on*!' bawled Kingsland, tearing himself loose.

'Look!' said Hazzard, pointing shakily. 'L – look – look!'

The ball had landed ten yards short, and ricochetted toward the hole; slower and slower it spun; it brought up against the pin, caromed off, and lay there, glistening in the pale sunlight six inches from the cup.

Three frenzied maniacs surrounded Norton, pumping his hand and howling incoherent delight. Forgetful of his weakness – and he himself forgot it for a time – they pummeled him until he cried for mercy.

'You almost got a *one*!' shrieked Hazzard. 'A *one*! You missed it by an *inch*!'

'A wonderful shot – wonderful!'

'Let him alone – let him alone!' pleaded Kingsland. 'He's got a putt yet – come on!'

They raced down toward the pits as rapidly as Norton could run – afterwards he realized that he had been fool-hardy, but this was no occasion for squeamishness. They gained the green, and saw that Norton's ball was a narrow hand's breadth from the haven of the hole.

'I – I never made a one in my life,' he said ecstatically.

'I *wish* you'd got it!' mourned Hazzard. 'But, my Lord!'

'I don't,' said Norton, transported. 'I'd – it would have been a *horrible* fluke—'

'And instead of that,' put in Kingsland excitedly, 'it was just a beautiful, beautiful drive. . . .'

'It's a discreeminating seventy-eight,' said Peters.

Norton guffawed feverishly.

'Not yet, I – I may miss the putt!'

'Yes – it's likely!'

'Take your time, Billy! Sink it, now!'

'Just a minute,' said Norton. He walked impetuously to the grinning boy who had sponsored him and insured his victory. 'Now then, caddy,' said Norton, 'loan me your putter, will you? One putt, and I'll give it back to you.' He broke out laughing at the boy's bewilderment. 'I won't ever need 'em any more,' he added. 'They're yours – and there's some balls in the pocket, too. You can call it your war cross if you want to . . . don't look so rattled. . . . I'm making you a present . . . now loan me that putter!'

And tapped the ball for his seventy-eight, and a birdie to close the chapter.

In the clubhouse, when Norton was reclining, woefully exhausted in a leather chair, and avowing to himself that the doctors were indubitably sound in their decree, Hazzard came to him, and clasped his hand tightly, and showed by the futility of his speech what affection he had for Norton.

'But I'd give anything I own,' he concluded, 'to have seen you make a one on that last hole. I would, really.'

Norton smiled in the beatitude of golden reminiscence.

'Well, Bunker,' he said, languidly, 'that's one way of looking at it – but consider the other side. It's all over – *finis coronat* Norton! And when I think about it, I can remember always and always that I wound up with a birdie . . . and nothing could be pleasanter than that. But . . . well, how'd *you* feel if you'd been in my shoes today? As it is, people will know I broke eighty. I hadn't played for weeks and weeks, and I wasn't very fit – and I broke eighty. That's all they'll say. I broke eighty. And … how would it be if people said: "Hear about Billy Norton's finish? Luck of the devil, wasn't it? *But he always was lucky, wasn't he?*" '

'Then … then you must have *wanted* that ball to stay out of the cup … when it was coming so close. That's funny. I—'

'I prayed for it to stay out,' said Norton simply. 'I prayed for it … *a one isn't golf!*' He leaned back wearily, and closed his eyes. Hazzard, after a moment, moved stealthily away. A mile to the northward, a tousled caddy was displaying a kit of clubs in a wondrous bag to a mother who was charmed and proud, and most inquisitive.

'But *why*?' she persisted. 'What d'you *do*? He must 'a' had *some* reason.'

'I dunno,' said the caddy, reciprocally dazzled and nonplussed. 'I dunno. He's a peacherino – he shot a seventy-eight. I didn't do nothin'. He just give 'em to me!'

BERNARD DARWIN

THE WOODEN PUTTER

IT WAS NOT for want of clubs that Mr Polwinkle's handicap obstinately refused to fall below 16. His rack full of them extended round three sides of the smoking room. In addition, there was an enormous box resembling a sarcophagus on the floor, and in one corner was a large loose heap of clubs. To get one out of the heap without sending the others crashing to the ground was as delicate and difficult as a game of spillikins, and the housemaid had bestowed on it many an early-morning malediction.

The rack along one side of the wall was clearly of a peculiarly sacred character. The clips holding the clubs were of plush, and behind each clip there was pasted on the wall an inscription in Mr Polwinkle's meticulously neat handwriting. There was a driver stated to have belonged to the great James Braid; a mashie of J. H. Taylor's; a spoon of Herd's.

Nor were illustrious amateurs unrepresented; indeed, these were the greatest treasures in Mr Polwinkle's collection, because they had been harder to come by. The mid-iron had quite a long pedigree, passing through a number of obscure and intermediate stages, and ending in a blaze of glory with the awful name of Mr John Ball, who was alleged once to have played a shot with it at the request of an admirer. A putting cleek with a rather long, old-fashioned head and a battered grip bore the scrupulous inscription: ATTRIBUTED TO THE LATE MR F. G. TAIT.

Mr Polwinkle always sighed when he came to that cleek. Its authenticity was, he had to admit, doubtful. There were so many Freddie Tait putters. Half the clubhouses in England seemed to possess one; they could hardly all be genuine. His Hilton he no longer even pretended to believe in.

'I bought that,' he would say, 'when I was a very young collector, and I'm afraid I was imposed upon.' But, at any rate, there was no doubt about his latest acquisition, before which he now paused lovingly. Here was the whole story, written down by a man, who knew another man, who knew the people with whom Mr Wethered had been staying. Mr Wethered had overslept himself, packed up his clubs in a hurry, and left his irons behind; so he had borrowed this one, and had graciously remarked that it was a very nice one.

It must not be supposed that Mr Polwinkle was ever so daring as to play with these sacred clubs. He contented himself with gazing and, on rare occasions, with a reverent waggle.

Mr Polwinkle, as I have said, was not a good player. He was aware of not playing consistently up to his 16-handicap. If he did not always insist on his rights of giving two strokes to his friend Buffery, he might. He was conscious, having suffered the indignity of being beaten level by an 18-handicap player; and with all this nonsense about scratch scores and a raising of the standard, he saw before him the horrid certainty of soon being 18 himself.

This evening he was feeling particularly depressed. It had been a bad day. Buffery had won by five and four without using either of his strokes, and had hinted pretty strongly that he did not propose to accept them any more. Confound the tactless creature!

Mr Polwinkle tried to soothe himself by looking at his treasures; Ah! If only he could just for one day be endued with the slash and power of those who had played with them. If only something of their virtue could have passed into their clubs, what a splendid heritage! Such a miracle might even be possible if he had but faith enough. Coué-suggestion – better and better and better – how wonderful it would be!

Suddenly he felt a glow of new hope and inspiration. Greatly daring, he took from the rack the driver 'WITH WHICH' as the inscription lyrically proclaimed 'JAMES BRAID WON THE CHAMPIONSHIP AT PRESTWICK IN 1908, WITH THE UNEXAMPLED SCORE OF 291; EIGHT STROKES BETTER THAN THE SECOND SCORE, AND PLAYING SUCH GOLF AS HAD NEVER BEEN SEEN BEFORE ON THAT CLASSIC GOLF COURSE.'

He took one glance to see that his feet were in the right place – long practice enabled him to judge to an inch of the position in which the furniture was safe – and then he swung.

Gracious goodness! What had happened? Back went the club, instinct with speed and power, and he felt a violent and unaccustomed wrenching round of his hips. Down it came more swiftly than ever, his knees seemed to crumple under him with the vehemence of the blow, and swish went the clubhead, right out and round in a glorious finish. A shower of glass fell all over him and he was left in darkness.

Never had he experienced anything before in the least like that tremendous sensation; the electric light had always been perfectly safe. With trembling fingers he struck a match and groped his way, crunching glass as he walked, to the two candles on the chimney piece. Once more he swung the club up; then paused at the top of the swing, as he had done so many hundreds of times before, and gazed at himself in the glass. Could it really be?

He rushed to the bookshelf; tore down *Advanced Golf,*

turned to the appropriate page, and again allowed the club to swing and wrench him in its grip. There could be no doubt about it. Allowing for differences of form and feature he was Braid to the very life – the poise, the turn of the body, the very knuckles – all were the same.

The miracle had happened with one club. Would it happen with all? Out came the Taylor mashie from the rack. As he picked it up his head seemed to shake formidably, his wrists felt suddenly as if they were made of whipcord, his boots seemed to swell and clutch the ground; another second – crash! – down came the club and out came a divot of carpet, hurtling across the room while Mr Polwinkle's eyes were fixed in a burning and furious gaze on the gaping rent that was left.

Then it really was all right. If he could swing the club like the great masters, he could surely hit the ball like them, and the next time he played Buffery, by Jove, it would not be only two strokes he could give him.

He was in the middle of being Mr Wethered when the door opened and Buffery walked in. Mr Polwinkle had got his feet so wide apart in his admirable impersonation that he could not move; for a perceptible moment he could only straddle and stare.

'They told me you were in, old chap,' began Buffery, 'so I just walked in. What on earth are you at? I always said that light would get it in the neck some day!' Buffery's heartiness, though well meant, was sometimes hard to bear. 'However, he went on, while Mr Polwinkle was still speechless, 'what I came about was this. You remember you said you'd come down to Sandwich with me some day. Well, I suddenly find I can get off for three days. Will you come?'

Mr Polwinkle hesitated a moment. He did not feel very kindly disposed toward Buffery. He should like to practice

his new styles a little before crushing him; but still, Sandwich! And he had never seen it.

'All right,' he said; 'I'll come.'

'Topping!' cried Buffery. 'We'll have some great matches,
and I'm going to beat you level – you see if I don't!'

Mr Polwinkle gathered himself together for an effort.

'I will give you,' he said slowly and distinctly, 'a stroke a
hole, and I'll play you for' – and he hesitated on the brink
of something still wilder – 'five pounds!'

Buffery guffawed with laughter. He had never heard Mr
Polwinkle make so good a joke before.

The next evening saw them safely arrived and installed at the
Bell. The journey, though slow, had been for Mr Polwinkle
full of romance. When he changed at Minster he snuffed the
air and thought that already he could smell the sea. His mind
was a jumble of old championships and of the wondrous
shots he was going to play on the morrow. At dinner he managed to make Buffery understand that he really did mean to
give him a stroke a hole. And Buffery, when at last convinced
that it was not a joke, merely observed that a fiver would be
a pleasant little help toward his expenses.

After dinner he felt too restless and excited to sit still, and
leaving Buffery to play bridge, wandered stealthily into the
hall to see if his precious clubs were safe. He felt a momentary shiver of horror when he found someone examining his
bag. Had news of the match been spread abroad? Was this a
backer of Buffery's tampering with his clubs?

No; he appeared a harmless, friendly creature, and apologized very nicely. He was merely, he said, amusing himself
by looking at the different sets of clubs.

'You've got some jolly good ones,' he went on, making Mr
Polwinkle blush with pleasure. 'And look here, your mashie

and mine might be twins – they're as like as two peas!' And he produced his own from a neighboring bag. They certainly were exactly alike; both bore the signature of their great maker; in weight and balance they were identical. 'Taylor used to play with mine himself,' said Mr Polwinkle in a voice of pride and awe. 'And this is Herd's spoon, and here's a putter of . . .'

'I expect he'd have played just as well with mine,' cut in the stranger – Jones was the unobtrusive name on his bag – with regrettable flippancy. 'Anyhow, they're both good clubs. Wish I could play like Taylor with mine. Well, I'm going to turn in early – good night!'

Mr Polwinkle, a little sad that Jones did not want to hear all about his collection, fastened up his bag, and thought he would go to bed, too. He lay awake for some time, for the cocks crow as persistently by night in the town of Sandwich as the larks sing by day upon the links; moreover he was a little excited. Still, he slept at last, and dreamed of mashie shots with so much backspin on them that they pitched on Prince's and came back into the hole on St George's.

'Well,' said Buffery, as they stood next morning on the first tee at St George's, 'it's your honor – you're the giver of strokes,' he added in a rather bitter tone.

Mr Polwinkle took out the Braid driver with as nonchalant an air as he could muster. He could not help feeling horribly frightened, but no doubt the club would help him through. He gave one waggle with the menacing little shake of the club that Walton Heath knows so well, and then the ball sped away an incredible distance. It was far over the 'kitchen,' that grassy hollow that has caught and stopped so many hundreds of balls; but it had a decided hook on it, and ran on and on till it finished in the rough on the left.

One of the caddies gave a prolonged whistle of surprise and admiration. Who was this new, unknown, and infinitely mild-looking champion who made the club hum through the air like a hornet? Buffery, too, was palpably taken aback.

'I say, old chap,' he remarked, 'you seem to have been putting a lot on to your drive. Was that what you had up your sleeve?'

However, he managed to hit a very decent shot himself into the kitchen, and then, narrowly escaping that trappy little bunker on the right with his second, lay in a good strategic position in front of the big cross bunker.

Meanwhile, Mr Polwinkle was following up his own vast tee shot in an agitated state of mind. Of course, he reflected, Braid can hook. It was, he had read, the one human weakness to which the great man was occasionally prone, but it seemed hard that this should be the occasion. The ball lay very heavy in the rough, and worse than all he had only his own niblick, with which he was singularly ineffective. He had once had the chance of acquiring a genuine Ray, but niblicks were clumsy, ugly things and did not interest him. Why had he been such a fool?

His first effort was a lamentable top. His second only just got the ball out of the rough, with a gaping wound in its vitals. Still, there was a hope if Herd's spoon would behave itself as it should, and he addressed himself to the shot with a desperate composure.

Heavens, what was the matter with him? Was he never going to hit the ball? He felt himself growing dizzy with all those waggles, a fierce little glance at the hole between each of them. There could be no possible doubt that this spoon was a genuine Herd. Just as he felt that he must scream if it went on much longer, up went the club; and away went the ball – the most divine spoon shot ever seen – cut up into the wind to perfection. The ball pitched over the bunker, gave a dying kick or two; and lay within a yard of the hole.

Even the ranks of Tuscany could scarce forbear to cheer. 'Good shot!' growled Buffery grudgingly.

That was four – he would be down in five. The enemy with his stroke had three for the hole, but the big cross bunker yawned between him and the green. Drat the man, he had not topped it. He had pitched well over, and his approach putt lay so dead that Mr Polwinkle, though in no generous mood, had to give it to him. One down.

At the second hole at Sandwich, as all the world knows, there is a long and joyous carry from the tee. A really fine shot will soar over the bunker and the hilltop beyond, and the ball will be in a little green valley, to be pitched home on to the green; but the short driver must make a wide tack to the right and will have a more difficult second.

Buffery, inspired by his previous win despite his opponent's mighty drive, decided to 'go for it.' And plump went his ball into the bunker.

The Braid driver was on its best behavior this time – a magnificent shot, straight as an arrow and far over the hill.

'H'm,' said Buffery, looking discontentedly at the face of his driver. 'Is that any new patent kind of ball you are playing with?'

'No,' returned Mr Polwinkle funnily. 'You can weigh it after the round if you like.' And they walked on in stony silence.

Buffery had to hack his ball out backward, and his third was away to the right of the green.

'Just a little flick with the mashie, sir,' said Mr Polwinkle's caddie, putting the club in his hand.

He took the mashie, but somehow he did not feel

comfortable. He shifted and wriggled, and finally his eye was high in the heavens long before the ball was struck. When he looked down to earth again he found the ball had only moved about three yards forward – a total and ignominious fluff. He tried again; another fluff moved it forward but a few painful inches; again, and a third precisely similar shot deposited it in the bunker in front of his nose. Then he went berserk with his niblick, irretrievably ruined a second new ball and gave up the hole.

'Let me look at the mashie!' he said to his caddie as he walked on toward the next tee – and after microscopically examining its head; 'I see what it is!' he exclaimed, in frantic accents. 'It's that fellow – what's his damned name, who was looking at my clubs last night – he's mixed them up. He's got my mashie and I've got his! Do you know Mr Jones by sight?' And he turned to his caddie.

'Yes, sir. I knows him. And that's a funny thing if you've got his mashie. I was just thinking to myself that them shots of yours was just like what he plays. "Joneses," his friends call them. He'll play like a blooming pro, for a bit, and then fluff two or three . . .'

'Where is he now? Is he in front of us?' Mr Polwinkle interrupted. Yes, Jones had started some time ago.

'Then run as hard as you can and tell him I'm playing an important match and insist on having my mashie back Quick now, run!' as the caddie was going to say something. 'I'll carry the clubs!' And the caddie disappeared reluctantly in the sand hills.

'Bad luck, old man!' said Buffery, his complacency restored by that wonderfully soothing medicine of two holes up. 'But I'll tell you where to go. Now this is the Sahara. The hole's over there,' pointing to the left, 'but it's too long a carry for you and me – we must go round to the right.'

'Which line would Braid take?' asked Mr Polwinkle. 'Straight at the flag, would he? Then I shall go straight for the flag!'

'Please yourself!' answered Buffery with a shrug, and played away to the right – a mild little shot and rather sliced, but still clear of the sand. Mr Polwinkle followed with another superb tee shot. Far over all that tumultuous mass of rolling sand hills the ball flew, and was last seen swooping down on to the green. Buffery's second was weak and caught in the hollow; his third was half topped and ran well past; his fourth put him within a yard or so of the hole.

The best he could do would be a five, and all the while there stood Mr Polwinkle, calm, silent, and majestic six yards from the flag in one. He had only to get down in two putts to win the hole; but he had not had a putt, and which putter was he to use – the Tait or the Harry Vardon? He decided on the Tait. A moment later he wished he had not, for his putt was the feeblest imaginable, and the ball finished a good five feet short. Still he persevered, and again was pitifully short.

'By Jove, that's a let-off, old chap!' said the tactless one, and popped his own ball into the hole.

'I'll give you that one!' He added magnanimously, and picked up Mr Polwinkle's ball, which was reposing some three inches from the hole.

'I was always afraid it was a forgery!' murmured Mr Polwinkle, mechanically accepting the ball. 'Freddie Tait was never short with his putts – the books all say that!'

Buffery looked at him wonderingly, opened his mouth as if to make some jocular comment, then thought better of it and led the way to the tee.

Much the same thing happened at the fourth. Two magnicent shots by Braid and Herd respectively, right up to the edge of the little plateau, where it stands defiantly with the black railings in the background; a series of four scrambles and scuffles by Buffery, which just escaped perdition. Two for the hole again, and this time the Vardon putter was tried. The first putt was beautiful. How sweetly and smoothly and with what a free wrist it was taken back! The ball, perfectly struck, seemed in, then it just slipped past and lay two feet away.

'Ah!' he said to himself with a long sigh of satisfaction, 'at any rate this is genuine!'

Alas! It was but too true, for when it came to the short putt, Mr Polwinkle's wrist seemed suddenly to become locked, there was a quick little jerk of the club and – yes, somehow or other the ball had missed the hole. Buffery was down in his two putts again; and it was another halve, this time in five to six.

'I ought to have been all square by now if I could have putted as well as an old lady with a broomstick!' said poor Mr Polwinkle.

'Well, I like that!' answered the other truculently. 'I ought to have been four up if I could have played a decent second either time!' And this time there was a lasting silence.

Mr Polwinkle felt depressed and miserable. Still his heart rose a little when he contemplated the bunker that had to be carried from the tee at the fifth, and beyond it the formidable Maiden with its black terraces. And, sure enough, Buffery got into the bunker in three – not into the black terraces, because, sad to say, men do not now play over the Maiden's crown, but only over the lower spurs – touching, as it were, but the skirts of her sandy garment. Still, he was in the bunker, and Mr Polwinkle had only a pitch to reach the green. Here it was that he wanted a good caddie to put an iron in his hand – to put anything there but the mashie that had played him false. But Mr Polwinkle was flustered.

'After all,' he thought, 'a mashie is a mashie, even if it is not a genuine Taylor, and if I keep my eye on the ball...'

Clean off the socket this time the ball flew away toward cover point, and buried itself in a clump of bents. Why did he not deem it unplayable, I do not know. But since Mr Horace Hutchinson once ruined a medal round and probably lost the St George's Vase at the Maiden by forgetting that he could tee and lose two, Mr Polwinkle may be forgiven. When his ball ultimately emerged from the bents he had played five; they holed out in nine apiece, for Buffery had also had his adventures and the stroke settled in. Three down.

Worse was to come, for at the sixth Buffery had the impudence to get a three – a perfect tee shot and two putts; no one could give a stroke to that. At the seventh Mr Polwinkle, club in hand, walked forward with elaborate care to survey the ground, walked backward, his eye still fixed on the green – and heeled his ball smartly backward like a rugby forward. For a moment he was bewildered. Then he looked at his club. His Wethered iron! Of course. It was the tragedy of the Open Championship at St Andrews over again!

At Hades his Vardon putter again misbehaved at short range, and Mr Polwinkle looked at it reproachfully.

'I always thought it belonged to a bad period!' he groaned, remembering some of those tragic years in which the greatest of all golfers could do everything but hole a yard putt. He would use the Vardon no more. But, then, what on earth was he to putt with? He tried the pseudo-Tait again at the ninth, and by dint of taking only three putts got a half; but still he was six down.

There was one ray of comfort. There was his caddie waiting for him, having no doubt run the villain Jones to earth, and under his arm protruded the handle of a club.

'Well,' he shouted, 'have you got it?'

'No, sir,' the caddie answered – and embarrassment and amusement seemed to struggle together in his voice. 'Mr Jones says he's playing an important match, too, and as you didn't send back his mashie he's going on with yours. Said they were just the same, he did, and he wouldn't know any difference between yours and his own.'

'Then what's that club you've got there?' demanded Mr Polwinkle.

'The gentleman lent you this to make up, so he said,' the caddie replied, producing a wooden putter. 'I was particularly to tell you it belonged to someone who used it in a great match, and blessed if I haven't forgotten who it was.'

Mr Polwinkle took the putter in his hand and could not disguise from himself that it had no apparent merits of any description. The shaft was warped, not bent in an upward curve as a well-bred wooden putter should be, and decidedly springy; no name whatever was discernible on the head. Still, he badly needed a putter and if it had been used by an eminent hand . . .

'Think, man, think!' he exclaimed vehemently. 'You must remember!' But the caddie racked his brain in vain. And then . . .

'Really,' said Buffery, 'we can't wait all day while your caddie tries to remember ancient history. This is the match we're thinking about, and I'm six up!' And he drove off – a bad hook into the thick and benty rough on the left.

And now, thank goodness, I have reached the end of Mr Polwinkle's misfortunes. The tide is about to turn. At the second shot Mr Wethered's iron, I regret to have to say, made another error. It just pulled the ball into the horrid trappy bunker that waits voraciously at the left-hand corner of the plateau green – and that after Buffery had played three and was not on the green.

Mr Polwinkle's temper had been badly shaken once or twice, and now it gave out entirely.

'Give me any dashed club you like!' he snarled, seized the first that came handy and plunged into the bunker.

'Good sort of club to get out of a bunker with!' he said to himself, finding that he had a mid-iron in his hand, and then – out came the ball, as if it was the easiest thing in the world, and sat down within four yards of the hole.

How had it happened? Why, it was Mr Ball's iron – and did not the hero of Hoylake habitually pitch out of bunkers with a straight-faced iron? Of course he did – and played his ordinary pitches with it as well. What a thing it was to know history! Here at once was a magic niblick and a substitute for the mashie rolled into one. And just then his caddie smacked himself loudly and suddenly on the thigh.

'I've remembered it, sir. It was Tommy something – young Tommy, I think.'

'Young Tom Morris?' gasped Mr Polwinkle breathlessly.

'Ah!' said caddie. 'Morris – that was it!'

'Give me the wooden putter!' said Mr Polwinkle – and the ball rattled against the back of the tin. That was a four against Buffery's six. Down to five with eight to play.

It is a well-known fact that when golf is faultless there is next to nothing to write about it. The golfing reporter may say that So-and-So pushed his drive and pulled his second; but the real fact is that the great So-and-So was on the course with his tee shot, on the green with his second, and down in two putts – and kept on doing it. That is all the reporter need have said but he says more because he has his living to earn. So have I; but, nevertheless, I shall not describe Mr Polwinkle's homecoming at full length. More brilliantly faultless golf never was seen. Braid drove magnificently, Mr Ball did all the pitching to perfection and even Mr Wethered behaved impeccably. As for the wooden putter, most of the putts went in, and even those that did not gave Buffery a cold shiver down his spine. What could poor 18-handicap Buffery do against it? He must need wilt under such an onslaught. If he did a respectable five, Mr Polwinkle did a 'birdie' three. If he did a long hole in six, as he did at the Suez Canal, that wooden putter holed one for a four.

Here, for those who know the course, are the figures of Mr Polwinkle's first eight holes coming home: four, three, three, four, four, four, two, four. That was enough. Buffery was a crushed man; hole after hole slipped away, and when he had reached the 17th green in eight, there was nothing for it but to give up the match. Six up at the turn and beaten by two and one!

As Mr Polwinkle walked triumphantly into the clubhouse he met Jones, and almost fell on his neck.

'My dear fellow,' he cried, 'I can't thank you enough for that putter. I holed everything. Never saw anything like it! I suppose,' he went on with a sudden desperate boldness, 'there's no chance of your selling it me, is there?'

'Oh no, I won't sell it!' began Jones.

'I knew it was too much to ask!' said Mr Polwinkle dejectedly.

'But I'll give it to you with pleasure!'

'Oh, but I couldn't let you do that! Give me it for nothing – a putter that belonged to young Tommy – the greatest putter that ever . . .'

'Well, you see,' said Jones, 'I only told the caddie to tell you that because I thought it might put you on your putting. And, by George, it seems to have done it, too. Wonderful what a little confidence will do. You're perfectly welcome to the putter – I bought it in a toy shop for 18 pence!'

Mr Polwinkle fell swooning to the floor.

F. SCOTT FITZGERALD

WINTER DREAMS

SOME OF THE caddies were poor as sin and lived in one-room houses with a neurasthenic cow in the front yard, but Dexter Green's father owned the second best grocery-store in Black Bear – the best one was 'The Hub,' patronized by the wealthy people from Sherry Island – and Dexter caddied only for pocket-money.

In the fall when the days became crisp and gray, and the long Minnesota winter shut down like the white lid of a box, Dexter's skis moved over the snow that hid the fairways of the golf course. At these times the country gave him a feeling of profound melancholy – it offended him that the links should lie in enforced fallowness, haunted by ragged sparrows for the long season. It was dreary, too, that on the tees where the gay colors fluttered in summer there were now only the desolate sand-boxes knee-deep in crusted ice. When he crossed the hills the wind blew cold as misery, and if the sun was out he tramped with his eyes squinted up against the hard dimensionless glare.

In April the winter ceased abruptly. The snow ran down into Black Bear Lake scarcely tarrying for the early golfers to brave the season with red and black balls. Without elation, without an interval of moist glory, the cold was gone.

Dexter knew that there was something dismal about this Northern spring, just as he knew there was something gorgeous about the fall. Fall made him clinch his hands and tremble and repeat idiotic sentences to himself, and make brisk abrupt gestures of command to imaginary audiences and armies. October filled him with hope which November raised to a sort of ecstatic triumph, and in this mood the fleeting brilliant impressions of the summer at Sherry Island were ready grist to his mill. He became a golf champion and defeated Mr T. A. Hedrick in a marvelous match played a hundred times over the fairways of his imagination, a match each detail of which he changed about untiringly – sometimes he won with almost laughable ease, sometimes he came up magnificently from behind. Again, stepping from a Pierce-Arrow automobile, like Mr Mortimer Jones, he strolled frigidly into the lounge of the Sherry Island Golf Club – or perhaps, surrounded by an admiring crowd, he gave an exhibition of fancy diving from the spring-board of the club raft. . . . Among those who watched him in open-mouthed wonder was Mr Mortimer Jones.

And one day it came to pass that Mr Jones – himself and not his ghost – came up to Dexter with tears in his eyes and said that Dexter was the — best caddy in the club, and wouldn't he decide not to quit if Mr Jones made it worth his while, because every other — caddy in the club lost one ball a hole for him – regularly –

'No, sir,' said Dexter decisively, 'I don't want to caddy any more.' Then, after a pause: 'I'm too old.'

'You're not more than fourteen. Why the devil did you decide just this morning that you wanted to quit? You promised that next week you'd go over to the State tournament with me.'

'I decided I was too old.'

Dexter handed in his 'A Class' badge, collected what money was due him from the caddy master, and walked home to Black Bear Village.

'The best — caddy I ever saw,' shouted Mr Mortimer Jones over a drink that afternoon. 'Never lost a ball! Willing! Intelligent! Quiet! Honest! Grateful!'

The little girl who had done this was eleven – beautifully ugly as little girls are apt to be who are destined after a few years to be inexpressibly lovely and bring no end of misery to a great number of men. The spark, however, was perceptible. There was a general ungodliness in the way her lips twisted down at the corners when she smiled, and in the – Heaven help us! – in the almost passionate quality of her eyes. Vitality is born early in such women. It was utterly in evidence now, shining through her thin frame in a sort of glow.

She had come eagerly out on to the course at nine o'clock with a white linen nurse and five small new golf-clubs in a white canvas bag which the nurse was carrying. When Dexter first saw her she was standing by the caddy house, rather ill at ease and trying to conceal the fact by engaging her nurse in an obviously unnatural conversation graced by startling and irrelevant grimaces from herself.

'Well, it's certainly a nice day, Hilda,' Dexter heard her say. She drew down the corners of her mouth, smiled, and glanced furtively around, her eyes in transit falling for an instant on Dexter.

Then to the nurse:

'Well, I guess there aren't very many people out here this morning, are there?'

The smile again – radiant, blatantly artificial – convincing.

'I don't know what we're supposed to do now,' said the nurse looking nowhere in particular.

'Oh, that's all right. I'll fix it up.'

Dexter stood perfectly still, his mouth slightly ajar. He knew that if he moved forward a step his stare would be in her line of vision – if he moved backward he would lose his full view of her face. For a moment he had not realized how young she was. Now he remembered having seen her several times the year before – in bloomers.

Suddenly, involuntarily, he laughed, a short abrupt laugh – then, startled by himself, he turned and began to walk quickly away.

'Boy!'

Dexter stopped.

'Boy—'

Beyond question he was addressed. Not only that, but he was treated to that absurd smile, that preposterous smile – the memory of which at least a dozen men were to carry into middle age.

'Boy, do you know where the golf teacher is?'

'He's giving a lesson.'

'Well, do you know where the caddy-master is?'

'He isn't here yet this morning.'

'Oh.' For a moment this baffled her. She stood alternately on her right and left foot.

'We'd like to get a caddy,' said the nurse. 'Mrs Mortimer Jones sent us out to play golf, and we don't know how without we get a caddy.'

Here she was stopped by an ominous glance from Miss Jones, followed immediately by the smile.

'There aren't any caddies here except me,' said Dexter to the nurse, 'and I got to stay here in charge until the caddy-master gets here.'

'Oh.'

Miss Jones and her retinue now withdrew, and at a proper distance from Dexter became involved in a heated conversation, which was concluded by Miss Jones taking one of the clubs and hitting it on the ground with violence. For further emphasis she raised it again and was about to bring it down smartly upon the nurse's bosom, when the nurse seized the club and twisted it from her hands.

'You damn little mean old *thing*!' cried Miss Jones wildly.

Another argument ensued. Realizing that the elements of comedy were implied in the scene, Dexter several times began to laugh, but each time restrained the laugh before it reached audibility. He could not resist the monstrous conviction that the little girl was justified in beating the nurse.

The situation was resolved by the fortuitous appearance of the caddy-master, who was appealed to immediately by the nurse.

'Miss Jones is to have a little caddy, and this one says he can't go.'

'Mr McKenna said I was to wait here till you came,' said Dexter quickly.

'Well, he's here now.' Miss Jones smiled cheerfully at the caddy-master. Then she dropped her bag and set off at a haughty mince toward the first tee.

'Well?' The caddy-master turned to Dexter. 'What you standing there like a dummy for? Go pick up the young lady's clubs.'

'I don't think I'll go out today,' said Dexter.

'You don't—'

'I think I'll quit.'

The enormity of his decision frightened him. He was a favorite caddy, and the thirty dollars a month he earned through the summer were not to be made elsewhere around the lake. But he had received a strong emotional shock, and his perturbation required a violent and immediate outlet.

It is not so simple as that, either. As so frequently would be the case in the future, Dexter was unconsciously dictated to by his winter dreams.

II

Now, of course, the quality and the seasonability of these winter dreams varied, but the stuff of them remained. They persuaded Dexter several years later to pass up a business course at the State university – his father, prospering now, would have paid his way – for the precarious advantage of attending an older and more famous university in the East, where he was bothered by his scanty funds. But do not get the impression, because his winter dreams happened to be concerned at first with musings on the rich, that there was anything merely snobbish in the boy. He wanted not association with glittering things and glittering people – he wanted the glittering things themselves. Often he reached out for the best without knowing why he wanted it – and sometimes he ran up against the mysterious denials and prohibitions in which life indulges. It is with one of those denials and not with his career as a whole that this story deals.

He made money. It was rather amazing. After college he went to the city from which Black Bear Lake draws its wealthy patrons. When he was only twenty-three and had been there not quite two years, there were already people who liked to say: 'Now *there's* a boy—' All about him rich men's sons were peddling bonds precariously, or investing patrimonies precariously, or plodding through the two dozen volumes of the 'George Washington Commercial Course,' but Dexter borrowed a thousand dollars on his college degree and his confident mouth, and bought a partnership in a laundry.

It was a small laundry when he went into it, but Dexter made a specialty of learning how the English washed fine woolen golfstockings without shrinking them, and within a year he was catering to the trade that wore knickerbockers.

Men were insisting that their Shetland hose and sweaters go to his laundry, just as they had insisted on a caddy who could find golf-balls. A little later he was doing their wives' lingerie as well – and running five branches in different parts of the city. Before he was twenty-seven he owned the largest string of laundries in his section of the country. It was then that he sold out and went to New York. But the part of his story that concerns us goes back to the days when he was making his first big success.

When he was twenty-three Mr Hart – one of the gray-haired men who liked to say 'Now there's a boy' – gave him a guest card to the Sherry Island Golf Club for a week-end. So he signed his name one day on the register, and that after-noon played golf in a foursome with Mr Hart and Mr Sand-wood and Mr T. A. Hedrick. He did not consider it necessary to remark that he had once carried Mr Hart's bag over this same links, and that he knew every trap and gully with his eyes shut – but he found himself glancing at the four caddies who trailed them, trying to catch a gleam or gesture that would remind him of himself, that would lessen the gap which lay between his present and his past.

It was a curious day, slashed abruptly with fleeting, famil-iar impressions. One minute he had the sense of being a trespasser – in the next he was impressed by the tremendous superiority he felt toward Mr T. A. Hedrick, who was a bore and not even a good golfer any more.

Then, because of a ball Mr Hart lost near the fifteenth green, an enormous thing happened. While they were search-ing the stiff grasses of the rough there was a clear call of 'Fore!' from behind a hill in their rear. And as they all turned abruptly from their search a bright new ball sliced abruptly over the hill and caught Mr T. A. Hedrick in the abdomen.

'By Gad!' cried Mr T. A. Hedrick, 'they ought to put

some of these crazy women off the course. It's getting to be outrageous.'

A head and a voice came up together over the hill:

'Do you mind if we go through?'

'You hit me in the stomach!' declared Mr Hedrick wildly.

'Did I?' The girl approached the group of men. 'I'm sorry. I yelled "Fore!"'

Her glance fell casually on each of the men – then scanned the fairway for her ball.

'Did I bounce into the rough?'

It was impossible to determine whether this question was ingenuous or malicious. In a moment, however, she left no doubt, for as her partner came up over the hill she called cheerfully:

'Here I am! I'd have gone on the green except that I hit something.'

As she took her stance for a short mashie shot, Dexter looked at her closely. She wore a blue gingham dress, rimmed at throat and shoulders with a white edging that accentuated her tan. The quality of exaggeration, of thinness, which had made her passionate eyes and downturning mouth absurd at eleven, was gone now. She was arrestingly beautiful. The color in her cheeks was centered like the color in a picture – it was not a 'high' color, but a sort of fluctuating and feverish warmth, so shaded that it seemed at any moment it would recede and disappear. This color and the mobility of her mouth gave a continual impression of flux, of intense life, of passionate vitality – balanced only partially by the sad luxury of her eyes.

She swung her mashie impatiently and without interest, pitching the ball into a sand-pit on the other side of the green. With a quick, insincere smile and a careless 'Thank you!' she went on after it.

'That Judy Jones!' remarked Mr Hedrick on the next tee, as they waited – some moments – for her to play on ahead. 'All she needs is to be turned up and spanked for six months and then to be married off to an old-fashioned cavalry captain.'

'My God, she's good-looking!' said Mr Sandwood, who was just over thirty.

'Good-looking!' cried Mr Hedrick contemptuously. 'She always looks as if she wanted to be kissed! Turning those big cow-eyes on every calf in town!'

It was doubtful if Mr Hedrick intended a reference to the maternal instinct.

'She'd play pretty good golf if she'd try,' said Mr Sandwood.

'She has no form,' said Mr Hedrick solemnly.

'She has a nice figure,' said Mr Sandwood.

'Better thank the Lord she doesn't drive a swifter ball,' said Mr Hart, winking at Dexter.

Later in the afternoon the sun went down with a riotous swirl of gold and varying blues and scarlets, and left the dry, rustling night of Western summer. Dexter watched from the veranda of the Golf Club, watched the even overlap of the waters in the little wind, silver molasses under the harvest-moon. Then the moon held a finger to her lips and the lake became a clear pool, pale and quiet. Dexter put on his bathing-suit and swam out to the farthest raft, where he stretched dripping on the wet canvas of the springboard.

There was a fish jumping and a star shining and the lights around the lake were gleaming. Over on a dark peninsula a piano was playing the songs of last summer and of summers before that – songs from 'Chin-Chin' and 'The Count of Luxemburg' and 'The Chocolate Soldier' – and because the sound of a piano over a stretch of water had always seemed beautiful to Dexter he lay perfectly quiet and listened.

The tune the piano was playing at that moment had been gay and new five years before when Dexter was a sophomore at college. They had played it at a prom once when he could not afford the luxury of proms, and he had stood outside the gymnasium and listened. The sound of the tune precipitated in him a sort of ecstasy and it was with that ecstasy he viewed what happened to him now. It was a mood of intense appreciation, a sense that, for once, he was magnificently attuned to life and that everything about him was radiating a brightness and a glamor he might never know again.

A low, pale oblong detached itself suddenly from the darkness of the Island, spitting forth the reverberated sound of a racing motorboat. Two white streamers of cleft water rolled themselves out behind it and almost immediately the boat was beside him, drowning out the hot tinkle of the piano in the drone of its spray. Dexter raising himself on his arms was aware of a figure standing at the wheel, of two dark eyes regarding him over the lengthening space of water – then the boat had gone by and was sweeping in an immense and purposeless circle of spray round and round in the middle of the lake. With equal eccentricity one of the circles flattened out and headed back toward the raft.

'Who's that?' she called, shutting off her motor. She was so near now that Dexter could see her bathing suit, which consisted apparently of pink rompers.

The nose of the boat bumped the raft, and as the latter tilted rakishly he was precipitated toward her. With different degrees of interest they recognized each other.

'Aren't you one of those men we played through this afternoon?' she demanded.

He was.

'Well, do you know how to drive a motorboat? Because if you do I wish you'd drive this one so I can ride on the surfboard behind. My name is Judy Jones' – she favored him with an absurd smirk – rather, what tried to be a smirk, for, twist her mouth as she might, it was not grotesque, it was merely beautiful – 'and I live in a house over there on the Island, and in that house there is a man waiting for me. When he drove up at the door I drove out of the dock because he says I'm his ideal.'

There was a fish jumping and a star shining and the lights around the lake were gleaming. Dexter sat beside Judy Jones and she explained how her boat was driven. Then she was in the water, swimming to the floating surf-board with a sinuous crawl. Watching her was without effort to the eye, watching a branch waving or a sea-gull flying. Her arms, burned to butternut, moved sinuously among the dull platinum ripples, elbow appearing first, casting the forearm back with a cadence of falling water, then reaching out and down, stabbing a path ahead.

They moved out into the lake; turning, Dexter saw that she was kneeling on the low rear of the now uptilted surfboard.

'Go faster,' she called, 'fast as it'll go.'

Obediently he jammed the lever forward and the white spray mounted at the bow. When he looked around again the girl was standing up on the rushing board, her arms spread wide, her eyes lifted toward the moon.

'It's awful cold,' she shouted. 'What's your name?'

He told her.

'Well, why don't you come to dinner tomorrow night?'

His heart turned over like a fly-wheel of the boat, and, for the second time, her casual whim gave a new direction to his life.

III

Next evening while he waited for her to come down-stairs, Dexter peopled the soft deep summer room and the sun-porch that opened from it with the men who had already loved Judy Jones. He knew the sort of men they were – the men who when he first went to college had entered from the great prep schools with graceful clothes and the deep tan of healthy summers. He had seen that, in one sense, he was better than these men. He was newer and stronger. Yet in acknowledging to himself that he wished his children to be like them he was admitting that he was but the rough, strong stuff from which they eternally sprang.

When the time had come for him to wear good clothes, he had known who were the best tailors in America, and the best tailors in America had made him the suit he wore this evening. He had acquired that particular reserve peculiar to his university, that set it off from other universities. He recognized the value to him of such a mannerism and he had adopted it; he knew that to be careless in dress and manner required more confidence than to be careful. But carelessness was for his children. His mother's name had been Krimslich. She was a Bohemian of the peasant class and she had talked broken English to the end of her days. Her son must keep to the set patterns.

At a little after seven Judy Jones came down-stairs. She wore a blue silk afternoon dress, and he was disappointed at first that she had not put on something more elaborate. This feeling was accentuated when, after a brief greeting, she went to the door of a butler's pantry and pushing it open called: 'You can serve dinner, Martha.' He had rather expected that a butler would announce dinner, that there would be a cocktail. Then he put these thoughts behind him as they sat down side by side on a lounge and looked at each other.

'Father and mother won't be here,' she said thoughtfully.

He remembered the last time he had seen her father, and he was glad the parents were not to be here tonight – they might wonder who he was. He had been born in Keeble, a Minnesota village fifty miles farther north, and he always gave Keeble as his home instead of Black Bear Village. Country towns were well enough to come from if they weren't inconveniently in sight and used as footstools by fashionable lakes.

They talked of his university, which she had visited frequently during the past two years, and of the near-by city which supplied Sherry Island with its patrons, and whither Dexter would return next day to his prospering laundries.

During dinner she slipped into a moody depression which gave Dexter a feeling of uneasiness. Whatever petulance she uttered in her throaty voice worried him. Whatever she smiled at – at him, at a chicken liver, at nothing – it disturbed him that her smile could have no root in mirth, or even in amusement. When the scarlet corners of her lips curved down, it was less a smile than an invitation to a kiss.

Then, after dinner, she led him out on the dark sun-porch and deliberately changed the atmosphere.

'Do you mind if I weep a little?' she said.

'I'm afraid I'm boring you,' he responded quickly.

'You're not. I like you. But I've just had a terrible afternoon. There was a man I cared about, and this afternoon he told me out of a clear sky that he was poor as a churchmouse. He'd never even hinted it before. Does this sound horribly mundane?'

'Perhaps he was afraid to tell you.'

'Suppose he was,' she answered. 'He didn't start right. You

see, if I'd thought of him as poor – well, I've been mad about loads of poor men, and fully intended to marry them all. But in this case, I hadn't thought of him that way, and my interest in him wasn't strong enough to survive the shock. As if a girl calmly informed her fiancé that she was a widow. He might not object to widows, but—

'Let's start right,' she interrupted herself suddenly. 'Who are you, anyhow?'

For a moment Dexter hesitated. Then:

'I'm nobody,' he announced. 'My career is largely a matter of futures.'

'Are you poor?'

'No,' he said frankly, 'I'm probably making more money than any man my age in the Northwest. I know that's an obnoxious remark, but you advised me to start right.'

There was a pause. Then she smiled and the corners of her mouth drooped and an almost imperceptible sway brought her closer to him, looking up into his eyes. A lump rose in Dexter's throat, and he waited breathless for the experiment, facing the unpredictable compound that would form mysteriously from the elements of their lips. Then he saw – she communicated her excitement to him, lavishly, deeply, with kisses that were not a promise but a fulfillment. They aroused in him not hunger demanding renewal but surfeit that would demand more surfeit . . . kisses that were like charity, creating want by holding back nothing at all.

It did not take him many hours to decide that he had wanted Judy Jones ever since he was a proud, desirous little boy.

IV

It began like that – and continued, with varying shades of intensity, on such a note right up to the dénouement. Dexter surrendered a part of himself to the most direct and unprincipled personality with which he had ever come in contact. Whatever Judy wanted, she went after with the full pressure of her charm. There was no divergence of method, no jockeying for position or premeditation of effects – there was a very little mental side to any of her affairs. She simply made men conscious to the highest degree of her physical loveliness. Dexter had no desire to change her. Her deficiencies were knit up with a passionate energy that transcended and justified them.

When, as Judy's head lay against his shoulders that first night, she whispered, 'I don't know what's the matter with me. Last night I thought I was in love with a man and tonight I think I'm in love with you—' – it seemed to him a beautiful and romantic thing to say. It was the exquisite excitability that for the moment he controlled and owned. But a week later he was compelled to view this same quality in a different light. She took him in her roadster to a picnic supper, and after supper she disappeared, likewise in her roadster, with another man. Dexter became enormously upset and was scarcely able to be decently civil to the other people present. When she assured him that she had not kissed the other man, he knew she was lying – yet he was glad that she had taken the trouble to lie to him.

He was, as he found before the summer ended, one of a varying dozen who circulated about her. Each of them had at one time been favored above all others – about half of them still basked in the solace of occasional sentimental revivals. Whenever one showed signs of dropping out through long neglect, she granted him a brief honeyed hour, which encouraged him to tag along for a year or so longer. Judy made these forays upon the helpless and defeated without malice, indeed half unconscious that there was anything mischievous in what she did.

When a new man came to town every one dropped out – dates were automatically canceled.

The helpless part of trying to do anything about it was that she did it all herself. She was not a girl who could be 'won' in the kinetic sense – she was proof against cleverness, she was proof against charm; if any of these assailed her too strongly she would immediately resolve the affair to a physical basis, and under the magic of her physical splendor the strong as well as the brilliant played her game and not their own. She was entertained only by the gratification of her desires and by the direct exercise of her own charm. Perhaps from so much youthful love, so many youthful lovers, she had come, in self-defense, to nourish herself wholly from within.

Succeeding Dexter's first exhilaration came restlessness and dissatisfaction. The helpless ecstasy of losing himself in her was opiate rather than tonic. It was fortunate for his work during the winter that those moments of ecstasy came infrequently. Early in their acquaintance it had seemed for a while that there was a deep and spontaneous mutual attraction – that first August, for example – three days of long evenings on her dusky veranda, of strange wan kisses through the late afternoon, in shadowy alcoves or behind the protecting trellises of the garden arbors, of mornings when she was fresh as a dream and almost shy at meeting him in the clarity of the rising day. There was all the ecstasy of an engagement about it, sharpened by his realization that there was no engagement. It was during those three days that, for the first time, he had asked her to marry him. She said 'Maybe some day,' she said 'kiss me,' she said 'I'd like to marry you,' she said 'I love you' – she said – nothing.

The three days were interrupted by the arrival of a New York man who visited at her house for half September. To Dexter's agony, rumor engaged them. The man was the son of the president of a great trust company. But at the end of a month it was reported that Judy was yawning. At a dance one night she sat all evening in a motorboat with a local beau, while the New Yorker searched the club for her frantically. She told the local beau that she was bored with her visitor, and two days later he left. She was seen with him at the station, and it was reported that he looked very mournful indeed.

On this note the summer ended. Dexter was twenty-four, and he found himself increasingly in a position to do as he wished. He joined two clubs in the city and lived at one of them. Though he was by no means an integral part of the stag-lines at these clubs, he managed to be on hand at dances where Judy Jones was likely to appear. He could have gone out socially as much as he liked – he was an eligible young man, now, and popular with down-town fathers. His confessed devotion to Judy Jones had rather solidified his position. But he had no social aspirations and rather despised the dancing men who were always on tap for the Thursday or Saturday parties and who filled in at dinners with the younger married set. Already he was playing with the idea of going East to New York. He wanted to take Judy Jones with him. No disillusion as to the world in which she had grown up could cure his illusion as to her desirability.

Remember that – for only in the light of it can what he did for her be understood.

Eighteen months after he first met Judy Jones he became

engaged to another girl. Her name was Irene Scheerer, and her father was one of the men who had always believed in Dexter. Irene was light-haired and sweet and honorable, and a little stout, and she had two suitors whom she pleasantly relinquished when Dexter formally asked her to marry him.

Summer, fall, winter, spring, another summer, another fall – so much he had given of his active life to the incorrigible lips of Judy Jones. She had treated him with interest, with encouragement, with malice, with indifference, with contempt. She had inflicted on him the innumerable little slights and indignities possible in such a case – as if in revenge for having ever cared for him at all. She had beckoned him and yawned at him and beckoned him again and he had responded often with bitterness and narrowed eyes. She had brought him ecstatic happiness and intolerable agony of spirit. She had caused him untold inconvenience and not a little trouble. She had insulted him, and she had ridden over him, and she had played his interest in her against his interest in his work – for fun. She had done everything to him except to criticize him – this she had not done – it seemed to him only because it might have sullied the utter indifference she manifested and sincerely felt toward him.

When autumn had come and gone again it occurred to him that he could not have Judy Jones. He had to beat this into his mind but he convinced himself at last. He lay awake at night for a while and argued it over. He told himself the trouble and the pain she had caused him, he enumerated her glaring deficiencies as a wife. Then he said to himself that he loved her, and after a while he fell asleep. For a week, lest he imagine her husky voice over the telephone or her eyes opposite him at lunch, he worked hard and late, and at night he went to his office and plotted out his years.

At the end of a week he went to a dance and cut in on her

once. For almost the first time since they had met he did not ask her to sit out with him or tell her that she was lovely. It hurt him that she did not miss these things – that was all. He was not jealous when he saw that there was a new man tonight. He had been hardened against jealousy long before.

He stayed late at the dance. He sat for an hour with Irene Scheerer and talked about books and about music. He knew very little about either. But he was beginning to be master of his own time now, and he had a rather priggish notion that he – the young and already fabulously successful Dexter Green – should know more about such things.

That was in October, when he was twenty-five. In January, Dexter and Irene became engaged. It was to be announced in June, and they were to be married three months later.

The Minnesota winter prolonged itself interminably, and it was almost May when the winds came soft and the snow ran down into Black Bear Lake at last. For the first time in over a year Dexter was enjoying a certain tranquility of spirit. Judy Jones had been in Florida, and afterward in Hot Springs, and somewhere she had been engaged, and some-where she had broken it off. At first, when Dexter had defi-nitely given her up, it had made him sad that people still linked them together and asked for news of her, but when he began to be placed at dinner next to Irene Scheerer people didn't ask him about her any more – they told him about her. He ceased to be an authority on her.

May at last. Dexter walked the streets at night when the darkness was damp as rain, wondering that so soon, with so little done, so much of ecstasy had gone from him. May one year back had been marked by Judy's poignant, unforgivable, yet forgiven turbulence – it had been one of those rare times when he fancied she had grown to care for him. That old penny's worth of happiness he had spent for this bushel of content. He knew that Irene would be no more than a curtain spread behind him, a hand moving among gleaming teacups, a voice calling to children . . . fire and loveliness were gone, the magic of nights and the wonder of the varying hours and seasons . . . slender lips, down-turning, dropping to his lips and bearing him up into a heaven of eyes. . . . The thing was deep in him. He was too strong and alive for it to die lightly.

In the middle of May when the weather balanced for a few days on the thin bridge that led to deep summer he turned in one night at Irene's house. Their engagement was to be announced in a week now – no one would be surprised at it. And tonight they would sit together on the lounge at the University Club and look on for an hour at the dancers. It gave him a sense of solidity to go with her – she was so sturdily popular, so intensely 'great.'

He mounted the steps of the brownstone house and stepped inside.

'Irene,' he called.

Mrs Scheerer came out of the living-room to meet him.

'Dexter,' she said, 'Irene's gone up-stairs with a splitting headache. She wanted to go with you but I made her go to bed.'

'Nothing serious, I—'

'Oh, no. She's going to play golf with you in the morning. You can spare her for just one night, can't you, Dexter?'

Her smile was kind. She and Dexter liked each other. In the living-room he talked for a moment before he said good-night.

Returning to the University Club, where he had rooms, he stood in the doorway for a moment and watched the dancers. He leaned against the door-post, nodded at a man or two – yawned.

'Hello, darling.'

The familiar voice at his elbow startled him. Judy Jones had left a man and crossed the room to him – Judy Jones, a slender enameled doll in cloth of gold: gold in a band at her head, gold in two slipper points at her dress's hem. The fragile glow of her face seemed to blossom as she smiled at him. A breeze of warmth and light blew through the room. His hands in the pockets of his dinner-jacket tightened spasmodically. He was filled with a sudden excitement.

'When did you get back?' he asked casually.

'Come here and I'll tell you about it.'

She turned and he followed her. She had been away – he could have wept at the wonder of her return. She had passed through enchanted streets, doing things that were like provocative music. All mysterious happenings, all fresh and quickening hopes, had gone away with her, come back with her now.

She turned in the doorway.

'Have you a car here? If you haven't, I have.'

'I have a coupé.'

In then, with a rustle of golden cloth. He slammed the door. Into so many cars she had stepped – like this – like that – her back against the leather, so – her elbow resting on the door – waiting. She would have been soiled long since had there been anything to soil her – except herself – but this was her own self outpouring.

With an effort he forced himself to start the car and back into the street. This was nothing, he must remember. She had done this before, and he had put her behind him, as he would have crossed a bad account from his books.

He drove slowly down-town and, affecting abstraction, traversed the deserted streets of the business section, peopled here and there where a movie was giving out its crowd or where consumptive or pugilistic youth lounged in front of pool halls. The clink of glasses and the slap of hands on the bars issued from saloons, cloisters of glazed glass and dirty yellow light.

She was watching closely and the silence was embarrassing, yet in this crisis he could find no casual word with which to profane the hour. At a convenient turning he began to zigzag back toward the University Club.

'Have you missed me?' she asked suddenly.

'Everybody missed you.'

He wondered if she knew of Irene Scheerer. She had been back only a day – her absence had been almost contemporaneous with his engagement.

'What a remark!' Judy laughed sadly – without sadness. She looked at him searchingly. He became absorbed in the dashboard.

'You're handsomer than you used to be,' she said thoughtfully. 'Dexter, you have the most rememberable eyes.'

He could have laughed at this, but he did not laugh. It was the sort of thing that was said to sophomores. Yet it stabbed at him.

'I'm awfully tired of everything, darling.' She called everyone darling, endowing the endearment with careless, individual comradery. 'I wish you'd marry me.'

The directness of this confused him. He should have told her now that he was going to marry another girl, but he could not tell her. He could as easily have sworn that he had never loved her.

'I think we'd get along,' she continued, on the same note, 'unless probably you've forgotten me and fallen in love with another girl.'

Her confidence was obviously enormous. She had said, in effect, that she found such a thing impossible to believe, that if it were true he had merely committed a childish indiscretion – and probably to show off. She would forgive him, because it was not a matter of any moment but rather something to be brushed aside lightly.

'Of course you could never love anybody but me,' she continued, 'I like the way you love me. Oh, Dexter, have you forgotten last year?'

'No, I haven't forgotten.'

'Neither have I!'

Was she sincerely moved – or was she carried along by the wave of her own acting?

'I wish we could be like that again,' she said, and he forced himself to answer:

'I don't think we can.'

'I suppose not. . . . I hear you're giving Irene Scheerer a violent rush.'

There was not the faintest emphasis on the name, yet Dexter was suddenly ashamed.

'Oh, take me home,' cried Judy suddenly; 'I don't want to go back to that idiotic dance – with those children.'

Then, as he turned up the street that led to the residence district, Judy began to cry quietly to herself. He had never seen her cry before.

The dark street lightened, the dwellings of the rich loomed up around them, he stopped his coupé in front of the great white bulk of the Mortimer Joneses' house, somnolent, gorgeous, drenched with the splendor of the damp moonlight. Its solidity startled him. The strong walls, the steel of the girders, the breadth and beam and pomp of it were there only to bring out the contrast with the young beauty beside him. It was sturdy to accentuate her slightness – as if to show what a breeze could be generated by a butterfly's wing.

He sat perfectly quiet, his nerves in wild clamor, afraid

that if he moved he would find her irresistibly in his arms. Two tears had rolled down her wet face and trembled on her upper lip.

'I'm more beautiful than anybody else,' she said brokenly, 'why can't I be happy?' Her moist eyes tore at his stability – her mouth turned slowly downward with an exquisite sadness: 'I'd like to marry you if you'll have me, Dexter. I suppose you think I'm not worth having, but I'll be so beautiful for you, Dexter.'

A million phrases of anger, pride, passion, hatred, tenderness fought on his lips. Then a perfect wave of emotion washed over him, carrying off with it a sediment of wisdom, of convention, of doubt, of honor. This was his girl who was speaking, his own, his beautiful, his pride.

'Won't you come in?' He heard her draw in her breath sharply.

Waiting.

'All right,' his voice was trembling, 'I'll come in.'

V

It was strange that neither when it was over nor a long time afterward did he regret that night. Looking at it from the perspective of ten years, the fact that Judy's flare for him endured just one month seemed of little importance. Nor did it matter that by his yielding he subjected himself to a deeper agony in the end and gave serious hurt to Irene Scheerer and to Irene's parents, who had befriended him. There was nothing sufficiently pictorial about Irene's grief to stamp itself on his mind.

Dexter was at bottom hard-minded. The attitude of the city on his action was of no importance to him, not because he was going to leave the city, but because any outside attitude on the situation seemed superficial. He was completely indifferent to popular opinion. Nor, when he had seen that it was no use, that he did not possess in himself the power to move fundamentally or to hold Judy Jones, did he bear any malice toward her. He loved her, and he would love her until the day he was too old for loving – but he could not have her. So he tasted the deep pain that is reserved only for the strong, just as he had tasted for a little while the deep happiness.

Even the ultimate falsity of the grounds upon which Judy terminated the engagement – that she did not want to 'take him away' from Irene – Judy, who had wanted nothing else – did not revolt him. He was beyond any revulsion or any amusement.

He went East in February with the intention of selling out his laundries and settling in New York – but the war came to America in March and changed his plans. He returned to the West, handed over the management of the business to his partner, and went into the first officers' training-camp in late April. He was one of those young thousands who greeted the war with a certain amount of relief, welcoming the liberation from webs of tangled emotion.

VI

This story is not his biography, remember, although things creep into it which have nothing to do with those dreams he had when he was young. We are almost done with them and with him now. There is only one more incident to be related here, and it happens seven years farther on.

It took place in New York, where he had done well – so well that there were no barriers too high for him. He was thirty-two years old, and, except for one flying trip immediately after the war, he had not been West in seven years. A man named Devlin from Detroit came into his office to see him in a business way, and then and there this incident occurred, and closed out, so to speak, this particular side of his life.

'So you're from the Middle West,' said the man Devlin with careless curiosity. 'That's funny – I thought men like you were probably born and raised on Wall Street. You know – wife of one of my best friends in Detroit came from your city. I was an usher at the wedding.'

Dexter waited with no apprehension of what was coming.

'Judy Simms,' said Devlin with no particular interest; 'Judy Jones she was once.'

'Yes, I knew her.' A dull impatience spread over him. He had heard, of course, that she was married – perhaps deliberately he had heard no more.

'Awfully nice girl,' brooded Devlin meaninglessly, 'I'm sort of sorry for her.'

'Why?' Something in Dexter was alert, receptive, at once.

'Oh, Lud Simms has gone to pieces in a way. I don't mean he ill-uses her, but he drinks and runs around—'

'Doesn't she run around?'

'No. Stays at home with her kids.'

'Oh.'

'She's a little too old for him,' said Devlin.

'Too old!' cried Dexter. 'Why, man, she's only twenty-seven.'

He was possessed with a wild notion of rushing out into the streets and taking a train to Detroit. He rose to his feet spasmodically.

'I guess you're busy,' Devlin apologized quickly. 'I didn't realize—'

'No, I'm not busy,' said Dexter, steadying his voice. 'I'm

not busy at all. Not busy at all. Did you say she was – twenty-seven? No, I said she was twenty-seven.'

'Yes, you did,' agreed Devlin dryly.

'Go on, then. Go on.'

'What do you mean?'

'About Judy Jones.'

Devlin looked at him helplessly.

'Well, that's – I told you all there is to it. He treats her like the devil. Oh, they're not going to get divorced or anything. When he's particularly outrageous she forgives him. In fact, I'm inclined to think she loves him. She was a pretty girl when she first came to Detroit.'

A pretty girl! The phrase struck Dexter as ludicrous.

'Isn't she – a pretty girl, any more?'

'Oh, she's all right.'

'Look here,' said Dexter, sitting down suddenly. 'I don't understand. You say she was a "pretty girl" and now you say she's "all right." I don't understand what you mean – Judy Jones wasn't a pretty girl, at all. She was a great beauty. Why, I knew her, I knew her. She was—'

Devlin laughed pleasantly.

'I'm not trying to start a row,' he said. 'I think Judy's a nice girl and I like her. I can't understand how a man like Lud Simms could fall madly in love with her, but he did.' Then he added: 'Most of the women like her.'

Dexter looked closely at Devlin, thinking wildly that there must be a reason for this, some insensitivity in the man or some private malice.

'Lots of women fade just like *that*,' Devlin snapped his fingers. 'You must have seen it happen. Perhaps I've forgotten how pretty she was at her wedding. I've seen her so much since then, you see. She has nice eyes.'

A sort of dullness settled down upon Dexter. For the first

time in his life he felt like getting very drunk. He knew that he was laughing loudly at something Devlin had said, but he did not know what it was or why it was funny. When, in a few minutes, Devlin went he lay down on his lounge and looked out the window at the New York sky-line into which the sun was sinking in dull lovely shades of pink and gold.

He had thought that having nothing else to lose he was invulnerable at last – but he knew that he had just lost something more, as surely as if he had married Judy Jones and seen her fade away before his eyes.

The dream was gone. Something had been taken from him. In a sort of panic he pushed the palms of his hands into his eyes and tried to bring up a picture of the waters lapping on Sherry Island and the moonlit veranda, and gingham on the golf-links and the dry sun and the gold color of her neck's soft down. And her mouth damp to his kisses and her eyes plaintive with melancholy and her freshness like a new fine linen in the morning. Why, these things were no longer in the world! They had existed and they existed no longer.

For the first time in years the tears were streaming down his face. But they were for himself now. He did not care about mouth and eyes and moving hands. He wanted to care, and he could not care. For he had gone away and he could never go back any more. The gates were closed, the sun was gone down, and there was no beauty but the gray beauty of steel that withstands all time. Even the grief he could have borne was left behind in the country of illusion, of youth, of the richness of life, where his winter dreams had flourished.

'Long ago,' he said, 'long ago, there was something in me, but now that thing is gone. Now that thing is gone, that thing is gone. I cannot cry. I cannot care. That thing will come back no more.'

RING LARDNER

MR FRISBIE

I AM MR ALLEN FRISBIE'S chauffeur. Allen Frisbie is a name I made up because they tell me that if I used the real name of the man I am employed by that he might take offense and start trouble though I am sure he will never see what I am writing as he does not read anything except the *American Golfer* but of course some of his friends might call his attention to it. If you knew who the real name of the man is it would make more interesting reading as he is one of the 10 most wealthiest men in the United States and a man who everybody is interested in because he is so famous and the newspapers are always writing articles about him and sending high salary reporters to interview him but he is a very hard man to reproach or get an interview with and when they do he never tells them anything.

That is how I come to be writing this article because about two weeks ago a Mr Kirk had an appointment to interview Mr Frisbie for one of the newspapers and I drove him to the station after the interview was over and he said to me your boss is certainly a tough egg to interview and getting a word out of him is like pulling turnips.

'The public do not know anything about the man,' said Mr Kirk. 'They know he is very rich and has got a wife and a son and a daughter and what their names are but as to his private life and his likes and dislikes he might just as well be a monk in a convent.'

'The public knows he likes golf,' I said.

'They do not know what kind of a game he plays.'

'He plays pretty good,' I said.

'How good?' said Mr Kirk.

'About 88 or 90,' I said.

'So is your grandmother,' said Mr Kirk.

He only meant the remark as a comparison but had either of my grandmothers lived they would both have been over 90. Mr Kirk did not believe I was telling the truth about Mr Frisbie's game and he was right though was I using real names I would not admit it as Mr Frisbie is very sensitive in regards to his golf.

Mr Kirk kept pumping at me but I am used to being pumped at and Mr Kirk finally gave up pumping at me as he found me as closed mouth as Mr Frisbie himself but he made the remark that he wished he was in my place for a few days and as close to the old man as I am and he would then be able to write the first real article which had ever been written about the old man. He called Mr Frisbie the old man.

He said it was too bad I am not a writer so I could write up a few instance about Mr Frisbie from the human side on account of being his caddy at golf and some paper or magazine would pay me big. He said if you would tell me a few instance I would write them up and split with you but I said no I could not think of anything which would make an article but after Mr Kirk had gone I got to thinking it over and thought to myself maybe I could be a writer if I tried and at least there is no harm in trying so for the week after Mr Kirk's visit I spent all my spare time writing down about Mr Frisbie only at first I used his real name but when I showed the article they said for me not to use real names but the public would guess who it was anyway and that was just as good as using real names.

So I have gone over the writing again and changed the

name to Allen Frisbie and other changes and here is the article using Allen Frisbie.

When I say I am Mr Frisbie's chauffeur I mean I am his personal chauffeur. There are two other chauffeurs who drive for the rest of the family and run errands. Had I nothing else to do only drive I might well be turned a man of leisure as Mr Frisbie seldom never goes in to the city more than twice a week and even less oftener than that does he pay social visits.

His golf links is right on the place an easy walk from the house to the first tee and here is where he spends a good part of each and every day playing alone with myself in the roll of caddy. So one would not be far from amiss to refer to me as Mr Frisbie's caddy rather than his chauffeur but it was as a chauffeur that I was engaged and can flatter myself that there are very few men of my calling who would not gladly exchange their salary and position for mine.

Mr Frisbie is a man just this side of 60 years of age. Almost 10 years ago he retired from active business with money enough to put him in a class with the richest men in the United States and since then his investments have increased their value to such an extent so that now he is in a class with the richest men in the United States.

It was soon after his retirement that he bought the Peter Vischer estate near Westbury, Long Island. On this estate there was a 9 hole golf course in good condition and considered one of the best private 9 hole golf courses in the United States but Mr Frisbie would have had it plowed up and the land used for some other usage only for a stroke of chance which was when Mrs Frisbie's brother came over from England for a visit.

It was during while this brother-in-law was visiting Mr Frisbie that I entered the last named employee and was an onlooker when Mr Frisbie's brother-in-law persuaded his brother-in-law to try the game of golf. As luck would have it Mr Frisbie's first drive was so good that his brother-in-law would not believe he was a new beginner till he had seen Mr Frisbie shoot again but that first perfect drive made Mr Frisbie a slave of the game and without which there would be no such instance as I am about to relate.

I would better explain at this junction that I am not a golfer but I have learned quite a lot of knowledge about the game by cadding for Mr Frisbie and also once or twice in company with my employer have picked up some knowledge of the game by witnessing players like Bobby Jones and Hagen and Sarazen and Smith in some of their matches. I have only tried it myself on a very few occasions when I was sure Mr Frisbie could not observe me and will confide that in my own mind I am convinced that with a little practise that I would have little trouble defeating Mr Frisbie but will never seek to prove same for reasons which I will leave it to the reader to guess the reasons.

One day shortly after Mr Frisbie's brother-in-law had ended his visit I was cadding for Mr Frisbie and as had become my custom keeping the score for him when a question arose as to whether he had taken 7 or 8 strokes on the last hole. A 7 would have given him a total of 63 for the 9 holes while a 8 would have made it 64. Mr Frisbie tried to recall the different strokes but was not certain and asked me to help him.

As I remembered it he had sliced his 4th wooden shot in to a trap but had recovered well and got on to the green and then had taken 3 putts which would make him a 8 but by some slip of the tongue when I started to say 8 I said 7 and before I could correct myself Mr Frisbie said yes you are right it was a 7.

'That is even 7s,' said Mr Frisbie.

'Yes,' I said.

On the way back to the house he asked me what was my salary which I told him and he said well I think you are worth more than that and from now on you will get $25.00 more per week.

On another occasion when 9 more holes had been added to the course and Mr Frisbie was playing the 18 holes regular every day he came to the last hole needing a 5 to break 112 which was his best score.

The 18th hole is only 120 yards with a big green but a brook in front and traps in back of it. Mr Frisbie got across the brook with his second but the ball went over in to the trap and it looked like bad business because Mr Frisbie is even worse with a niblick than almost any other club except maybe the No. 3 and 4 irons and the wood.

Well I happened to get to the ball ahead of him and it laid there burred in the deep sand about a foot from a straight up and down bank 8 foot high where it would have been impossible for any man alive to oust it in one stroke but as luck would have it I stumbled and gave the ball a little kick and by chance it struck the side of the bank and stuck in the grass and Mr Frisbie got it up on the green in one stroke and was down in 2 putts for his 5.

'Well that is my record 111 or 3 over 6s,' he said.

Now my brother had a couple of tickets for the polo at Meadowbrook the next afternoon and I am a great lover of horses flesh so I said to Mr Frisbie can I go to the polo tomorrow afternoon and he said certainly any time you want a afternoon off do not hesitate to ask me but a little while later there was a friend of mine going to get married at Atlantic City and Mr Frisbie had just shot a 128 and broke his spoon besides and when I mentioned about going to Atlantic City for my friend's wedding he snapped at me like a wolf and said what did I think it was the xmas holidays.

Personally I am a man of simple tastes and few wants and it is very seldom when I am not satisfied to take my life and work as they come and not seek fear or favor but of course there are times in every man's life when they desire something a little out of the ordinary in the way of a little vacation or perhaps a financial accommodation of some kind and in such cases I have found Mr Frisbie a king amongst men provide it one uses discretion in choosing the moment of their reproach but a variable tyrant if one uses bad judgment in choosing the moment of their reproach.

You can count on him granting any reasonable request just after he has made a good score or even a good shot where as a person seeking a favor when he is off his game might just swell ask President Coolidge to do the split.

I wish to state that having learned my lesson along these lines I did not use my knowledge to benefit myself alone but have on the other hand utilized same mostly to the advantage of others especially the members of Mr Frisbie's own family. Mr Frisbie's wife and son and daughter all realized early in my employment that I could handle Mr Frisbie better than anyone else and without me ever exactly divulging the secret of my methods they just naturally began to take it for granted that I could succeed with him where they failed and it became their habit when they sought something from their respective spouse and father to summons me as their adviser and advocate.

As an example of the above I will first sight an example in connection with Mrs Frisbie. This occurred many years ago and was the instance which convinced her beyond all doubt that I was a expert on the subject of managing her husband.

Mrs Frisbie is a great lover of music but unable to perform

on any instrument herself. It was her hope that one of the children would be a pianiste and a great deal of money was spent on piano lessons for both Robert the son and Florence the daughter but all in vain as neither of the two showed any talent and their teachers one after another gave them up in despair.

Mrs Frisbie at last became desirous of purchasing a player piano and of course would consider none but the best but when she brooched the subject to Mr Frisbie he turned a deaf ear as he said pianos were made to be played by hand and people who could not learn same did not deserve music in the home.

I do not know how often Mr and Mrs Frisbie disgust the matter pro and con.

Personally they disgust it in my presence any number of times and finally being a great admirer of music myself and seeing no reason why a man of Mr Frisbie's great wealth should deny his wife a harmless pleasure such as a player piano I suggested to the madam that possibly if she would leave matters to me the entire proposition might be put over. I can no more than fail I told her and I do not think I will fail so she instructed me to go ahead as I could not do worse than fail which she had already done herself.

I will relate the success of my plan as briefly as possible. Between the house and the golf course there was a summer house in which Mrs Frisbie sat reading while Mr Frisbie played golf. In this summer house she could sit so as to not be visible from the golf course. She was to sit there till she heard me whistle the strains of 'Over There' where at she was to appear on the scene like she had come direct from the house and the fruits of our scheme would then be known.

For two days Mrs Frisbie had to console herself with her book as Mr Frisbie's golf was terrible and there was no moment when I felt like it would not be courting disaster to summons her on the scene but during the 3rd afternoon his game suddenly improved and he had shot the 1st 9 holes in 53 and started out on the 10th with a pretty drive when I realized the time had come.

Mrs Frisbie appeared promptly in answer to my whistling and walked rapidly up to Mr Frisbie like she had hurried from the house and said there is a man at the house from that player piano company and he says he will take $50.00 off the regular price if I order today and please let me order one as I want one so much.

'Why certainly dear go ahead and get it dear,' said Mr Frisbie and that is the way Mrs Frisbie got her way in regards to a player piano. Had I not whistled when I did but waited a little longer it would have spelt ruination to our schemes as Mr Frisbie took a 12 on the 11th hole and would have bashed his wife over the head with a No. 1 iron had she even asked him for a toy drum.

I have been of assistance to young Mr Robert Frisbie the son with reference to several items of which I will only take time to touch on one item with reference to Mr Robert wanting to drive a car. Before Mr Robert was 16 years of age he was always after Mr Frisbie to allow him to drive one of the cars and Mr Frisbie always said him nay on the ground that it is against the law for a person under 16 years of age to drive a car.

When Mr Robert reached the age of 16 years old however this excuse no longer held good and yet Mr Frisbie continued to say Mr Robert nay in regards to driving a car. There is plenty of chauffeurs at your beckon call said Mr Frisbie to drive you where ever and when ever you wish to go but of course Mr Robert like all youngsters wanted to drive himself and personally I could see no harm in it as I personally could not drive for him and the other 2 chauffeurs in Mr Frisbie's employee at the time were just as lightly to wreck a car as Mr Robert so I promised Mr Robert that I would do my best towards helping him towards obtaining permission to drive one of the cars.

'Leave it to me' was my bequest to Mr Robert and sure enough my little strategy turned the trick though Mr Robert did not have the patience like his mother to wait in the summer house till a favorable moment arrived so it was necessary for me to carry through the entire proposition by myself.

The 16th hole on our course is perhaps the most difficult hole on our course at least it has always been a variable tartar for Mr Frisbie.

It is about 350 yards long in length and it is what is called a blind hole as you can not see the green from the tee as you drive from the tee up over a hill with a direction flag as the only guide and down at the bottom of the hill there is a brook a little over 225 yards from the tee which is the same brook which you come to again on the last hole and in all the times Mr Frisbie has played around the course he has seldom never made this 16th hole in less than 7 strokes or more as his tee shot just barely skins the top of the hill giving him a down hill lie which upsets him so that he will miss the 2nd shot entirely or top it and go in to the brook.

Well I generally always stand up on top of the hill to watch where his tee shot goes and on the occasion referred to he got a pretty good tee shot which struck on top of the hill and rolled halfway down and I hurried to the ball before he could see me and I picked it up and threw it across the brook and when he climbed to the top of the hill I pointed to where the ball laid the other side of the brook and shouted good shot Mr Frisbie. He was overjoyed and beamed with joy and did not suspect anything out of the way though in realty he could not hit a ball more than 160 yards if it was teed on the summit of Pike's Peak.

Fate was on my side at this junction and Mr Frisbie hit a perfect mashie shot on to the green and sunk his 2nd putt for the only 4 of his career on this hole. He was almost delirious with joy and you may be sure I took advantage of the situation and before we were fairly off the green I said to him Mr Frisbie if you do not need me tomorrow morning do you not think it would be a good time for me to learn Mr Robert to drive a car.

'Why certainly he is old enough now to drive a car and it is time he learned.'

I now come to the main instance of my article which is in regards to Miss Florence Frisbie who is now Mrs Henry Craig and of course Craig is not the real name but you will soon see that what I was able to do for her was no such childs play like gaining consent for Mr Robert to run a automobile or Mrs Frisbie to purchase a player piano but this was a matter of the up most importance and I am sure the reader will not consider me a vain bragger when I claim that I handled it with some skill.

Miss Florence is a very pretty and handsome girl who has always had a host of suiters who paid court to her on account of being pretty as much as her great wealth and I believe there has been times when no less than half a dozen or more young men were paying court to her at one time. Well about 2 years ago she lost her heart to young Henry Craig and at the same time Mr Frisbie told her in no uncertain turns that she must throw young Craig over board and marry his own choice young junior Holt or he would cut her off without a dime.

Holt and Craig are not the real names of the two young

134

men referred to though I am using their real first names namely Junior and Henry. Young Holt is a son of Mr Frisbie's former partner in business and a young man who does not drink or smoke and has got plenty of money in his own rights and a young man who any father would feel safe in trusting their daughter in the bands of matrimony. Young Craig at that time had no money and no position and his parents had both died leaving nothing but debts.

'Craig is just a tramp and will never amount to anything,' said Mr Frisbie. 'I have had inquirys made and I understand he drinks when anyone will furnish him the drinks. He has never worked and never will. Junior Holt is a model young man from all accounts and comes of good stock and is the only young man I know whose conduct and habits are such that I would consider him fit to marry my daughter.'

Miss Florence said that Craig was not a tramp and she loved him and would not marry anyone else and as for Holt he was terrible but even if he was not terrible she would never consider undergoing the bands of matrimony with a man named Junior.

'I will elope with Henry if you do not give in,' she said.

Mr Frisbie was not alarmed by this threat as Miss Florence has a little common sense and would not be lightly to elope with a young man who could hardly finance a honeymoon trip on the subway. But neither was she showing any signs of yielding in regards to his wishes in regards to young Holt and things began to take on the appearance of a dead lock between father and daughter with neither side showing any signs of yielding.

Miss Florence grew pale and thin and spent most of her time in her room instead of seeking enjoyment amongst her friends as was her custom. As for Mr Frisbie he was always a man of iron will and things began to take on the appearance of a dead lock with neither side showing any signs of yielding.

It was when it looked like Miss Florence was on the verge of a serious illness when Mrs Frisbie came to me and said we all realize that you have more influence with Mr Frisbie than anyone else and is there any way you can think of to get him to change his status toward Florence and these 2 young men because if something is not done right away I am afraid of what will happen. Miss Florence likes you and has a great deal of confidence in you said Mrs Frisbie so will you see her and talk matters over with her and see if you can not think up some plan between you which will put a end to this situation before my poor little girl dies.

So I went to see Miss Florence in her bedroom and she was a sad sight with her eyes red from weeping and so pale and thin and yet her face lit up with a smile when I entered the room and she shook hands with me like I was a long lost friend.

'I asked my mother to send you,' said Miss Florence. 'This case looks hopeless but I know you are a great fixer as far as Father is concerned and you can fix it if anyone can. Now I have got a idea which I will tell you and if you like it it will be up to you to carry it out.'

'What is your idea?'

'Well,' said Miss Florence, 'I think that if Mr Craig the man I love could do Father a favor why Father would not be so set against him.'

'What kind of a favor?'

'Well Mr Craig plays a very good game of golf and he might give Father some pointers which would improve Father's game.'

'Your father will not play golf with anyone and certainly not with a good player and besides that your father is not the kind of a man that wants anyone giving him pointers. Personally I would just as leaf go up and tickle him as tell him that his stance is wrong.'

'Then I guess my idea is not so good.'

'No,' I said and then all of a sudden I had a idea of my own. 'Listen Miss Florence does the other one play golf?'

'Who?'

'Young Junior Holt.'

'Even better than Mr Craig.'

'Does your father know that?'

'Father does not know anything about him or he would not like him so well.'

Well I said I have got a scheme which may work or may not work but no harm to try and the first thing to be done is for you to spruce up and pretend like you do not feel so unkindly towards young Holt after all. The next thing is to tell your father that Mr Holt never played golf and never even saw it played but would like to watch your father play so he can get the hang of the game.

And then after that you must get Mr Holt to ask your father to let him follow him around the course and very secretly you must tip Mr Holt off that your father wants his advice. When ever your father does anything wrong Mr Holt is to correct him. Tell him your father is crazy to improve his golf but is shy in regards to asking for help.

There is a lot of things that may happen to this scheme but if it should go through why I will guarantee that at least half your troubles will be over.

Well as I said there was a lot of things that might have happened to spoil my scheme but nothing did happen and the very next afternoon Mr Frisbie confided in me that Miss Florence seemed to feel much better and seemed to have changed her mind in regards to Mr Holt and also said that the last named had expressed a desire to follow Mr Frisbie around the golf course and learn something about the game.

Mr Holt was a kind of a fat pudgy young man with a kind of a sneering smile and the first minute I saw him I wished him the worst.

For a second before Mr Frisbie started to play I was certain we were lost as Mr Frisbie remarked where have you been keeping yourself Junior that you never watched golf before. But luckily young Holt took the remark as a joke and made no reply. Right afterwards the storm clouds began to gather in the sky. Mr Frisbie sliced his tee shot.

'Mr Frisbie,' said Young Holt, 'there was several things the matter with you then but the main trouble was that you stood too close to the ball and cut across it with your club head and besides that you swang back faster than Alex Smith and you were off your balance and you gripped too hard and you jerked instead of hitting with a smooth follow through.'

Well, Mr Frisbie gave him a queer look and then made up his mind that Junior was trying to be humorous and he frowned at him so as he would not try it again but when we located the ball in the rough and Mr Frisbie asked me for his spoon young Holt said Oh take your mashie Mr Frisbie never use a wooden club in a place like that and Mr Frisbie scowled and mumbled under his breath and missed the ball with his spoon and missed it again and then took a mid-iron and just dribbled it on to the fairway and finally got on the green in 7 and took 3 putts.

I suppose you might say that this was one of the quickest golf matches on record as it ended on the 2nd tee. Mr Frisbie tried to drive and sliced again. Then young Holt took a ball from my pocket and a club from the bag and said here let me show you the swing and drove the ball 250 yards straight down the middle of the course.

I looked at Mr Frisbie's face and it was puffed out and a kind of a purple black color. Then he burst and I will only repeat a few of the more friendlier of his remarks.

'Get to hell and gone of my place. Do not never darken my doors again. Just show up around here one more time and I will blow out what you have got instead of brains. You lied to my girl and you tried to make a fool out of me. Get out before I sick my dogs on you and tear you to pieces.'

Junior most lightly wanted to offer some word of explanation or to demand one on his own account but saw at a glance how useless same would be. I heard later that he saw Miss Florence and that she just laughed at him.

'I made a mistake about Junior Holt,' said Mr Frisbie that evening. 'He is no good and must never come to this house again.'

'Oh Father and just when I was beginning to like him,' said Miss Florence.

Well like him or not like him she and the other young man Henry Craig were married soon afterwards which I suppose Mr Frisbie permitted the bands in the hopes that same would rile Junior Holt.

Mr Frisbie admitted he had made a mistake in regards to the last named but he certainly was not mistaken when he said that young Craig was a tramp and would never amount to anything.

Well I guess I have rambled on long enough about Mr Frisbie.

STEPHEN LEACOCK

THE
GOLFOMANIAC

WE RIDE IN and out pretty often together, he and I, on a suburban train.

That's how I came to talk to him. 'Fine morning,' I said as I sat down beside him yesterday and opened a newspaper.

'Great!' he answered. 'The grass is drying out fast now and the greens will soon be all right to play.'

'Yes,' I said, 'the sun is getting higher and the days are decidedly lengthening.'

'For the matter of that,' said my friend, 'a man could begin to play at six in the morning easily. In fact, I've often wondered that there is little golf played before breakfast. We happened to be talking about golf, a few of us last night – I don't know how it came up – and we were saying that it seems a pity that some of the best part of the day, say, from five o'clock to seven-thirty, is never used.'

'That's true,' I answered, and then, to shift the subject, I said, looking out of the window:

'It's a pretty bit of country just here, isn't it?'

'It is,' he replied, 'but it seems a shame they make no use of it – just a few market gardens and things like that. Why, I noticed along here acres and acres of just glass – some kind of houses for plants or something – and whole fields of lettuce and things like that. It's a pity they don't make something of it. I was remarking only the other day as I came along in the train with a friend of mine, that you could easily lay out an eighteen-hole course anywhere here.'

'Could you?' I said.

'Oh, yes. This ground, you know, is an excellent light soil to shovel up into bunkers. You could drive some ditches through it and make one or two deep holes – the kind they have on some of the French links. In fact, improve it to any extent.'

I glanced at my morning paper. 'I see,' I said, 'that it is again rumoured that Lloyd George is at least definitely to retire.'

'Funny thing about Lloyd George,' answered my friend. 'He never played, you know; most extraordinary thing – don't you think? – for a man in his position. Balfour, of course, was very different: I remember when I was over in Scotland last summer I had the honour of going around the course at Dumfries just after Lord Balfour. Pretty interesting experience, don't you think?'

'Were you over on business?' I asked.

'No, not exactly. I went to get a golf ball, a particular golf ball. Of course, I didn't go merely for that. I wanted to get a mashie as well. The only way, you know, to get just what you want is to go to Scotland for it.'

'Did you see much of Scotland?'

'I saw it all. I was on the links at St Andrews and I visited the Loch Lomond course and the course at Inverness. In fact, I saw everything.'

'It's an interesting country, isn't it, historically?'

'It certainly is. Do you know they have played there for over five hundred years! Think of it! They showed me at Loch Lomond the place where they said Robert the Bruce played the Red Douglas (I think that was the other party – at any rate, Bruce was one of them), and I saw where Bonnie Prince Charlie disguised himself as a caddie when the Duke of Cumberland's soldiers were looking for him. Oh, it's a wonderful country historically.'

After that I let a silence intervene so as to get a new start. Then I looked up again from my newspaper.

'Look at this,' I said pointing to a headline, *United States Navy Ordered Again to Nicaragua*. 'Looks like more trouble, doesn't it?'

'Did you see in the paper a while back,' said my companion, 'that the United States Navy Department is now making golf compulsory at the training school at Annapolis? That's progressive, isn't it? I suppose it will have to mean shorter cruises at sea; in fact, probably lessen the use of the Navy for sea purposes. But it will raise the standard.'

'I suppose so,' I answered. 'Did you read about this extraordinary murder case in Long Island?'

'No,' he said. 'I never read murder cases. They don't interest me. In fact, I think this whole continent is getting over-preoccupied with them—'

'Yes, but this case had such odd features—'

'Oh, they all have,' he replied, with an air of weariness. 'Each one is just boomed by the papers to make a sensation—'

'I know, but in this case it seems that the man was killed with a blow from a golf club.'

'What's that? Eh, what's that? Killed with a blow from a golf club!'

'Yes, some kind of club—'

'I wonder if it was an iron – let me see the paper – though, for the matter of that, I imagine that a blow from even a wooden driver, let alone one of the steel-handled drivers – where does it say it? – pshaw, it only just says "a blow with a golf club". It's a pity the papers don't write these things up with more detail, isn't it? But perhaps it will be better in the afternoon paper—'

'Have you played golf much?' I inquired. I saw it was no use to talk of anything else.

'No,' answered my companion, 'I am sorry to say I haven't. You see, I began late. I've only played twenty years, twenty-one if you count the year that's beginning in May. I don't know what I was doing. I wasted about half my life. In fact, it wasn't till I was well over thirty that I caught on to the game. I suppose a lot of us look back over our lives that way and realize what we have lost.

'And even as it is,' he continued, 'I don't get much chance to play. At the best I can only manage about four afternoons a week, though of course I get most of Saturday and all Sunday. I get my holiday in the summer, but it's only a month, and that's nothing. In the winter I manage to take a run south for a game once or twice and perhaps a little swack at it around Easter, but only a week at a time. I'm too busy – that's the plain truth of it.' He sighed. 'It's hard to leave the office before two,' he said. 'Something always turns up.'

And after that he went on to tell me something of the technique of the game, illustrate it with a golf ball on the seat of the car, and the peculiar mental poise needed for driving, and the neat, quick action of the wrist (he showed me how it worked) that is needed to undercut a ball so that it flies straight up in the air. He explained to me how you can do practically anything with a golf ball, provided that you keep your mind absolutely poised and your eye in shape, and your body a trained machine. It appears that even Bobby Jones of Atlanta and people like that fall short very often from the high standard set by my golfing friend in the suburban car.

So, later in the day, meeting someone in my club who was a person of authority on such things, I made inquiry about my friend. 'I rode into town with Llewellyn Smith,' I said.

'I think he belongs to your golf club. He's a great player, isn't he?'

'A great player!' laughed the expert. 'Llewellyn Smith? Why, he can hardly hit a ball! And anyway, he's only played about twenty years!'

E. C. BENTLEY

THE SWEET SHOT

'NO; I HAPPENED to be abroad at the time,' Philip Trent said. 'I wasn't in the way of seeing the English papers, so until I came here this week I never heard anything about your mystery.'

Captain Royden, a small, spare, brown-faced man, was engaged in the delicate – and forbidden – task of taking his automatic telephone instrument to pieces. He now suspended his labours and reached for the tobacco jar. The large window of his office in the Kempshill clubhouse looked down upon the eighteenth green of that delectable golf course, and his eye roved over the whin-clad slopes beyond as he called on his recollection.

'Well, if you call it a mystery,' he said as he filled a pipe. 'Some people do, because they like mysteries, I suppose. For instance, Colin Hunt, the man you're staying with, calls it that. Others won't have it, and say there was a perfectly natural explanation. I could tell you as much as anybody could about it, I dare say.'

'As being secretary here, you mean?'

'Not only that. I was one of the two people who were in at the death, so to speak – or next door to it,' Captain Royden said. He limped to the mantelshelf and took down a silver box embossed on the lid with the crest and mottoes of the Corps of Royal Engineers. 'Try one of these cigarettes, Mr Trent. If you'd like to hear the yarn, I'll give it you. You have heard something about Arthur Freer, I suppose?'

'Hardly anything,' Trent said. 'I just gathered that he wasn't a very popular character.'

'No,' Captain Royden said with reserve. 'Did they tell you he was my brother-in-law? No? Well, now, it happened about four months ago, on a Monday – let me see – yes, the second Monday in May. Freer had a habit of playing nine holes before breakfast. Barring Sundays – he was strict about Sunday – he did it most days, even in the beastliest weather, going round all alone usually, carrying his own clubs, studying every shot as if his life depended on it. That helped to make him the very good player he was. His handicap here was two, and at Undershaw he used to be scratch, I believe.

'At a quarter to eight he'd be on the first tee, and by nine he'd be back at his house – it's only a few minutes from here. That Monday morning he started off as usual—'

'And at the usual time?'

'Just about. He had spent a few minutes in the clubhouse blowing up the steward about some trifle. And that was the last time he was seen alive by anybody – near enough to speak to, that is. No one else went off the first tee until a little after nine, when I started round with Browson – he's our local padre; I had been having breakfast with him at the Vicarage. He's got a game leg, like me, so we often play together when he can fit it in.

'We had holed out on the first green, and were walking on to the next tee, when Browson said, "Great Scot! Look there. Something's happened." He pointed down the fairway of the second hole; and there we could see a man lying sprawled on the turf, face down and motionless. Now there is this point about the second hole – the first half of it is in a dip in the land, just deep enough to be out of sight from any other point on the course, unless you're standing right above it –

you'll see when you go round yourself. Well, on the tee, you *are* right above it; and we saw this man lying. We ran to the spot.

'It was Freer, as I had known it must be at that hour. He was dead, lying in a disjointed sort of way no live man could have lain in. His clothing was torn to ribbons, and it was singed too. So was his hair – he used to play bareheaded – and his face and hands. His bag of clubs was lying a few yards away, and the brassie, which he had just been using, was close by the body.

'There wasn't any wound showing, and I had seen far worse things often enough, but the padre was looking sickish, so I asked him to go back to the clubhouse and send for a doctor and the police while I mounted guard. They weren't long coming, and after they had done their job the body was taken away in an ambulance. Well, that's about all I can tell you at first hand, Mr Trent. If you are staying with Hunt, you'll have heard about the inquest and all that probably.'

Trent shook his head. 'No,' he said. 'Colin was just beginning to tell me, after breakfast this morning, about Freer having been killed on the course in some incomprehensible way, when a man came to see him about something. So, as I was going to apply for a fortnight's run of the course, I thought I would ask you about the affair.'

'All right,' Captain Royden said. 'I can tell you about the inquest anyhow – had to be there to speak my own little piece, about finding the body. As for what happened to Freer, the medical evidence was rather confusing. It was agreed that he had been killed by some tremendous shock, which had jolted his whole system to pieces and dislocated several joints, but had been not quite violent enough to cause any visible wound. Apart from that, there was a disagreement. Freer's own doctor, who saw the body first, declared he must

153

have been struck by lightning. He said it was true there hadn't been a thunderstorm, but that there had been thunder about all that weekend, and that sometimes lightning did act in that way. But the police surgeon, Collins, said there would be no such displacement of the organs from a lightning stroke, even if it did ever happen that way in our climate, which he doubted. And he said that if it had been lightning, it would have struck the steel-headed clubs; but the clubs lay there in their bag quite undamaged. Collins thought there must have been some kind of explosion, though he couldn't suggest what kind.'

Trent shook his head. 'I don't suppose that impressed the court,' he said. 'All the same, it may have been all the honest opinion he could give.' He smoked in silence a few moments, while Captain Royden attended to the troubles of his telephone instrument with a camel-hair brush. 'But surely,' Trent said at length, 'if there had been such an explosion as that, somebody would have heard the sound of it.'

'Lots of people would have heard it,' Captain Royden answered. 'But there you are, you see nobody notices the sound of explosions just about here. There's the quarry on the other side of the road there, and anytime after 7 a.m. there's liable to be a noise of blasting.'

'A dull, sickening thud?'

'Jolly sickening,' Captain Royden said, 'for all of us living nearby. And so that point wasn't raised. Well, Collins is a very sound man; but as you say, his evidence didn't really explain the thing, and the other fellow's did, whether it was right or wrong. Besides, the coroner and the jury had heard about a bolt from a clear sky, and the notion appealed to them. Anyhow, they brought it in death from misadventure.'

'Which nobody could deny, as the song says,' Trent remarked. 'And was there no other evidence?'

'Yes, some. But Hunt can tell you about it as well as I can; he was there. I shall have to ask you to excuse me now,' Captain Royden said. 'I have an appointment in the town. The steward will sign you on for a fortnight, and probably get you a game too, if you want one today.'

Colin Hunt and his wife, when Trent returned to their house for luncheon, were very willing to complete the tale. The verdict, they declared, was tripe. Dr Collins knew his job, whereas Dr Hoyle was an old footler, and Freer's death had never been reasonably explained.

As for the other evidence, it had, they agreed, been interesting, though it didn't help at all. Freer had been seen after he had played his tee shot at the second hole, when he was walking down to the bottom of the dip toward the spot where he met his death.

'But according to Royden,' Trent said, 'that was a place where he couldn't be seen, unless one was right above him.'

'Well, this witness *was* right above him,' Hunt rejoined. 'Over one thousand feet above him, so he said. He was an RAF man, piloting a bomber from Bexford Camp, not far from here. He was up doing some sort of exercise, and passed over the course just at that time. He didn't know Freer but he spotted a man walking down from the second tee, because he was the only living soul visible on the course. Gossett, the other man in the plane, is a temporary member here, and he did know Freer quite well – or as well as anybody cared to know him – but he never saw him. However, the pilot was quite clear that he saw a man just at the time in question, and they took his evidence so as to prove that Freer was absolutely alone just before his death. The only other person who saw Freer was another man who knew him well; used to be a caddy here, and then got a job at the quarry. He was at work on the hillside, and he watched Freer play the first hole and go on to the second – nobody with him, of course.'

'Well, that was pretty well-established then,' Trent remarked. 'He was about as alone as he could be, it seems. Yet something happened somehow.'

Mrs Hunt sniffed sceptically, and lighted a cigarette. 'Yes, it did,' she said. 'However, I didn't worry much about it, for one. Edith – Mrs Freer, that is: Royden's sister – must have had a terrible life of it with a man like that. Not that she ever said anything – she wouldn't. She is not that sort.'

'She is a jolly good sort, anyhow,' Hunt declared.

'Yes, she is: too good for most men. I can tell you,' Mrs Hunt added for the benefit of Trent, 'if Colin ever took to cursing me and knocking me about, my well-known loyalty wouldn't stand the strain for very long.'

'That's why I don't do it. It's the fear of exposure that makes me the perfect husband, Phil. She would tie a can to me before I knew what was happening. As for Edith, it's true she never said anything, but the change in her since it happened tells the story well enough. Since she's been living with her brother she has been looking far better and happier than she ever succeeded in doing while Freer was alive.'

'She won't be living with him for very long, I dare say,' Mrs Hunt intimated darkly.

'No. I'd marry her myself if I had the chance,' Hunt agreed cordially.

'Pooh! You wouldn't be in the first six,' his wife said. 'It will be Rennie, or Gossett, or possibly Sandy Butler – you'll see. But perhaps you've had enough of the local tittle-tattle, Phil. Did you fix up a game for this afternoon?'

'Yes – with the Jarman Professor of Chemistry in the University of Cambridge,' Trent said. 'He looked at me as if he thought a bath of vitriol would do me good, but he agreed to play me.'

'You've got a tough job,' Hunt observed. 'I believe he is almost as old as he looks, but he is a devil at the short game, and he knows the course blindfold, which you don't. And he isn't so cantankerous as he pretends to be. By the way, he was the man who saw the finish of the last shot Freer ever played – a sweet shot if ever there was one. Get him to tell you.'

'I shall try to,' Trent said. 'The steward told me about that, and that was why I asked the professor for a game.'

Colin Hunt's prediction was fulfilled that afternoon. Professor Hyde, receiving five strokes, was one up at the seventeenth, and at the last hole sent down a four-foot putt to win the match. As they left the green he remarked, as if in answer to something Trent had that moment said, 'Yes, I can tell you a curious circumstance about Freer's death.'

Trent's eye brightened; for the professor had not said a dozen words during the game, and Trent's tentative allusion to the subject after the second hole had been met merely by an intimidating grunt.

'I saw the finish of the last shot he played,' the old gentleman went on, 'without seeing the man himself at all. A lovely brassie it was, too – though lucky. Rolled to within two feet of the pin.'

Trent considered. 'I see,' he said, 'what you mean. You were near the second green, and the ball came over the ridge and ran down to the hole.'

'Just so,' Professor Hyde said. 'That's how you play it – if you can. You might have done it yourself today, if your second shot had been thirty yards longer. I've never done it; but Freer often did. After a really good drive, you play a long

157

second, blind, over the ridge; and with a perfect shot, you may get the green. Well, my house is quite near that green. I was pottering about in the garden before breakfast, and just as I happened to be looking toward the green a ball came hopping down the slope and trickled right across to the hole. Of course, I knew whose it must be – Freer always came along about that time. If it had been anyone else, I'd have waited to see him get his three, and congratulate him. As it was, I went indoors, and didn't hear of his death until long afterward.'

'And you never saw him play the shot?' Trent said thoughtfully.

The professor turned a choleric blue eye on him. 'How the deuce could I?' he said huffily. 'I can't see through a mass of solid earth.'

'I know, I know,' Trent said. 'I was only trying to follow your mental process. Without seeing him play the shot, you knew it was his second – you say he would have been putting for a three. And you said too – didn't you? – that it was a brassie shot.'

'Simply because, my young friend' – the professor was severe – 'I happened to know the man's game. I had played that nine holes with him before breakfast often, until one day he lost his temper more than usual, and made himself impossible. I knew he practically always carried the ridge with his second – I won't say he always got the green – and his brassie was the only club that would do it. It is conceivable, I admit,' Professor Hyde added a little stiffly, 'that some mishap took place and that the shot in question was not actually Freer's second; but it did not occur to me to allow for that highly speculative contingency.'

On the next day, after those playing a morning round were started on their perambulation, Trent indulged himself with an hour's practice, mainly on the unsurveyed stretch of the second hole. Afterward he had a word with the caddy master; then visited the professional's shop, and won the regard of that expert by furnishing himself with a new mid-iron. Soon he brought up the subject of the last shot played by Arthur Freer. A dozen times that morning, he said, he had tried, after a satisfying drive, to reach the green with his second; but in vain. Fergus MacAdam shook his head. Not many, he said, could strike the ball with yon force. He could get there himself, whiles, but never for certainty. Mr Freer had the strength, and he kenned how to use it forbye.

What sort of clubs, Trent asked, had Freer preferred? 'Lang and heavy, like himsel'. Noo ye mention it,' MacAdam said, 'I hae them here. They were brocht here after the ahccident.' He reached up to the top of a rack. 'Ay, here they are. They shouldna be, of course; but naebody came to claim them, and it juist slippit ma mind.'

Trent, extracting the brassie, looked thoughtfully at the heavy head with the strip of hard white material inlaid in the face. 'It's a powerful weapon, sure enough,' he remarked.

'Ay, for a man that could control it,' MacAdam said. 'I dinna care for yon ivorine face mysel'. Some fowk think it gies mair reseelience, ye ken; but there's naething in it.'

'He didn't get it from you, then,' Trent suggested, still closely examining the head.

'Ay, but he did. I had a lot down from Nelsons while the fashion for them was on. Ye'll find my name,' MacAdam added, 'stampit on the wood in the usual place, if yer een are seein' richt.'

'Well, I don't – that's just it. The stamp is quite illegible.'

'Tod! Let's see,' the professional said, taking the club in hand. 'Guid reason for its being illegible,' he went on after a brief scrutiny. 'It's been obleeterated – that's easy seen. Who ever saw sic a daft-like thing! The wood has juist been crushed some gait – in a vice, I wouldna wonder. Noo, why would onybody want to dae a thing like yon?'

'Unaccountable, isn't it?' Trent said. 'Still, it doesn't matter, I suppose. And anyhow, we shall never know.'

It was twelve days later that Trent, looking in at the open door of the secretary's office, saw Captain Royden happily engaged with the separated parts of some mechanism in which coils of wire appeared to be the leading motive.

'I see you're busy,' Trent said.

'Come in! Come in!' Royden said heartily. 'I can do this anytime – another hour's work will finish it.' He laid down a pair of sharp-nosed pliers. 'The electricity people have just changed us over to A.C., and I've got to rewind the motor of our vacuum cleaner. Beastly nuisance,' he added, looking down affectionately at the bewildering jumble of disarticulated apparatus on his table.

'You bear your sorrow like a man,' Trent remarked; and Royden laughed as he wiped his hands on a towel.

'Yes,' he said, 'I do love tinkering about with mechanical jobs, and if I do say it myself, I'd rather do a thing like this with my own hands than risk having it faultily done by a careless workman. Too many of them about. Why, about a year ago the company sent a man here to fit a new main fuse box, and he made a short-circuit with his screwdriver that knocked him right across the kitchen and might very well have killed him.' He reached down his cigarette box and offered it to Trent, who helped himself; then looked down thoughtfully at the device on the lid.

'Thanks very much. When I saw this box before, I put you down for an R.E. man. *Ubique*, and *Quo fas et gloria ducunt*. H'm! I wonder why Engineers were given that motto in particular.'

'Lord knows,' the captain said. 'In my experience, Sappers don't exactly go where right and glory lead. The dirtiest of all the jobs and precious little of the glory – that's what they get.'

'Still, they have the consolation,' Trent pointed out, 'of feeling that they are at home in a scientific age, and that all the rest of the Army are amateurs compared with them. That's what one of them once told me, anyhow. Well now, Captain, I have to be off this evening. I've looked in just to say how much I've enjoyed myself here.'

'Very glad you did,' Captain Royden said. 'You'll come again, I hope, now you know that the golf here is not so bad.'

'I like it immensely. Also the members. And the secretary.' Trent paused to light his cigarette. 'I found the mystery rather interesting, too.'

Captain Royden's eyebrows lifted slightly. 'You mean about Freer's death? So you made up your mind it *was* a mystery.'

'Why yes,' Trent said. 'Because I made up my mind he had been killed by somebody, and probably killed intentionally. Then, when I had looked into the thing a little, I washed out the "probably".'

Captain Royden took up a penknife from his desk and began mechanically to sharpen a pencil. 'So you don't agree with the coroner's jury?'

'No, as the verdict seems to have been meant to rule out murder or any sort of human agency, I don't. The lightning idea, which apparently satisfied them, or some of them, was not a very bright one, I thought. I was told what Dr Collins had said against it at the inquest; and it seemed to me he had disposed of it completely when he said that Freer's clubs, most of them steel ones, were quite undamaged. A man carrying his clubs puts them down, when he plays a shot, a few feet away at most; yet Freer was supposed to have been electrocuted without any notice having been taken of them, so to speak.'

'H'm! No, it doesn't seem likely. I don't know that that quite decides the point, though,' the captain said. 'Lightning plays funny tricks, you know. I've seen a small tree struck when it was surrounded by trees twice the size. All the same, I quite agree there didn't seem to be any sense in the lightning notion. It was thundery weather, but there wasn't any storm that morning in this neighbourhood.'

'Just so. But when I considered what had been said about Freer's clubs, it suddenly occurred to me that nobody had said anything about *the* club, so far as my information about the inquest went. It seemed clear, from what you and the parson saw, that he had just played a shot with his brassie when he was struck down; it was lying near him, not in the bag. Besides, old Hyde actually saw the ball he had hit roll down the slope onto the green. Now, it's a good rule to study every little detail when you are on a problem of this kind. There weren't many left to study, of course, since the thing had happened four months before; but I knew Freer's clubs must be somewhere, and I thought of one or two places where they were likely to have been taken, in the circumstances, so I tried them. First, I reconnoitred the caddy master's shed, asking if I could leave my bag there for a day or two; but I was told that the regular place to leave them was the pro's shop. So I went and had a chat with MacAdam, and sure enough it soon came out that Freer's bag was still in his rack. I had a look at the clubs, too.'

'And did you notice anything peculiar about them?' Captain Royden asked.

'Just one little thing. But it was enough to set me thinking, and next day I drove up to London, where I paid

162

a visit to Nelsons, the sporting outfitters. You know the firm, of course.'

Captain Royden, carefully fining down the point of his pencil, nodded. 'Everybody knows Nelsons.'

'Yes, and MacAdam, I knew, had an account there for his stocks. I wanted to look over some clubs of a particular make – a brassie, with a slip of ivorine let into the face, such as they had supplied to MacAdam. Freer had had one of them from him.'

Again Royden nodded.

'I saw the man who shows clubs at Nelsons. We had a talk, and then – you know how little things come out in the course of conversation—'

'Especially,' put in the captain with a cheerful grin, 'when the conversation is being steered by an expert.'

'You flatter me,' Trent said. 'Anyhow, it did transpire that a club of that particular make had been bought some months before by a customer whom the man was able to remember. Why he remembered him was because, in the first place, he insisted on a club of rather unusual length and weight – much too long and heavy for himself to use, as he was neither a tall man nor of powerful build. The salesman had suggested as much in a delicate way; but the customer said no, he knew exactly what suited him, and he bought the club and took it away with him.'

'Rather an ass, I should say,' Royden observed thought-fully.

'I don't think he was an ass, really. He was capable of making a mistake, though, like the rest of us. There were some other things, by the way, that the salesman recalled about him. He had a slight limp, and he was, or had been, an Army officer. The salesman was an ex-Service man, and he couldn't be mistaken, he said, about that.'

Captain Royden had drawn a sheet of paper toward him, and was slowly drawing little geometrical figures as he listened. 'Go on, Mr Trent,' he said quietly.

'Well, to come back to the subject of Freer's death. I think he was killed by someone who knew Freer never played on Sunday, so that his clubs would be – or ought to be, shall we say? – in his locker all that day. All the following night, too, of course – in case the job took a long time. And I think this man was in a position to have access to the lockers in this clubhouse at any time he chose, and to possess a master key to those lockers. I think he was a skilful amateur craftsman. I think he had a good practical knowledge of high explosives. There is a branch of the Army' – Trent paused a moment and looked at the cigarette box on the table – 'in which that sort of knowledge is specially necessary, I believe.'

Hastily, as if just reminded of the duty of hospitality, Royden lifted the lid of the box and pushed it toward Trent. 'Do have another,' he urged.

Trent did so with thanks. 'They have to have it in the Royal Engineers,' he went on, 'because – so I'm told – demolition work is an important part of their job.'

'Quite right,' Captain Royden observed, delicately shading one side of a cube.

'*Ubique!*' Trent mused, staring at the box lid. 'If you are "everywhere", I take it you can be in two places at the same time. You could kill a man in one place, and at the same time be having breakfast with a friend a mile away. Well, to return to our subject yet once more; you can see the kind of idea I was led to form about what happened to Freer. I believe that his brassie was taken from his locker on the Sunday before his death. I believe the ivorine face of it was taken off and a cavity hollowed out behind it; and in that cavity a charge of explosive was placed. Where it came from

164

I don't know, for it isn't the sort of thing that is easy to come by, I imagine.'

'Oh, there would be no difficulty about that,' the captain remarked. 'If this man you're speaking of knew all about H.E., as you say, he could have compounded the stuff himself from materials anybody can buy. For instance, he could easily make tetranitroaniline – that would be just the thing for him, I should say.'

'I see. Then perhaps there would be a tiny detonator attached to the inner side of the ivorine face, so that a good smack with the brassie would set it off. Then the face would be fixed on again. It would be a delicate job, because the weight of the club head would have to be exactly right. The feel and balance of the club would have to be just the same as before the operation.'

'A delicate job, yes,' the captain agreed. 'But not an impossible one. There would be rather more to it than you say, as a matter of fact; the face would have to be shaved down thin, for instance. Still, it could be done.'

'Well, I imagine it done. Now, this man I have in mind knew there was no work for a brassie at the short first hole, and that the first time it would come out of the bag was at the second hole, down at the bottom of the dip, where no one could see what happened. What certainly did happen was that Freer played a sweet shot, slap on to the green. What else happened at the same moment we don't know for certain, but we can make a reasonable guess. And then, of course, there's the question of what happened to the club – or what was left of it; the handle, say. But it isn't a difficult question, I think, if we remember how the body was found.'

'How do you mean?' Royden asked.

'I mean, by whom it was found. One of the two players who found it was too much upset to notice very much. He hurried back to the clubhouse; and the other was left alone with the body for, as I estimate it, at least fifteen minutes. When the police came on the scene, they found lying near the body a perfectly good brassie, an unusually long and heavy club, exactly like Freer's brassie in every respect except one. The name stamped on the wood of the club head had been obliterated by crushing. That name, I think, was not F. MacAdam, but W. J. Nelson; and the club had been taken out of a bag that was not Freer's – a bag which had the remains, if any, of Freer's brassie at the bottom of it. And I believe that's all.' Trent got to his feet and stretched his arms. 'You can see what I meant when I said I found the mystery interesting.'

For some moments Captain Royden gazed thoughtfully out of the window; then he met Trent's inquiring eye. 'If there was such a fellow as you imagine,' he said coolly, 'he seems to have been careful enough – lucky enough too, if you like – to leave nothing at all of what you could call proof against him. And probably he had personal and private reasons for what he did. Suppose that somebody whom he was much attached to was in the power of a foul-tempered, bullying brute; and suppose he found that the bullying had gone to the length of physical violence; and suppose that the situation was hell by day and by night to this man of yours; and suppose there was no way on earth of putting an end to it except the way he took. Yes, Mr Trent, suppose all that!'

'I will – I do!' Trent said. 'That man – if he exists at all – must have been driven pretty hard, and what he did is no business of mine anyway. And now – still in the conditional mood – suppose I take myself off.'

JOHN P. MARQUAND

CADDIE CRISIS

DEAR ALBERT:

I know what you are going to say when you receive this letter. You are going to say that you cannot constantly be called upon to bail out the Happy Knoll Country Club. You are going to add that during the past year there have been too many fiscal crises and contingencies. You are going to ask, as you do always, why it is that certain members of our group who can afford it better than you, invariably run out of ready cash whenever the hat is passed. You are also going to say that only last week you contributed generously toward a new set of dentures for Old Tim because his last ones were broken while on duty in the men's locker room when he was seized with a fit of laughter at a practical joke played by one of our many pranksters. Although you remarked at the time that it was hard for you to see how this could be called an employee's injury in line of duty, you also added that you would contribute to anything, however indirect, which might improve Old Tim's personal appearance. When holes were burned in the new Oriental rug in the Pendleton Room during the recent celebration of Benny Muldoon's victory in the Invitation Tournament, you contributed toward the repair bills, only making the obvious remark that it might be safer in the future not to have Oriental rugs in the Pendleton Room. When the rear porch of the clubhouse unexpectedly collapsed as the new deep-freeze unit, to which you also subscribed, was being moved across it to the kitchen, you only sent a rhetorical question with your check which was, If the club building is falling to pieces, why not let it?

You must not think that the Board of Governors, not to mention the whole Happy Knoll membership, is not deeply appreciative of both your generosity and your suggestions. In fact, we are acutely embarrassed that so many new contingencies have recently arisen. I know you will say, having gone this far with this communication, that I would not have extolled your generosity if something new and serious had not transpired, and in this case, as almost always, you are right.

I need not remind you of your benign and almost paternal interest in the caddie situation at Happy Knoll, which is only exceeded by that of the young advertising executive, Mr Bob Lawton, who, I must have told you, should never have been made a member of the Board of Governors. Unfortunately, if I may say so, you both react toward our caddie problem as though you were demagogic politicians in a welfare state. Yet, though I have sometimes disagreed, I have never violently objected to your eleemosynary steps in this direction because I, too, have found many of the boys who have spent their adolescence on the links at Happy Knoll individually beguiling. I hope that you will be as shocked as we on the Board of Governors were when we learned from Benny Muldoon and from Pete, the caddie master, that the caddie house situation, in spite of all the palliatives you have attempted, is deteriorating as rapidly as the world situation. We stand, at Happy Knoll, like our own great country – thinking of the money that has been spent, reviewing our good-will missions and the panel discussions, and then wondering what under the sun has happened.

What, you may ask, *has* happened? Nothing that may not be inevitable in this changing world, but the news is, according to Pete and Benny Muldoon, who are both themselves in a state of deep unrest, that the caddies are leaving Happy Knoll for other places, and that, if this regressive movement is not very shortly checked, members will begin pulling golf carts at Happy Knoll.

I know very well how strongly you feel about this contingency and how often you have said that a boy carrying the bag and replacing divots, even though he is afflicted by hiccoughs, is an essential part of a golf match. When he has disappeared, you have often said, a human element and a human hazard has also left the game. We know how the specter of pulling a golf cart has always haunted you, and we know also that your aversion does not arise because of class distinction, but because of your innate fondness for the game. We know the extraordinary steps you have taken in order to avoid this danger. It was you who had plumbing, something which none of us quite frankly had ever thought of associating with caddies, added to the caddie house. It was you, too, when this change was made, who defrayed from your own pocket the cost of a caddie room equipped with easy chairs, magazines and checkerboards. It is not your fault that the chairs are hardly ever used or the checkerboards, either, because the young men, when inside, are invariably on their knees shooting craps. It may disturb you, but also interest you, that a recent delegation from the Board of Governors to the caddie room discovered there a five-cent gambling machine contributed by Old Ned, who oversees its operation. In fact, we believe that this explains why Old Ned has been so anxious lately to convert nickels into dollar bills, and why all the tills at Happy Knoll are filled with only nickels. I do not like to use the word 'racket' in connection with Old Ned – but then, perhaps the Happy Knoll Country Club is merely the Great World in microcosm. It further appeared, when our committee looked into the affairs at the caddie house, that certain of the young men have been selling packets of recently invented 'non-anxiety pills' for nervous and unsteady players. This seemed preposterous until pills were discovered behind a pile of *National Geographic* magazines in your caddie rest room. When analyzed, they proved to be salt tablets; but young Tommy Bailey said that Old Ned was selling the tablets, and arranging for their distribution. Upon being informed of this story, both Benny Muldoon and Pete said that the Bailey boy had been reading too many comic books, and when we attempted to question the Bailey boy again, he had entirely disappeared.

Unfortunately, not your rest room, nor the gambling facilities, nor pill peddling, nor all combined, are any longer sufficient to keep caddies at Happy Knoll. It is true you envisaged the problem, and we all have faced the question of what could be done now that teen-agers can pick up eight or ten dollars for mowing a lawn. Our answer was to make life more glamorous for caddies; and I may say Benny and Pete have been doing their best to make Happy Knoll the cradle of the Hogans of tomorrow by giving useful golf advice. And Tuesday is Caddies' Day. It was Bob Lawton, I believe, who inaugurated the Caddies' Tournament, and the green Caddie Hat with H.K. embroidered on it; and Benny Muldoon himself has made personal calls on caddies' mothers to explain to them the high moral atmosphere of Happy Knoll and its golfers.

Why is it, you may ask, that these intelligent and expensive efforts have borne so little fruit? Some of the Golf

Committee have begun blaming the increasing lack of caddie interest on television, and it may be that the American boy is becoming effeminate or beginning to tire of the game of golf – but frankly, I believe the caddie shortage can be explained in a single word, namely: competition. Frankly, Albert, there are too many golf courses in this area, and too few boys when the caddie potential is being cut by wage inflation and other forms of entertainment. Unfortunately, too, other country clubs have also thought of the devices for caddie happiness that have occurred to us here at Happy Knoll, and the Hard Hollow Country Club is a painful illustration. Hard Hollow caddie caps, we have discovered, not only have a handsome H.H. but an embroidered figure of an American eagle that Hard Hollow has spuriously adopted as an emblem. In some unexplained manner, Mr Benton Follen, the only really big stockbroker in Hard Hollow, has discovered a lawyer who has convinced the Bureau of Internal Revenue that a caddie's recreation room is a boys' school and consequently tax exempt. This has enabled Mr Follen to pour a huge portion of his paper profits into a building whose tiled showers and foam-rubber chairs make your effort at Happy Knoll meager; and I am sorry to say there is a Hard Hollow pinball concession which is somehow classed as charity. But what is still more disturbing is the growing aggressiveness of individual Hard Hollow members. It has been revealed by our investigation that an intensive canvassing of potential caddies' parents has been made, not by their professional, Jerry Scalponi, but actually by a members' committee. These individuals have not only verbally extolled the advantages of Hard Hollow, but have also made unfair and defamatory attacks on Happy Knoll. The rumor, believe it or not, is being spread that the Hard Hollow environment is more salubrious for boys than

Happy Knoll – and to prove it, a transcript has been made of the golf language of certain Happy Knoll members, including, we have learned, your own. Old Ned and his pills have not come off unscathed, either, and several mothers were told by a Hard Hollow member, in front of the meat counter of an A & P store, that Benny Muldoon and Pete run crap games. It was also said in the A & P store that Jerry Scalponi is more interested in teaching caddies golf and is a better instructor and was once an Eagle Scout.

I know that such subversions will infuriate you as much as they have the rest of us and we all dislike to have you disturbed while you are still waiting for the final report on your last medical checkup, but something must be done immediately. The immediacy, I regret, is all the greater because of an agreement which our fellow governor, Bob Lawton – who had no business to speak in behalf of the whole club membership – made with Mr Conrad Richtover, who, as you know, is now the president of Hard Hollow. Unfortunately, the ideas of Mr Lawton are frequently as unsound as they are dangerous, and his enthusiasm constantly outruns his intelligence. It appears that he and Mr Richtover met one afternoon at a cocktail party somewhere on Foxrun Road, where Mr Richtover stated, facetiously I hope, that the only reason any caddie ever worked at Happy Knoll was due to the preposterous tips given them by certain wealthy members. Naturally, Mr Richtover said, I hope facetiously, caddies were drawn to Happy Knoll by the Jaguars, Cadillacs and Bentleys in the parking lot. It seems, according to the somewhat garbled account of Mr Lawton, that he expressed indignation. Tipping, he said, was impossible for the upstanding American boys who came to Happy Knoll. In fact, he was sure that it did not exist and he was sure that all our Board of Governors would be glad to make a gentlemen's agreement with Hard Hollow that members of neither club should tip, however great should be the temptation. You will say, and I will agree with you, that anything said at a Foxrun cocktail party means nothing, but unfortunately Mr Lawton brought up the question at the recent annual meeting, where it was voted on favorably with the help of our tennis, swimming, backgammon and bridge membership, and there it stands. It means that our last leverage to hold caddies at Happy Knoll has been pulled out from under us by, frankly, the lack of alcoholic capacity of one of our newer governors. Personally I had no idea how important the incentive motive was until the 'No Tipping' regulation was suddenly put into practice. It may be a degrading institution, but effective. Without it, Albert, I am very much afraid that the golf cart is here unless immediate measures are taken.

You cannot say that we are not ready with an answer. Some of Happy Knoll's best lawyers have been working on one all last week, and here it is. There will be no tipping but there will be what is known as a Revolving Incentive Fund for Deserving Caddies. This fund will be divided at the end of the season, according to merit, to pay for caddies' schoolbooks and other school expenses; and thus it is our hope, although no promise can be made as yet, that the Bureau of Internal Revenue will pass it as an effort as educational and as tax exempt as that of the caddies' room at Hard Hollow. When this plan goes into operation, as it must, a huge thermometer will be placed at the door of the golf shop showing the rising amount of dollars being subscribed for the Caddies' Revolving Incentive Fund. If this does not catch the interest of our local youth, we shall all be very much surprised. The moment the fund is created, each caddie will have a card with a point system to be signed by the member who employs him; one point for average work and three points for excellence – but there will also be demerits. These will be: talking, sniffling, coughing and sneezing, one demerit each; laughter, three; taking practice swings with the employer's clubs, four; and ten demerits for any caddie seen taking a full swing with a putter on any green. Think what this revolving incentive fund will mean. It will mean, frankly, that Happy Knoll, because of its financial position, should be able to outbid any effort of Hard Hollow in this direction, whether these contributions are tax exempt or not. It will mean far more skillful caddies as much pledged to do kind deeds as are Boy Scouts. It will mean dedicated boys and the pick of the market. Try to keep them away from Happy Knoll when there is a Revolving Incentive Fund for schoolbooks! Try to make their parents not send them, daily!

This idea, I may confess, is entirely my own and I can see you catching fire already. The secret of its success is of course the subscription of a large initial sum and I believe that you or I should start the ball rolling. It must, I am afraid, be something substantial, and I fear I cannot do what I should ordinarily because unfortunately the Government has found an error in my recent tax returns which will set me back for many months to come. But I am sure it is different with you, Albert. What we need is a thousand dollars as a starter, and we know you always lead the way, and don't forget that time is of the essence. Why not telegraph the money before you forget it, just as soon as you receive this letter?

With all our thanks in advance,

Most sincerely,

ROGER HORLICK

REX LARDNER

TRIUMPH AT CRESTWOOD

THE GALLERY FOR tournaments at Crestwood is not as large as those found at Baltusrol or Tam O'Shanter during championships, but it makes up in noise, knowledge of the game and partisanship for its comparative lack of numbers.

The screams of delight at the sinking of a long putt and murmurs of 'Oooooooh!' and 'Geeeeeeeez!' when long drives smoke off the tee are just as loud and spontaneous as the exclamations of fans who line the fairways and pursue their favorites at larger tournaments.

Moreover, the spectators at Crestwood, from practice, are generally much quicker on their feet than those who attend national-championship matches. It takes a fine low shot to fell a Crestwood galleryite.

While my wife chose to stay home – competition this grueling is too much for her nerves, she says – there was my own group of supporters who rooted for me, some backing their faith in my ability to cream this outstanding field with modest wagers at respectable odds.

Unlike most other tournaments at the club, which take two or three days to run off, this was a sudden-death medal affair, with low score for 18 holes – less handicap – determining the winner.

It meant that some of us would be fighting like the very devil and using every shot in the book to equalize the advantage given other players who had been accorded monstrous handicaps by the handicap committee – of which I happened to be a member.

As luck would have it, the cards I had been turning in for the past two rating periods had caused the committee to raise my own handicap somewhat higher than my standard of play would seem to require or deserve – but I had it, and I needs must abide by it. 'Ours not to reason why,' as Tennyson so sagely observed in his poem about the boo-boo at Balaclava.

The subject of the tournament was naturally on everyone's lips in the locker room and the bar during the week preceding. The feeling was that it might well be a three-way battle down to the wire, the other two players being Bob ('Fighting Bob') Lindsey and Albert ('Al' or 'Albie') Prentice. Bob had won it four years ago, while Prentice finished second to Bob's third last year. I had never finished better than seventh. Fortunately, the player who had won it three times running – Andy Barnes – was sick at home with the flu.

Toward the end of the week, when excitement about the tournament reached its zenith and it was sure that Andy would definitely not defend his championship, the group that supported me chuckled among themselves that with my ability and the handicap I had been given, Man-O'-War could have won the tournament. I felt their confidence was touching.

Indeed, the day before the tournament, my spirits had risen from the complete despair of the Sunday preceding to high optimism. Four days before, I had discovered High Tension as the secret of playing top-notch golf. Reflections on my analysis kept me in a reasonably annoyed state. On Wednesday I phoned my secretary to cancel all appointments and went to a driving range and banged drives and finessed pitches until my hands were blistered and I had knots in my arms. On Thursday I put in some time at the office, managing to persuade a few customers to decide whether it was going to be reconciliation or splitsville. In the afternoon I ducked over to the pro's studio where the canvas backdrop is that sounds like Big Bertha and hit a couple of hundred wood shots – *whack! whack! whack!* Sometimes the pro would look over at me enviously, wishing to God he could hit a ball that hard.

On Friday I canceled all my appointments and drove to Crestwood in the morning to put my theories to the acid test. To build up tension, I drove on the left lane of the right side of the boulevard, which is full of people who block traffic for miles while they wait to make a left turn. I could feel my back and shoulders surge with power as I blasted with the horn and bounced exhortations off the windows.

Moderately wound up, eager to prove my system in the arena, as it were, I dressed, hurried out on the course and played my most satisfactory round of the year. I went the entire 18 holes in less than two and a half hours. My score was respectable but not earthshaking. After lunch and a snooze I played another 18 – a single against a pretty good golfer. Pepito caddied for me. I wasn't trying for speed this time but concentrating more on score and trying not to lose too many balls. In the morning I had lost eight.

While I was not out for blood against this fellow, my game was so 'on' that I made mincemeat out of him – 4 up going into the 17th. I let him win the last two to build him up for a small wager some time in the future, which is nothing more than golf etiquette.

My morning round caused a great deal of comment and hubbub among the members, as you can imagine. I posted the speed record (which I am sure it was) on the clubroom bulletin board, a good-natured challenge to the rapid players in the club and calculated to give my opponents in the tournament something to stew over.

There is golf, as Jones says, and there is tournament golf.

While I was by no means fanatical about it, I tried to prepare myself for the latter in other ways besides hitting a golf ball. Lest I destroy the delicate balance I had effected between my left and right sides during the days preceding the tournament, I did no hammering or sawing, and I did not risk overdeveloping the muscles in my shoulders by moving the furniture around, which my wife likes to have done about once a week so guests will have something to talk about when they come over and drink my liquor.

When I ate, I alternated between right and left hands. I learned to butter rolls left-handed because I found I always wind my watch and turn on TV right-handed. I kept my hands out of hot water, except for washing, because hot water softens the palm muscles and gives you a hook. The swallowing muscles, being smack in the center of the body, cannot possibly throw your swing out of balance, however, and you do not have to worry about them.

On Saturday I rested, except for visiting a driving range to bang out a hundred or so drives and, as a change of pace, trying my luck on a miniature golf course. There, I am sure, I had the customers and manager buzzing with speculation as I made a monkey out of par with my fiendishly accurate putts, winning a chocolate ice-cream stick for getting an ace on the tricky 2nd hole, a par-2. Few sweets ever tasted better.

That night I pondered tournament strategy and examined the strengths and weaknesses of my opponents, one by one.

I had drawn the caustic Prentice, while Fighting Bob had drawn Josh Hilliard, a splendid stylist but a mediocre golfer. A possible dark horse in the tournament (there were eight of us altogether) was Norman Blount, who would go around with plodding George Kneezley; and the remaining pair were bespectacled Gene Teller and the long-hitting Buff Kowalski.

We were to start at half-hour intervals, beginning at ten. Teller-Kowalski were to start first, followed by the Blount team, then Bob-Josh and then Prentice and myself. The pressure was certainly on Al and me, since by the time those six got through chomping and chewing up the course there would hardly be a grassy square foot left.

The 72-year-old Blount had a psychological advantage over all of us in that he would be riding while we were afoot. He had consented to play in the tournament only if allowed to go around in his golf car. The committee had acceded to his request because they were determined to have a field of eight. But they drew the line when Blount wanted his score prorated for the 18 holes in the event he didn't finish. It was 18 or nothing, they said, and Blount grumpily acquiesced.

This was much tougher than match play because I had to defeat not one opponent but seven. Seven of the shrewdest and most tenacious golfers in the East, all eying the trophy like so many vultures. Under the merciless pressures of the tournament, any of them might be steeled to play superb, errorless golf. Who could say?

I wondered whether I should try to beat Old Man Par, not paying attention to my opponents' scores, or simply attempt to demolish Prentice, who, I felt, was the man most likely to triumph – not reckoning on the technical brilliance and heart of Fighting Bob Lindsey.

The last couple of hours I spent cutting down my twenty-three clubs to fourteen, since that rule would be strictly observed. It was a little like cutting out my own appendix.

This was not, of course, merely a test of my skill at golf; it was a test of the High-Tension theory. When we look back on the event, it is obvious that the system was *right*, if we are to judge by the results. But I was not so certain of it at the time.

In order not to be overawed by the task that lay ahead and to make sure my tension tanks were full to overflowing when I set foot on the first tee, I evolved the following program which the reader may at some time find useful:

1. I set the alarm late, so that I had to rush to get to the club on time.

2. I shaved with an old blade, managing to cut myself twice.

3. I woke my wife up and had some words with her about not having coffee ready. She went back to sleep.

4. There being no time to squeeze orange juice or anything, I shoveled a handful of granulated sugar in my mouth and chewed it while putting on my socks.

5. I put on my shoes in the car while stopping for red lights, possibly causing several other drivers to develop High Tension of their own.

Thus prepared, burning with the desire to plaster hell out of a golf ball and anything else that got in the way, I tore into the locker room. Prentice, double-knotting his laces, the picture of disdainful confidence, offered to shake hands in a theatrical way, but I merely gave him a cool wave and a nod. I would have been hypocritical when I intended to tear him to pieces a few minutes later on the course.

Hurriedly I got into sky-blue slacks, a tan polo shirt, an orange-and-blue baseball cap and brown-and-white shoes. My left-hand glove matched the visor of my cap.

By keeping to this pace I actually beat Prentice outside and walked briskly to the first tee. A gallery in holiday raiment and mood had assembled. They waved a greeting which I returned desultorily, absorbed in the business at hand. A few words with Pepito about general strategy, and then I chatted for a few seconds with E. K. G. Potter, the marshal, and Jock Murdoch, a member of the rules committee.

He likes to be called 'the' Murdoch in the manner of clan chieftains.

As I fumed slightly, waiting for Prentice, the Murdoch told me that Kneezley had got off to a bad start. It seemed he couldn't find his lucky hat, and they had to penalize him 2 strokes for holding up the tournament.

'How is Bob doing?' I asked, swinging several woods at the same time.

'Sae-sae,' said the Murdoch. 'He got a six on the first.'

'Teller?'

The Murdoch chuckled. 'He dropped thirty strokes to par on the first six,' he said.

'That won't hurt him,' I said. 'He has a pretty sizable handicap.' I was taking nothing for granted.

Al sauntered out, resplendent in Navy blue slacks, white polo shirt with a hawk embroidered on it, black-and-white shoes and a glove to match his slacks. Instead of a hat he wore a proofreader's visor, I presume for superstitious reasons.

When the gallery spotted him, they cheered in anticipation of the match starting. Solemnly we flipped for the honor and I won. Prentice sneered as I went over to discuss with Pepito what club to use on this important shot. I selected a driver and after three experimental swings, more for the gratification of the crowd than for any practical purpose, I signaled I was ready.

An announcement was made to impressive applause, and the gallery, ranging far down the fairway and curving slightly to the left, braced itself as I teed up.

It was a memorable moment. The sky was a hazy endless blue with a few blimplike cotton clouds, hardly a breeze stirring.

The crowd hushed, a few cameras went Bzzzzzt! Bzzzzzt!,

my opponent stared at me in a disgruntled way and the pin 198 yards off was beckoning. Bzzzzzt! Bzzzzzt! I murmured, imitating the James Wong Howes of the 16-millimeter. The defiant ball. I was going to let *everything* bother me today.

I set my feet, waggled, launched the club back and gave the ball a terrific swipe. 'Oooooooooh!' breathed the gallery in wonder and awe. The ball was one of those hard-hit shots that sometimes seem to defy the laws of physics. It started out far to the left, maintained a low trajectory, finally plumed upward a few feet, started to curve right, began to lose some of its initial momentum, rose a little more but kept curving to the right and finally lost its long battle to gravity, plunking down smack in the center of the fairway, 115 yards from the tee.

The gallery broke off its spontaneous applause as Al stepped up. Again there was a hush as he hoisted his brassie back and hammered a prosaic knock 10 yards beyond mine and to the left. In air-distance, however, mine was far longer.

I had nothing to fear from the trap on the right, since I was almost at right angles to it, so, as the gallery scampered ahead for a better view of the next shot, I aimed for the center of the narrow alley feeding the green. After topping once in-effectively except to improve my lie, I hit a superb shot that fell just short of the trap on the right of the green. Al socked a fine high shot that landed smack in the trap on the left.

A tiny chip and I was on the green. I was lucky, because in spite of not yet being warmed up I had got off several good shots. Usually a golfer in these circumstances will fritter away shots on the first few holes. It's the first few drives that put most tournament golfers in hot water. But High Tension was working out. Here I was, parked on the green, needing only to sink a 25-footer for a bogey. A moment later it developed

Al had a 3-footer to sink for the same score. I missed mine the first time but nailed it the second. He picked up a stroke.

The gallery cheered just before it broke and sped to the next hole.

I wasn't worried about Al's picking up a stroke so early. My handicap was 10 more than his, and he had a long way to go before catching me. He and Fighting Bob had the same handicap.

All I had to do, I figured, was play good, consistent, thinking golf, keep my head down, stay mad and I'd beat the both of them.

On the second – our water hole – I thought I'd pull a piece of strategy which I had worked before. If it came off it would break Al's back.

It was his honor. Because Pepito's shadow fell in front of him or perhaps because of some unnatural fear of water, Al hit a bad 4-wood – a shank that went about 30 feet and was stopped by a tree. Now my plan could go into effect.

After talking with Pepito, I made no secret of the fact that I was using a 3-iron. There was a gasp from the gallery followed by a hubba-hubba like that in a courtroom when the prosecutor shows up drunk and accuses the defendant of the wrong crime.

My intent was, by carefully cutting and finessing the shot, to drop it a little short of the pin. I knew that Al, who relies on other people's brains for many of his decisions, would then probably choose a 3-iron for his next shot – but, unable to control it, would blast the ball to hell-and-gone in the dense forest behind the green.

I did not make the green, however, with the shot. Instead I hit a long soaring curve with enough power to carry across the lake twice over had it gone straight but which flew sideways after heading 20 yards out and landed deep in the woods to the right.

Snorting and chortling to himself, Al now took out a 6-iron and plunked the ball over the lake smack into the middle of the green – where the unimaginative tournament committee had seen fit to place the pin.

By the time I got out of the woods and slammed the ball into the cup, I had a 9 to Al's par 3 and there went 6 more strokes.

I held him even by brilliant play on the 3rd, 4th and 5th. On the par-4 6th, one of the most treacherous holes in the course, we were both on in 5. I had a 5-foot putt, blocking his 9-footer. Here was a chance to earn back a stroke and turn the tide.

I carefully plotted the shot and waited, poised over the ball, my teeth beginning to itch, until the cameras should stop buzzing and Al stopped making explosive ticking noises by snapping his tongue at the roof of his mouth. Then I putted. The ball was perfectly hit, the break perfectly judged and it rolled straight and true directly toward the cup – and then seemingly looked into it and drew back. It was a heart-breaker. You could have heard the spectators moan a mile off.

'Too bad,' said Al with cheery commiseration.

'What do you mean "Too bad"?' I demanded, walking over to him rapidly. Pepito meanwhile was walking around the hole, studying the putt, banging his feet the way he does when he is concentrating. I was hoping there would be a tremor or hailstorm or something, but the sky stayed clear. After a minute of standing stock still lest he disturb the ball, Al tiptoed over to the Murdoch and complained.

I strode over to him, too.

'Look at the damn thing,' Al said in a low, slow voice. 'It's at least two inches from the cup.'

'But it's downhill, the—!' I said loudly. A couple of my partisans in the crowd started to holler. 'Let's at least wait and see if it's stopped rolling!' I tried to sound reasonable.

The Murdoch asked if anyone had a carpenter's level, but no one had. Pepito said he thought the green was downhill at this point, but Barney, who was caddying for Al and is almost as big as Pepito, said the pro once told him it was uphill at this point.

So we waited a few minutes and finally the Murdoch, peering down at it, ruled the ball had stopped – though I could swear I saw it move once or twice – and I had to putt out. Which I did without a bit of trouble.

Now Al prowled back and forth between the ball and the hole, picking out so many pieces of grass and lint it appeared he had constructed a valley to the cup. He finally putted and missed, then hit, and we had halved another.

I picked up a stroke on the 7th, lost it back on the 8th and we halved the 9th. We were both playing fantastic golf, bogeys and double bogeys dropping like flies, but an explosion seemed imminent. A couple of times, when he spent twenty minutes selecting a club or lining up 4- and 5-iron shots I felt like hitting him on the head with a number 5 wood. Surreptitiously, Pepito was giving him the horns, but without much effect.

Reports now began to filter back about other competitors' trials: Kneezley was hopelessly out of contention with a 200 and 4 holes yet to play; how Blount's battery had given out on the 17th, and he called Fred Conch, who runs the garage, terrible names because there were no recharge batteries available, and could likewise be eliminated; how Kowalski and Teller had got involved in a distance-hitting duel – Oooooooooh! – and had forgotten about making low scores. Some of Biff's drives had gone 350 yards into the woods and some of Gene's were landing on the wrong fairways, upsetting the competitors they came close to crowning.

There was no news about Fighting Bob except that he seemed to be shooting steady golf. As for Hilliard, he was nervous about the wild balls Gene hit and was blowing up at least once on every hole.

On the 13th – par 3, 260 yards – I got into trouble. This is a blind hole with trees and traps guarding the green. A huge bunker stands two-thirds of the way down the fairway to the right.

I hit a beautiful drive – thwack! – getting as big a gasp as Biff. The ball soared 145 yards down the fairway – not as long as some of his, but more crisply hit. Then, in trying to pancake a 3-iron onto the green, I dumped the ball into the bunker. It wound up in a fiendishly bad lie – somehow wedged under a projecting overhang, unable to be seen from a standing position.

As the gallery chatted among themselves, wondering how I would play the shot, I bent way down to look at the ball. Actually, it didn't look like mine.

'There's no rule that says you have to see a ball to hit it,' said Al, who came hurrying up, his face full of suspicion and greed.

The Murdoch was fifty yards behind him.

I straightened up and brushed off my slacks.

'Geez, Al,' I said dubiously, 'I wonder if that's my ball or not.'

He had flopped down suddenly to examine it. Some of his partisans were alarmed that he might have succumbed to the strain of tournament play. But I indicated with a wave that he was just nosing around.

He peered at it closely. 'Well, it's a gold ball with a monogramed RL on it,' he announced. 'It *could* be yours.'

I accepted the possibility. 'Are you sure?' I asked, wanting to be certain. 'The light's damn bad down there.'

He thought it was adequate.

'I'd like to see it in the light,' I said. I tried to maneuver around him, but his hulking frame blocked the way. 'Maybe Pepito—'

'Figure it out by elimination,' he interrupted. 'Did you start out with a gold ball with RL on it in red?'

'Gosh, Al,' I said cheerily. 'I don't recall. You know how I am about the ball I tee up. Nylon, rubber, English-made. They're all the same to me. Anyway, I think my shot went more to the right.'

He was willing to let me hunt for it while he rested in the shade of the bunker.

'Here's the Murdoch,' he said. 'Let him decide.'

Again the decision went against me. By the time I had finished chopping at it and banged it in the cup, we were all even, and it was root, hog or die.

Suddenly there was an indication that our worries were just beginning. As we made ready to tee off for the 14th, there was a roar from the gallery following Bob and Josh who were on the 16th. A few seconds later there was another roar. Somebody was getting hot and it could only be Bob. Al's and my gallery were beginning to desert and feed the mob around Lindsey.

'Now I know what a sinking ship feels like,' I told Al, but he has no sense of humor. 'Listen,' I told him in a friendly way, 'I notice your ball banks sharply to the right when you hit it. You suppose it's off-center after the terrific blasts you've been hitting?'

'It might be,' he said thoughtfully. 'You're getting nice wrist into your long ones yourself,' he added in a sudden gush of comradeship. Bob's spurt must have thawed him a little.

We soon got the unwelcome news that Bob was burning up the course. He had a bogey on the 16th and a fantastic par on the 17th, one of the most treacherous holes on the course. The pressure was on, all right. In a few minutes we would know Bob's final score, which would give us something to brood about in the home-stretch.

He picked up a 6 to my 7 on the par-4 15th and we made ready to attack the 16th with Al a stroke up. This par-4 280-yarder had several traps around the green and the route there is blocked by a huge pine tree. Al hit a soggy shot about 50 yards down the fairway, and I realized that now was the time to smash him to bits.

You have to go over the pine tree or around it, and I was determined to go over it. As about twenty of the faithful watched, I drew my brassie back and swung for height as well as distance. As the crowd gasped, I somehow hit the bottom of the ball with the toe of the club, and it sailed about 15 feet in the air and landed in a spectator's jacket pocket. He was as surprised as I was but assumed an expression of terror when I stalked over to him, club in hand.

'Lie down,' I told him. 'Lie down, dammit, and let me get a shot at the ball.' His features grew chalk-white as he turned appealingly to the ever-present the Murdoch. I recalled, if the Murdoch didn't, the situation had come up once before at Crestwood. It was solved (a non-tournament decision) by having the man lie down on his side with the ball facing up. The player who blooped the ball there then took a stroke at it. In fact, he took two strokes before his human tee got up and scampered away.

I was in favor of this fellow lying down and letting me do the same thing. I had lost too many strokes on bad breaks to be penalized now for some spectator's sluggishness.

'Let him take his change and keys and whatever he's got

out of his pocket,' I told the Murdoch. 'I'm entitled to a clear cut at the ball.' I believe the man would have darted away and complicated matters endlessly if I hadn't held him by the arm.

While the Murdoch was busy with the Solomon bit, I had a quick discussion with Pepito about the proper club. I wanted to use a cleek, but he thought a 6-iron was better. I figured if I used an open stance and kept my eye on the lump in the fellow's pocket, unless he had a projecting hipbone, I wouldn't have any trouble. I could get off a pretty respectable shot.

The Murdoch came to a decision, however, that threw my plans out the window but which worked to my advantage. He said the ball should be taken out of the man's pocket and placed where he'd been standing. There would be no stroke penalty. The man looked relieved as he fished the ball out of his pocket.

I poured a lot of frustration and pique into the 5-wood I hit and it sliced neatly around the tree instead of over it. The gallery's applause indicated they felt, as I did, that this was the most neatly finessed 5-wood of the entire tournament.

Al was on in 3, I was on in 4. I had a 5-footer on a green that went up and down like a corrugated roof, while he had a 12-footer. My ball blocked his, and I elected to putt out. Nervous, I was down in 2. If he sank his putt, he'd be 2 strokes up going to the 17th. It was a tricky situation. Again he took unconscionably long to size up a putt, making a furrow between the ball and the hole. Finally he bent over the ball as I tensely watched and the spectators bordering the green held their breath.

Suddenly I sprang up and shouted, 'Let it go through, let it go through!', running toward the spectators at the far side of the green and pushing them out of the way. I remembered one of Hagen's matches in England where a spectator stopping his opponent's ball had cost him a hole.

Making surprised noises, the gallery backed off.

'Dammit,' said Al irritably, 'I haven't putted yet.' He gave me a sour look. The fans who had scattered came back to their places. I admit I had erred, but Al did not seem to be bothered. He was down in three putts, and we had halved another.

At the 17th we got the bad news. Fighting Bob had finished with an amazing 86 (after his handicap had been subtracted). The other players were in the 100's – such are the pressures of tournament play. When we tallied our scores, under the Murdoch's watchful eye, it developed that Al, who was one stroke under me, would have to shoot the next two holes (par 3 and par 4) in 10 to beat Fighting Bob; while I would have to shoot them in 9!

Impossible? Naturally.

Bob's contingent and Bob himself now joined the growing gallery, his supporters practically counting their money. A huge crowd lined the fairway of the 191-yard 17th as we prepared to tee off.

This was where I had 'frozen' the week before – but I did not freeze today! After Al hit a long drive into a trap on the left, I studied the situation carefully and hit a low, well-placed slice into the woods on the right, but not too deep. Playing well under pressure, a mashie shot got me on the green in a fantastic 2, while Al was on in 3.

Now disaster struck. I with a chance for par, he with a chance for a bogey, we both had difficulty with our putts. It seemed we passed back and forth like sentinels on post, putting, putting, putting. I was dizzy from so much walking bent over with my arms held stiff so as not to lose my touch.

When the smoke had cleared and the two balls were finally

laid away, I had a 6 and he had an 11. The pressure had finally told on poor Al.

But I was almost as much out of contention as he was. As the gallery, now silent except for the muffled chortling of Bob and his elated friends, moved to the next hole, we all realized I had to get an incredible 3 on the 18th to win, a fantastic 4 to tie.

The chortling got on my nerves, needless to state, along with a kind of enveloping annoyance at getting so close to winning only to lose at the next-to-last hole, in addition to the idiots with their cameras who kept going Bzzzzzt! Bzzzzzt! at critical moments during our putts. When the tournament was over, I promised myself, I was going to clobber a few movie cameras with a 5-iron, that versatile club.

The 18th is a 420-yard par-4 which runs roughly parallel to the front of the clubhouse. It looks something like a crescent – bent the wrong way, to the left. A huge bunker lies in the middle of the fairway as you approach the bend, and two traps guard the left side and front of the green. To the right are woods and to the left is very dense rough, along with scattered trees. The green lies about 40 yards from the flagstone terrace, which is filled with natty metal tables and wicker chairs. Naturally, a sizable bunch of spectators had assembled there to see the homecoming – though it would appear to be anti-climactic.

It was my honor, and I was seething. Since I had to make the hole in 3, or at most 4, I extracted a driver without any discussion, gripped the handle for a hook, wound up, raised my head a fraction too soon on the downswing and missed the ball entirely.

The crowd gasped and groaned, particularly the diehards in my faction who had hoped I would somehow get a tie. Their groans increased when I missed it again.

It was no use hooking, I felt. The solution was to aim and purposely slice – slice with all the seething vehemence at my command – and get to the green *the back way.*

It demanded tremendous concentration, evaluation of wind, distance and angle. Facing somewhat left, I used an open stance, got my right wrist well under, lifted the left side quickly, kept my weight on my right heel and hit a tremendous spinning drive that soared up and up, broke sharply to the right in a sweeping arc, started to lose height, plummeted downward, bounced hard on the clubhouse roof, bounced off onto the caddie house roof, hit the flagstone terrace behind the club, smacked an oak behind the club, rebounded and was lost sight of for a few moments and then reappeared – according to cowering witnesses on the terrace – as it flew like a cannon blast out of a window in the ladies' shower room, bounced off an umbrella stand on one of the tables, rolled out onto the green, hesitated on the lip of the cup and toppled in.

The people on the terrace rose in wonder and awe.

In an incredible display of nerve and skill, I had canned my third shot from the tee for a birdie 3 and nailed the lid shut on the tournament!

My High-Tension system had proven itself in the stiffest kind of competition. The Kingston Trophy was mine.

Triumphantly we marched to the flag, my contingent leaping and shouting, followed by the marveling gallery. Bob and Al peered into the cup and then these two gallant competitors, who just didn't have it, shook hands with me and walked away shaking their heads. I thanked Pepito for his splendid job, thanked the Murdoch for his willing, if over-zealous, officiating, picked up the ball and, as is customary, tossed it to the crowd for a souvenir. Then I took off after some of those bastards with cameras.

IAN FLEMING

From GOLDFINGER

'GOOD AFTERNOON, BLACKING. All set?' The voice was casual, authoritative. 'I see there's a car outside. Not somebody looking for a game, I suppose?'

'I'm not sure, sir. It's an old member come back to have a club made up. Would you like me to ask him, sir?'

'Who is it? What's his name?'

Bond smiled grimly. He pricked his ears. He wanted to catch every inflection.

'A Mr Bond, sir.'

There was a pause. 'Bond?' The voice had not changed. It was politely interested. 'Met a fellow called Bond the other day. What's his first name?'

'James, sir.'

'Oh yes.' Now the pause was longer. 'Does he know I'm here?' Bond could sense Goldfinger's antennae probing the situation.

'He's in the workshop, sir. May have seen your car drive up.'

Bond thought: Alfred's never told a lie in his life. He's not going to start now.

'Might be an idea.' Now Goldfinger's voice unbent. He wanted something from Alfred Blacking, some information. 'What sort of a game does this chap play? What's his handicap?'

'Used to be quite useful when he was a boy, sir. Haven't seen his game since then.'

'Hm.'

Bond could feel the man weighing it all up. Bond smelled that the bait was going to be taken. He reached into his bag and pulled out his driver and started rubbing down the grip with a block of shellac. Might as well look busy. A board in the shop creaked. Bond honed away industriously, his back to the open door.

'I think we've met before.' The voice from the doorway was low, neutral.

Bond looked quickly over his shoulder. 'My God, you made me jump. Why,' recognition dawned, 'it's Gold, Gold-man . . . er, Goldfinger.' He hoped he wasn't over-playing it. He said with a hint of dislike, or mistrust, 'Where have you sprung from?'

'I told you I played down here. Remember?' Goldfinger was looking at him shrewdly. Now the eyes opened wide. The X-ray gaze pierced through to the back of Bond's skull.

'No.'

'Did not Miss Masterton give you my message?'

'No. What was it?'

'I said I would be over here and that I would like a game of golf with you.'

'Oh well,' Bond's voice was coldly polite, 'we must do that some day.'

'I was playing with the professional. I will play with you instead.' Goldfinger was stating a fact.

There was no doubt that Goldfinger was hooked. Now Bond must play hard to get.

'Why not some other time? I've come to order a club. Any-way I'm not in practice. There probably isn't a caddie.' Bond was being as rude as he could. Obviously, the last thing he wanted to do was play with Goldfinger.

'I also haven't played for some time.' (Bloody liar, thought Bond.) 'Ordering a club will not take a moment.' Goldfinger turned back into the shop. 'Blacking, have you got a caddie for Mr Bond?'

'Yes, sir.'

'Then that is arranged.'

Bond wearily thrust his driver back into his bag. 'Well, all right then.' He thought of a final way of putting Goldfinger off. He said roughly, 'But I warn you I like playing for money. I can't be bothered to knock a ball round just for the fun of it.' Bond felt pleased with the character he was building up for himself.

Was there a glint of triumph, quickly concealed, in Goldfinger's pale eyes? He said indifferently, 'That suits me. Anything you like. Off handicap, of course. I think you said you're 9.'

'Yes.'

Goldfinger said carefully, 'Where, may I ask?'

'Huntercombe.' Bond was also 9 at Sunningdale. Huntercombe was an easier course. Nine at Huntercombe wouldn't frighten Goldfinger.

'And I also am 9. Here. Up on the board. So it's a level game. Right?'

Bond shrugged. 'You'll be too good for me.'

'I doubt it. However,' Goldfinger was offhand, 'tell you what I'll do. That bit of money you removed from me in Miami. Remember? The big figure was 10. I like a gamble. It will be good for me to have to try. I will play you double or quits for that.'

Bond said indifferently, 'That's too much.' Then as if he thought better of it, thought he might win, he said – with just the right amount of craft mixed with reluctance – 'Of course you can say that was "found money". I won't miss it if it goes again. Oh, well, all right. Easy come, easy go. Level match. Ten thousand dollars it is.'

Goldfinger turned away. He said, and there was a sudden sweetness in the flat voice, 'That's all arranged then, Mr Blacking. Many thanks. Put your fee down on my account. Very sorry we shall be missing our game. Now, let me pay the caddie fees.'

Alfred Blacking came into the workroom and picked up Bond's clubs. He looked very directly at Bond. He said, 'Remember what I told you, sir.' One eye closed and opened again. 'I mean about that flat swing of yours. It needs watching – all the time.'

Bond smiled at him. Alfred had long ears. He might not have caught the figure, but he knew that somehow this was to be a key game. 'Thanks, Alfred. I won't forget. Four Penfolds – with hearts on them. And a dozen tees. I won't be a minute.'

Bond walked through the shop and out to his car. The bowler-hatted man was polishing the metal work of the Rolls with a cloth. Bond felt rather than saw him stop and watch Bond take out his zip bag and go into the clubhouse. The man had a square flat yellow face. One of the Koreans?

Bond paid his green fee to Hampton, the steward, and went into the changing room. It was just the same – the same tacky smell of old shoes and socks and last summer's sweat. Why was it a tradition of the most famous golf clubs that their standard of hygiene should be that of a Victorian private school? Bond changed his socks and put on the battered old pair of nailed Saxons. He took off the coat of his yellowing black-and-white hound's tooth suit and pulled on a faded black windcheater. Cigarettes? Lighter? He was ready to go.

Bond walked slowly out, preparing his mind for the game. On purpose he had needled this man into a high, tough match so that Goldfinger's respect for him should increase and Goldfinger's view of Bond – that he was the type of ruthless, hard adventurer who might be very useful to Goldfinger – would be confirmed. Bond had thought that perhaps a £100 nassau would be the form. But $10,000! There had probably never been such a high singles game in history – except in the finals of American championships or in the big amateur Calcutta Sweeps where it was the backers rather than the players who had the money on. Goldfinger's private accounting must have taken a nasty dent. He wouldn't have liked that. He would be aching to get some of his money back. When Bond had talked about playing high, Goldfinger had seen his chance. So be it. But one thing was certain, for a hundred reasons Bond could not afford to lose.

He turned into the shop and picked up the balls and tees from Alfred Blacking.

'Hawker's got the clubs, sir.'

Bond strolled out across the 500 yards of shaven seaside turf that led to the first tee. Goldfinger was practicing on the putting green. His caddie stood nearby, rolling balls to him. Goldfinger putted in the new fashion – between his legs with a mallet putter. Bond felt encouraged. He didn't believe in the system. He knew it was no good practicing himself. His old hickory Calamity Jane had its good days and its bad. There was nothing to do about it. He knew also that the St Marks practice green bore no resemblance, in speed and texture, to the greens on the course.

Bond caught up with the limping, insouciant figure of his caddie who was sauntering along chipping at an imaginary ball with Bond's blaster. 'Afternoon, Hawker.'

'Afternoon, sir.' Hawker handed Bond the blaster and threw down three used balls. His keen sardonic poacher's face split in a wry grin of welcome. 'How've you been keepin', sir? Played any golf in the last 20 years? Can you still put them on the roof of the starter's hut?' This referred to the day when Bond, trying to do just that before a match, had put two balls through the starter's window.

'Let's see.' Bond took the blaster and hefted it in his hand, gauging the distance. The tap of the balls on the practice green had ceased. Bond addressed the ball, swung quickly, lifted his head and shanked the ball almost at right angles. He tried again. This time it was a dunch. A foot of turf flew up. The ball went 10 yards. Bond turned to Hawker, who was looking his most sardonic. 'It's all right, Hawker. Those were for show. Now then, one for you.' He stepped up to the third ball, took his club back slowly and whipped the club head through. The ball soared 100 feet, paused elegantly, dropped 80 feet on to the thatched roof of the starter's hut and bounced down.

Bond handed back the club. Hawker's eyes were thoughtful, amused. He said nothing. He pulled out the driver and handed it to Bond. They walked together to the first tee, talking about Hawker's family.

Goldfinger joined them, relaxed, impassive. Bond greeted Goldfinger's caddie, an obsequious, talkative man called Foulks whom Bond had never liked. Bond glanced at Goldfinger's clubs. They were a brand new set of American Ben Hogans with smart St Marks leather covers for the woods. The bag was one of the stitched black leather holdalls favored by American pros. The clubs were in individual cardboard tubes for easy extraction. It was a pretentious outfit, but the best.

'Toss for honor?' Goldfinger flicked a coin.

'Tails.'

It was heads. Goldfinger took out his driver and unpeeled a new ball. He said 'Dunlop 65. No. 1. Always use the same ball. What's yours?'

'Penfold. Hearts.'

Goldfinger looked keenly at Bond. 'Strict Rules of Golf?'

'Naturally.'

'Right.' Goldfinger walked on to the tee and teed up. He took one or two careful, concentrated practice swings. It was a type of swing Bond knew well – the grooved, mechanical, repeating swing of someone who had studied the game with great care, read all the books and spent £5,000 on the finest pro teachers. It would be a good, scoring swing which might not collapse under pressure. Bond envied it.

Goldfinger took up his stance, waggled gracefully, took his clubhead back in a wide, slow arc and, with his eyes glued to the ball, broke his wrists correctly. He brought the club-head mechanically, effortlessly, down and through the ball and into a rather artificial, copybook finish. The ball went straight and true about 200 yards down the fairway.

It was an excellent, uninspiring shot. Bond knew that Goldfinger would be capable of repeating the same swing with different clubs again and again round the 18 holes.

Bond took his place, gave himself a lowish tee, addressed the ball with careful enmity and, with a flat, racket-player's swing in which there was just too much wrist for safety, lashed the ball away. It was a fine, attacking drive that landed past Goldfinger's ball and rolled on 50 yards. But it had had a shade of draw and ended on the edge of the left-hand rough.

They were two good drives. As Bond handed his club to Hawker and strolled off in the wake of the more impatient Goldfinger, he smelled the sweet smell of the beginning of a knock-down-and-drag-out game of golf on a beautiful day in May with the larks singing over the greatest seaside course in the world.

The first hole of the Royal St Marks is 450 yards long –

450 yards of undulating fairway with one central bunker to trap a mis-hit second shot and a chain of bunkers guarding three-quarters of the green to trap a well-hit one. You can slip through the unguarded quarter, but the fairway slopes to the right there and you are more likely to end up with a nasty first-chip-of-the-day out of the rough. Goldfinger was well placed to try for this opening. Bond watched him take what was probably a spoon, make his two practice swings and address the ball.

Many unlikely people play golf, including people who are blind, who have only one arm, or even no legs, and people often wear bizarre clothes to the game. Other golfers don't think them odd, for there are no rules of appearance of dress at golf. That is one of its minor pleasures. But Goldfinger had made an attempt to look smart at golf and that is the only way of dressing that is incongruous on a links. Everything matched in a blaze of rust-colored tweed, from the buttoned 'golfer's cap' centered on the huge, flaming red hair, to the brilliantly polished, almost orange shoes. The plus four suit was too well cut and the plus fours themselves had been pressed down the sides. The stockings were of a matching heather mixture and had green garter tabs. It was as if Goldfinger had gone to his tailor and said, 'Dress me for golf – you know, like they wear in Scotland.' Social errors made no impression on Bond, and for the matter of that he rarely noticed them. With Goldfinger it was different. Everything about the man had grated on Bond's teeth from the first moment he had seen him. The assertive blatancy of his clothes was just part of the malevolent animal magnetism that had affected Bond from the beginning.

Goldfinger executed his mechanical, faultless swing. The ball flew true but just failed to make the slope and curled off to the right to finish pin-high off the green in the short rough. Easy 5. A good chip could turn it into a 4, but it would have to be a good one.

Bond walked over to his ball. It was lying cocked up, just off the fairway. Bond took his 4-wood. Now for the 'all air route' – a soaring shot that would carry the cross bunkers and give him two putts for a 4. Bond remembered the dictum of the pros: 'It's never too early to start winning.' He took it easy, determined not to press for the long but comfortable carry.

As soon as Bond had hit the shot he knew it wouldn't do. The difference between a good golf shot and a bad one is the same as the difference between a beautiful and a plain woman – a matter of millimeters. In this case, the clubface had gone through just that one millimeter too low under the ball. The are of flight was high and soft – no legs. Why the hell hadn't he taken a spoon or a 2-iron off that lie? The ball hit the lip of the far bunker and fell back. Now it was the blaster and fighting for a halve.

Bond never worried too long about his bad or stupid shots. He put them behind him and thought of the next. He came up to the bunker, took his blaster and measured the distance to the pin. Twenty yards. The ball was lying well back. Should he splash it out with a wide stance and an out-side-in swing, or should he blast it and take plenty of sand? For safety's sake he would blast it out. Bond went down into the bunker. Head down and follow well through. The easiest shot in golf. Try and put it dead. The wish, halfway down his backswing, hurried the hands in front of the clubhead. The loft was killed and there was the ball rolling back off the face. Get it out, you bloody fool, and hole a long putt! Now Bond took too much sand. He was out, but barely on the green. Goldfinger bent to his chip and kept his head down until his ball was halfway to the hole. The ball stopped three inches from the pin. Without waiting to be given the putt, Goldfinger turned his back on Bond and walked off towards the second tee. Bond picked up his ball and took his driver from Hawker.

'What does he say his handicap is, sir?'

'Nine. It's a level match. Have to do better than that though. Ought to have taken my spoon for the second.'

Hawker said encouragingly, 'It's early days yet, sir.'

Bond knew it wasn't. It was always too early to start losing.

Goldfinger had already teed up. Bond walked slowly behind him, followed by Hawker. Bond stood and leant on his driver. He said, 'I thought you said we would be playing the strict rules of golf. But I'll give you that putt. That makes you one up.'

Goldfinger nodded curtly. He went through his practice routine and hit his usual excellent, safe drive.

The second hole is a 370-yard dogleg to the left with deep cross bunkers daring you to take the tiger's line. But there was a light, helping breeze. For Goldfinger it would now be a 5-iron for his second. Bond decided to try and make it easier for himself and only have a wedge to the green. He laid his ears back and hit the ball hard and straight for the bunkers. The breeze got under the slight draw and winged the ball on and over. The ball pitched and disappeared down into the gully just short of the green. A 4. Chance of a 3.

Goldfinger strode off without comment. Bond lengthened his stride and caught up. 'How's the agoraphobia? Doesn't all this wide open space bother it?'

'No.'

Goldfinger deviated to the right. He glanced at the distant, half-hidden flag, planning his second shot. He took his 5-iron and hit a good, careful shot which took a bad kick short of the green and ran down into the thick grass to the left. Bond knew that territory. Goldfinger would be lucky to get down in two. Bond walled up to his ball, took the wedge and flicked the ball onto the green with plenty of stop. The ball pulled up and lay a yard past the hole. Goldfinger executed a creditable pitch but missed the 12-foot putt. Bond had two for the hole from a yard. He didn't wait to be given the hole but walked up and putted. The ball stopped an inch short. Goldfinger walked off the green. Bond knocked the ball in. All square.

The third is a blind 240 yards, all carry, a difficult par 3. Bond chose his brassie and hit a good one. It would be on or near the green. Goldfinger's routine drive was well hit but would probably not have enough steam to carry the last of the rough and trickle down into the saucer of the green. Sure enough, Goldfinger's ball was on top of the protecting mound of rough. He had a nasty, cuppy lie, with a tuft just behind the ball. Goldfinger stood and looked at the lie. He seemed to make up his mind. He stepped past his ball to take a club from the caddie. His left foot came down just behind the ball, flattening the tuft. Goldfinger could now take his putter. He did so and trickled the ball down the bank towards the hole. It stopped three feet short.

Bond frowned. The only remedy against a cheat at golf is not to play with him again. But that was no good in this match. Bond had no intention of playing with the man again. And it was no good starting a you-did-I-didn't argument unless he caught Goldfinger doing something even more outrageous. Bond would just have to try and beat him, cheating and all.

Now Bond's 20-foot putt was no joke. There was no question of going for the hole. He would have to concentrate on laying it dead. As usual, when one plays to go dead, the ball stopped short – a good yard short. Bond took a lot of trouble about the putt and holed it, sweating. He knocked Gold-finger's ball away. He would go on giving Goldfinger miss-able putts until suddenly Bond would ask him to hole one. Then that one might look just a bit more difficult.

Still all square. The fourth is 460 yards. You drive over one of the tallest and deepest bunkers in the United Kingdom and then have a long second shot across an undulating hilly fairway to a plateau green guarded by a final steep slope which makes it easier to take three putts than two.

Bond picked up his usual 50 yards on the drive, and Gold-finger hit two of his respectable shots to the gully below the green. Bond, determined to get up, took a brassie instead of a spoon and went over the green and almost up against the boundary fence. From there he was glad to get down in three for a halve.

The fifth was again a long carry, followed by Bond's favorite second shot on the course – over bunkers and through a valley between high sand dunes to a distant, taunting flag. It is a testing hole for which the first essential is a well-placed drive. Bond stood on the tee, perched high up in the sand hills, and paused before the shot while he gazed at the glitter-ing distant sea and at the faraway crescent of white cliffs beyond Pegwell Bay. Then he took up his stance and visual-ized the tennis court of turf that was his target. He took the club back as slowly as he knew how and started down for the last terrific acceleration before the clubhead met the ball. There was a dull clang on his right. It was too late to stop. Desperately Bond focused the ball and tried to keep his swing all in one piece. There came the ugly clonk of a mis-hit ball. Bond's head shot up. It was a lofted hook. Would it have legs? Get on! Get on! The ball hit the top of a mountain of rough and bounced over. Would it reach the beginning of the fairway?

Bond turned toward Goldfinger and the caddies, his eyes fierce. Goldfinger was straightening up. He met Bond's eyes indifferently. 'Sorry. Dropped my driver.'

'Don't do it again,' said Bond curtly. He stood down off the tee and handed his driver to Hawker. Hawker shook his head sympathetically. Bond took out a cigarette and lit it. Goldfinger hit his drive the dead straight regulation 200 yards.

They walked down the hill in silence, which Goldfinger unexpectedly broke. 'What is the firm you work for?'

'Universal Export.'

'And where do they hang out?'

'London. Regent's Park.'

'What do they export?'

Bond woke up from his angry ruminations. Here, pay attention! This is work, not a game. All right, he put you off your drive, but you've got your cover to think about. Don't let him needle you into making mistakes about it. Build up your story. Bond said casually, 'Oh everything from sewing machines to tanks.'

'What's your specialty?'

Bond could feel Goldfinger's eyes on him. He said, 'I look after the small arms side. Spend most of my time selling miscellaneous ironmongery to sheiks and rajahs – anyone the Foreign Office decides doesn't want the stuff to shoot at us with.'

'Interesting work,' Goldfinger's voice was flat, bored.

'Not very. I'm thinking of quitting. Came down here for a week's holiday to think it out. Not much future in England. Rather like the idea of Canada.'

'Indeed?'

They were past the rough, and Bond was relieved to find that his ball had got a forward kick off the hill onto the fairway. The fairway curved slightly to the left, and Bond had even managed to pick up a few feet on Goldfinger. It was Goldfinger to play. Goldfinger took out his spoon. He wasn't going for the green but only to get over the bunkers and through the valley.

Bond waited for the usual safe shot. He looked at his own lie. Yes, he could take his brassie. There came the wooden thud of a mis-hit. Goldfinger's ball, hit off the heel, sped along the ground and into the stony wastes of Hell Bunker – the widest bunker and the only unkempt one, because of the pebbles, on the course.

For once Homer had nodded – or rather, lifted his head. Perhaps his mind had been half on what Bond had told him. Good show! But Goldfinger might still get down in three more. Bond took out his brassie. He couldn't afford to play safe. He addressed the ball, seeing in his mind's eye its 88-millimeter trajectory through the valley and then the two or three bounces that would take it on the green. He laid off a bit to the right to allow for his draw. Now!

There came a soft clinking away to his right. Bond stood away from his ball. Goldfinger had his back to Bond. He was gazing out to sea, rapt in its contemplation, while his right hand played 'unconsciously' with the money in his pocket.

Bond smiled grimly. He said, 'Could you stop shifting bullion till after my shot?'

Goldfinger didn't turn round or answer. The noise stopped.

Bond turned back to his shot, desperately trying to clear his mind again. Now the brassie was too much of a risk. It needed too good a shot. He handed it to Hawker and took his spoon and banged the ball safely through the valley. It ran on well and stopped on the apron. A 5, perhaps a 4.

Goldfinger got well out of the bunker and put his chip dead. Bond putted too hard and missed the one back. Still all square.

The sixth, appropriately called 'The Virgin,' is a famous short hole in the world of golf. A narrow green, almost ringed with bunkers, it can need anything from an 8- to a 2-iron according to the wind. Today, for Bond, it was a seven. He played a soaring shot, laid off to the right for the wind to bring it in. It ended 20 feet beyond the pin with a difficult putt over and down a shoulder. Should be 3. Goldfinger took his 5-iron and played it straight. The breeze took it, and it rolled down into the deep bunker on the left. Good news! That would be a hell of a difficult 3.

They walked in silence to the green. Bond glanced into the bunker. Goldfinger's ball was in a deep heel mark. Bond walked over to his ball and listened to the larks. This was going to put him 1 up. He looked for Hawker to take his putter, but Hawker was on the other side of the green, watching with intent concentration Goldfinger play his shot. Goldfinger got down into the bunker with his blaster. He jumped up to get a view of the hole and then settled himself for the shot. As his club went up Bond's heart lifted. He was going to try and flick it out – a hopeless technique from that buried lie. The only hope would have been to explode it. Down came the club, smoothly, without hurry. With hardly a handful of sand the ball curved up out of the deep bunker, bounced once and lay dead!

Bond swallowed. Blast his eyes! How the hell had Goldfinger managed that? Now, out of sour grapes, Bond must try for his two. He went for it, missed the hole by an inch and rolled a good yard past. Hell and damnation! Bond walked slowly up to the putt, knocking Goldfinger's ball away. Come on, you bloody fool! But the specter of the big swing – from an almost certain 1 up to a possible 1 down – made Bond wish the ball into the hole instead of tapping it in. The coaxed ball, lacking decision, slid past the lip. One down!

Now Bond was angry with himself. He, and he alone, had lost that hole. He had taken three putts from 20 feet. He really must pull himself together and get going.

At the seventh, 500 yards, they both hit good drives and Goldfinger's immaculate second lay 50 yards short of the green. Bond took his brassie. Now for the equalizer! But he hit from the top, his club head came down too far ahead of the hands and the smothered ball shot into one of the right-hand bunkers. Not a good lie, but he must put it on the green. Bond took a dangerous seven and failed to get it out. Goldfinger got his 5. Two down. They halved the short eighth in 3. At the ninth Bond, determined to turn only 1 down, again tried to do too much off a poor lie. Goldfinger got his 4 to Bond's 5. Three down at the turn! Not too good. Bond asked Hawker for a new ball. Hawker unwrapped it slowly, waiting for Goldfinger to walk over the hillock to the next tee. Hawker said softly, 'You saw what he did at The Virgin, sir?'

'Yes, damn him. It was an amazing shot.'

Hawker was surprised. 'Oh, you didn't see what he did in the bunker, sir?'

'No, what? I was too far away.'

The other two were out of sight over the rise. Hawker silently walked down into one of the bunkers guarding the ninth green, kicked a hole with his toe and dropped the ball in the hole. He then stood just behind the half-buried ball with his feet close together. He looked up at Bond. 'Remember he jumped up to look at the line to the hole, sir?'

'Yes.'

'Just watch this, sir.' Hawker looked towards the ninth pin and jumped, just as Goldfinger had done, as if to get the line. Then he looked up at Bond again and pointed to the ball at his feet. The heavy impact of the two feet just behind the ball had leveled the hole in which it had lain and had squeezed the ball out so that it was now perfectly teed for an easy shot – for just the easy cut-up shot which had seemed utterly impossible from Goldfinger's lie at The Virgin.

Bond looked at his caddie for a moment in silence. Then he said, 'Thanks, Hawker. Give me the bat and the ball. Somebody's going to be second in this match, and I'm damned if it's going to be me.'

'Yes, sir,' said Hawker stolidly. He limped off on the short cut that would take him halfway down the 10th fairway.

Bond sauntered slowly over the rise and down to the 10th tee. He hardly looked at Goldfinger who was standing on the tee swishing his driver impatiently. Bond was clearing his mind of everything but cold, offensive resolve. For the first time since the first tee, he felt supremely confident. All he needed was a sign from heaven and his game would catch fire.

The 10th at the Royal St Marks is the most dangerous hole on the course. The second shot, to the skiddy plateau green with cavernous bunkers to right and left and a steep hill beyond, has broken many hearts. Bond remembered that Philip Scrutton, out in four-under 4s in the Gold Bowl, had taken a 14 at this hole, seven of them ping-pong shots from one bunker to another, to and fro across the green. Bond knew that Goldfinger would play his second to the apron, or short of it, and be glad to get a 5. Bond must go for it and get his 4.

Two good drives and, sure enough, Goldfinger well up on the apron with his second. A possible 4. Bond took his seven, laid off plenty for the breeze and fired the ball off into the sky. At first he thought he had laid off too much, but then the ball began to float to the left. It pitched and stopped dead in the soft sand blown on to the green from the right-hand bunker. A nasty 15-foot putt. Bond would now be glad to get a half. Sure enough, Goldfinger putted up to within a yard. That, thought Bond as he squared up to his putt, he will have to hole. He hit his own putt fairly smartly to get it through the powdering of sand and was horrified to see it going like lightning across the skiddy green. God, he was going to have not a yard, but a two-yard putt back! But suddenly, as if drawn by a magnet, the ball swerved straight for the hole, hit the back of the tin, bounced up and fell into the cup with an audible rattle. The sign from heaven! Bond sent up to Hawker, winked at him and took his driver.

They left the caddies and walked down the slope and back to the next tee. Goldfinger said coldly, 'That putt ought to have run off the green.'

Bond said off-handedly, 'Always give the hole a chance!' He teed up his ball and hit his best drive of the day down the breeze. Wedge and one putt? Goldfinger hit his regulation shot and they walked off again. Bond said, 'By the way, what happened to that nice Miss Masterson?'

Goldfinger looked straight in front of him. 'She left my employ.'

Bond thought, good for her! He said, 'Oh, I must get in touch with her again. Where did she go to?'

'I couldn't say.' Goldfinger walked away from Bond toward his ball. Bond's drive was out of sight, over the ridge that bisected the fairway. It wouldn't be more than 50 yards from the pin. Bond thought he knew what would be in Gold-finger's mind, what is in most golfers' minds when they smell the first scent of a good lead melting away. Bond wouldn't be surprised to see that grooved swing quicken a trifle. It did. Goldfinger hooked into a bunker on the left of the green.

Now was the moment when it would be the end of the game if Bond made a mistake, let his man off the hook. He had a slightly downhill lie, otherwise an easy chip – but to the trickiest green on the course. Bond played it like a man. The ball ended six feet from the pin. Goldfinger played well out of his bunker, but missed the longish putt. Now Bond was only 1 down.

They halved the dogleg 12th in inglorious 5s and the long-ish 13th also in 5s, Goldfinger having to hole a good putt to do so.

Now a tiny cleft of concentration had appeared on Gold-finger's massive, unlined forehead. He took a drink of water from the tap beside the 14th tee. Bond waited for him. He didn't want a sharp clang from that tin cup when it was out-of-bounds over the fence to the right and the drive into the breeze favoring a slice! Bond brought his left hand over to increase his draw and slowed down his swing. The drive, well to the left, was only just adequate, but at least it had stayed in bounds. Goldfinger, apparently unmoved by the out-of-bounds hazard, hit his standard shot. They both negotiated the transverse canal without damage and it was another halve in 5. Still 1 down and now only four to play.

The 460-yard 15th is perhaps the only hole where the long hitter may hope to gain one clear shot. Two smashing woods will just get you over the line of bunkers that lie right up against the green. Goldfinger had to play short of them with his second. He could hardly improve on a 5, and it was up to Bond to hit a really godlike second shot from a barely adequate drive.

The sun was on its way down, and the shadows of the four men were beginning to lengthen. Bond had taken up his stance. It was a good lie. He had kept his driver. There was dead silence as he gave his two incisive waggles. This was going to be a vital stroke. Remember to pause at the top of the swing, come down slow and whip the clubhead through at the last second. Bond began to take the club back. Something moved at the corner of his right eye. From nowhere the shadow of Goldfinger's huge head approached the ball on the ground, engulfed it and moved on. Bond let his swing take itself to pieces in sections. Then he stood away from his ball and looked up. Goldfinger's feet were still moving. He was looking carefully up at the sky.

'Shades please, Goldfinger.' Bond's voice was furiously controlled.

Goldfinger stepped and looked slowly at Bond. The eyebrows were raised a fraction in inquiry. He moved back and stood still, saying nothing.

Bond went back to his ball. Now then, relax! To hell with Goldfinger. Slam that ball on to the green. Just stand still and hit it. There was a moment when the world stood still, then . . . then somehow Bond did hit it – on a low trajectory that mounted gracefully to carry the distant surf of the bunkers. The ball hit the bank below the green, bounced high with the impact and rolled out of sight into the saucer round the pin.

Hawker came up and took the driver out of Bond's hand. They walked on together. Hawker said seriously, 'That's one of the finest shots I've seen in 30 years.' He lowered his voice, 'I thought he'd fixed you then, sir.'

'He damned nearly did, Hawker. It was Alfred Blacking

that hit that ball, not me.' Bond took out his cigarettes, gave one to Hawker and lit his own. He said quietly, 'All square and three to play. We've got to watch those next three holes. Know what I mean?'

'Don't you worry, sir. I'll keep my eye on him.'

They came up with the green. Goldfinger had pitched on and had a long putt for a 4, but Bond's ball was only two inches away from the hole. Goldfinger picked up his ball and walked off the green. They halved the short 16th in good 3s. Now there were the two long holes home. Fours would win them. Bond hit a fine drive down the center. Goldfinger pushed his far out to the right into deep rough. Bond walked along trying not to be too jubilant, trying not to count his chickens. A win for him at this hole and he would only need a half at the 18th for the match. He prayed that Goldfinger's ball would be unplayable or, better still, lost.

Hawker had gone on ahead. He had already laid down his bag and was busily – far too busily to Bond's way of thinking – searching for Goldfinger's ball when they came up.

It was bad stuff – jungle country, deep thick luxuriant grass whose roots still held last night's dew. Unless they were very lucky, they couldn't hope to find the ball. After a few minutes' search Goldfinger and his caddie drifted away still wider to where the rough thinned out into isolated tufts. That's good, thought Bond. That wasn't anything like the line. Suddenly he trod on something. Hell and damnation. Should he stamp it in? He shrugged his shoulders, bent down and gently uncovered the ball so as not to improve the lie. Yes, it was a Dunlop 65. 'Here you are,' he called grudgingly. 'Oh no, sorry. You play with a No. 1, don't you?'

'Yes,' came back Goldfinger's voice impatiently.

'Well, this is a No. 7.' Bond picked it up and walked over to Goldfinger.

Goldfinger gave the ball a cursory glance. He said, 'Not mine,' and went poking among the tufts with the head of his driver.

It was a good ball, unmarked and almost new. Bond put it in his pocket and went back to his search. He glanced at this watch. The statutory five minutes was almost up. Another half-minute and by God he was going to claim the hole. Strict rules of golf, Goldfinger had stipulated. All right my friend, you shall have them!

Goldfinger was casting back toward Bond, diligently prodding and shuffling through the grass.

Bond said, 'Nearly time, I'm afraid.'

Goldfinger grunted. He started to say something when there came a cry from his caddie. 'Here you are, sir. No. 1 Dunlop.'

Bond followed Goldfinger over to where the caddie stood on a small plateau of higher ground. He was pointing down. Bond bent and inspected the ball. Yes, an almost new Dunlop 1 and in an astonishingly good lie. It was miraculous – more than miraculous. Bond stared hard from Goldfinger to his caddie. 'Must have had a hell of a lucky kick,' he said mildly.

The caddie shrugged his shoulders. Goldfinger's eyes were calm, untroubled. 'So it would seem.' He turned to his caddie. 'I think we can get a spoon to that one, Foulks.'

Bond walked thoughtfully away and then turned to watch the shot. It was one of Goldfinger's best. It soared over a far shoulder of rough towards the green. Might just have caught the bunker to the right.

Bond walked on to where Hawker, a long blade of grass dangling from his wry lips, was standing on the fairway watching the shot finish. Bond smiled bitterly at him. He said in a controlled voice, 'Is my good friend in the bunker, or is the bastard on the green?'

'Green, sir,' said Hawker unemotionally.

Bond went up to his ball. Now things had got tough again. Once more he was fighting for a half after having a certain win in his pocket. He glanced toward the pin, gauging the distance. This was a tricky one. He said, 'Five or six?'

'The six should do it, sir. Nice firm shot.' Hawker handed him the club.

Now then, clear your mind. Keep it slow and deliberate. It's an easy shot. Just punch it so that it's got plenty of zip to get up the bank and onto the green. Stand still and head down. Click! The ball, hit with a slightly closed face, went off on just the medium trajectory Bond had wanted. It pitched below the bank. It was perfect! No, damn it. It had hit the bank with its second bounce, stopped dead, hesitated and then rolled back and down again. Hells, bells! Was it Hagen who had said, 'You drive for show, but you putt for dough?' Getting dead from below that bank was one of the most difficult putts on the course. Bond reached for his cigarettes and lit one, already preparing his mind for the next crucial shot to save the hole – so long as that bastard Goldfinger didn't hole his from 30 feet!

Hawker walked along by his side. Bond said, 'Miracle finding that ball.'

'It wasn't his ball, sir.' Hawker was stating a fact.

'What do you mean?' Bond's voice was tense.

'Money passed, sir. White, probably a fiver. Foulks must have dropped that ball down his trouser leg.'

'Hawker!' Bond stopped in his tracks. He looked round. Goldfinger and his caddie were 50 yards away, walking slowly toward the green. Bond said fiercely, 'Do you swear to that? How can you be sure?'

Hawker gave a half-ashamed, lop-sided grin. But there was a crafty belligerence in his eye. 'Because his ball was lying under my bag of clubs, sir.' When he saw Bond's open-mouthed expression he added apologetically, 'Sorry, sir. Had to do it after what he's been doing to you. Wouldn't have mentioned it, but I had to let you know he's fixed you again.'

Bond had to laugh. He said admiringly, 'Well you are a card, Hawker. So you were going to win the match for me all on your own!' He added bitterly, 'But, by God, that man's the flaming limit. I've got to get him. I've simply got to. Now let's think!' They walked slowly on.

Bond's left hand was in his trousers pocket, absent-mindedly fingering the ball he had picked up in the rough. Suddenly the message went to his brain. Got it! He came closer to Hawker. He glanced across at the others. Goldfinger had stopped. His back was to Bond and he was taking the putter out of his bag. Bond nudged Hawker. 'Here, take this.' He slipped the ball into the gnarled hand. Bond said softly, urgently, 'Be certain you take the flag. When you pick up the balls from the green, whichever way the hole has gone, give Goldfinger this one. Right?'

Hawker walked stolidly forward. His face was expression-less. 'Got it, sir,' he said in his normal voice. 'Will you take the putter for this one?'

'Yes,' Bond walked up to his ball. 'Give me a line, would you?'

Hawker walked up on to the green. He stood sideways to the line of the putt and then stalked round to behind the flag and crouched. He got up. 'Inch outside the right lip, sir. Firm putt. Flag, sir?'

'No. Leave it in, would you.'

Hawker stood away. Goldfinger was standing by his ball on the right of the green. His caddie had stopped at the bottom of the slope. Bond bent to the putt. Come on, Calamity Jane! This one has to go dead or I'll put you across my knee. Stand still. Club head straight back on the line and follow through toward the hole. Give it a chance. Now! The ball, hit firmly in the middle of the club, had run up the bank and was on its way to the hole. But too hard, damn it! Hit the stick! Obediently the ball curved in, rapped the stick hard and bounced back three inches – dead as a doornail!

Bond let out a deep sigh and picked up his discarded cigarette. He looked over at Goldfinger. Now then, you bastard. Sweat that one out. And by God if you hole it! But Goldfinger couldn't afford to try. He stopped two feet short. 'All right, all right,' said Bond generously. 'All square and one to go.' It was vital that Hawker should pick up the balls. If he had made Goldfinger hole that short putt it would have been Goldfinger who would have picked the ball out of the hole. Anyway, Bond didn't want Goldfinger to miss that putt. That wasn't part of the plan.

Hawker bent down and picked up the balls. He rolled one toward Bond and handed the other to Goldfinger. They walked off the green, Goldfinger leading as usual. Bond noticed Hawker's hand go to his pocket. Now, so long as Goldfinger didn't notice anything on the tee!

But, with all square and one to go you don't scrutinize your ball. Your motions are more or less automatic. You are thinking of how to place your drive, or whether to go for the green with the second or play to the apron, of the strength of the wind – of the vital figure 4 that must somehow be achieved to win or at least to halve.

Considering that Bond could hardly wait for Goldfinger to follow him and hit, just once, that treacherous Dunlop No. 7 that looked so very like a No. 1, Bond's own drive down the 450-yard 18th was praiseworthy. If he wanted to, he could now reach the green – if he wanted to!

Now Goldfinger was on the tee. Now he had bent down.

The ball was on the peg, its lying face turned up at him. But Goldfinger had straightened, had stood back, was taking his two deliberate practice swings. He stepped up to the ball, cautiously, deliberately. Stood over it, waggled, focusing on the ball minutely. Surely he would see! Surely he would stop and bend down at the last minute to inspect the ball! Would the waggle never end? But now the club head was going back, coming down, the left knee bent correctly toward the ball, the left arm straight as a ramrod. Crack! The ball sailed off, a beautiful drive, as good as Goldfinger had hit, straight down the fairway.

Bond's head sang. Got you, you bastard! Got you! Blithely Bond stepped down from the tee and strolled off down the fairway planning the next steps which would now be as eccentric, as fiendish as he wished. Goldfinger was beaten already – hoist with his own petard! Now to roast him, slowly, exquisitely.

Bond had no compunction. Goldfinger had cheated him twice and got away with it. But for his cheats at The Virgin and the 17th, not to mention his improved lie at the third and the various times he had tried to put Bond off, Goldfinger would have been beaten by now. If it needed one cheat by Bond to rectify the scoresheet, that was only poetic justice. And besides, there was more to this than a game of golf. It was Bond's duty to win. By his reading of Goldfinger, he had to win. If he was beaten, the score between the two men would have been equalized. If he won the match, as he now had, he would be 2 up on Goldfinger – an intolerable state of affairs, Bond guessed, to a man who saw himself as all powerful. This man Bond, Goldfinger would say to himself, has something. He has qualities I can use. He is a tough adventurer with plenty of tricks up his sleeve. This is the sort of man I need for – for what? Bond didn't know. Perhaps there would be nothing for him. Perhaps his reading of Goldfinger was wrong, but there was certainly no other way of creeping up on the man.

Goldfinger cautiously took out his spoon for the longish second over crossbunkers to the narrow entrance to the green. He made one more practice swing than usual and then hit exactly the right, controlled shot up to the apron. A certain 5, probably a 4. Much good would it do him!

Bond, after a great show of taking pains, brought his hands down well ahead of the club and smothered his number 3-iron so that the topped ball barely scrambled over the crossbunkers. He then wedged the ball on to the green 20 feet past the pin. He was where he wanted to be – enough of a threat to make Goldfinger savor the sweet smell of victory, enough to make Goldfinger really sweat to get his 4.

And now Goldfinger really was sweating. There was a savage grin of concentration and greed as he bent to the long putt up the bank and down to the hole. Not too hard, not too soft. Bond could read every anxious thought that would be running through the man's mind. Goldfinger straightened up again, walked deliberately across the green to behind the flag to verify his line. He walked slowly back beside his line, brushing away – carefully, with the back of his hand – a wisp or two of grass, a speck of topdressing. He bent again and made one or two practice swings and then stood to the putt, the veins standing out on his temples, the cleft of concentration deep between his eyes.

Goldfinger hit the putt and followed through on the line. It was a beautiful putt that stopped six inches past the pin. Now Goldfinger would be sure that unless Bond sank his difficult 20-footer, the match was his!

Bond went through a long rigmarole of sizing up his putt.

He took his time, letting the suspense gather like a thunder cloud round the long shadows on the livid, fateful green.

'Flag out, please. I'm going to sink this one.' Bond charged the words with a deadly certitude, while debating whether to miss the hole to the right or the left or leave it short. He bent to the putt and missed the hole well on the right.

'Missed it, by God!' Bond put bitterness and rage into his voice. He walked over to the hole and picked up the two balls, keeping them in full view.

Goldfinger came up. His face was glistening with triumph. 'Well, thanks for the game. Seems I was just too good for you after all.'

'You're a good 9-handicap,' said Bond with just sufficient sourness. He glanced at the balls in his hand to pick out Goldfinger's and hand it to him. He gave a start of surprise. 'Hullo!' He looked sharply at Goldfinger. 'You play a No. 1 Dunlop don't you?'

'Yes, of course.' A sixth sense of disaster wiped the triumph off Goldfinger's face. 'What is it? What's the matter?'

'Well,' said Bond apologetically. ''Fraid you've been playing with the wrong ball. Here's my Penfold Hearts, and this is a No. 7 Dunlop.' He handed both balls to Goldfinger. Goldfinger tore them off his palm and examined them feverishly.

Slowly the color flooded over Goldfinger's face. He stood, his mouth working, looking from the balls to Bond and back to the balls.

Bond said softly, 'Too bad we were playing to the rules. Afraid that means you lose the hole. And, of course, the match.' Bond's eyes observed Goldfinger impassively.

'But, but . . .'

This was what Bond had been looking forward to – the cup dashed from the lips. He stood and waited, saying nothing.

Rage suddenly burst Goldfinger's usually relaxed face like a bomb. 'It was a Dunlop 7 you found in the rough. It was your caddie that gave me this ball. On the 17th green. He gave me the wrong ball on purpose, the damned che—'

'Here, steady on,' said Bond mildly. 'You'll get slander action on your hands if you aren't careful. Hawker, did you give Mr Goldfinger the wrong ball by mistake or anything?'

'No, sir.' Hawker's face was stolid. He said indifferently, 'If you want my opinion, sir, the mistake may have been made at the 17th when the gentleman found his ball pretty far off the line we'd all marked it on. A 7 looks very much like a 1. I'd say that's what happened, sir. It would have been a miracle for the gentleman's ball to have ended up as wide as where it was found.'

'Tommy rot!' Goldfinger gave a snort of disgust. He turned angrily on Bond. 'You saw that was a No. 1 my caddie found.'

Bond shook his head doubtfully. 'I didn't really look closely, I'm afraid. However,' Bond's voice became brisk, businesslike, 'it's really the job of the player to make certain he's using the right ball, isn't it? I can't see that anyone else can be blamed if you tee the wrong ball up and play three shots with it. Anyway,' he started walking off the green, 'many thanks for the match. We must have it again one day.'

Goldfinger, lit with glory by the setting sun, but with a long black shadow tied to his heels, followed Bond slowly, his eyes fixed thoughtfully on Bond's back.

HERBERT WARREN WIND

HARRY SPRAGUE MEETS THE MASTERS

MARCH 21, 1960

Mr Amos A. Tabor
Entre Les Iles Country Club
Fort-de-France
Martinique, French West Indies

Dear Mr Tabor,
Now that I am moving it again and radeemed myself last
week with that fifth place in the St Pete Open, you are hearing from me again, because the idea of telling my troubles
out loud to a steno doesn't bother a fellow when he's got
none. So there's no need for you to fly in a plane down to
Florida for a talk with me like you kindly made the suggestion; you just stay planted where you are down there among
the sweltering palms, not that I don't appreciate your thinking of me like a son like you wrote and wondering why you
didn't get a letter from me for so long.

Not only is my game back but my personality is once
again back in the groove, which I knew for sure yesterday
afternoon after my practice round in the Seminole Pro-Am
here in Palm Beach when I went out for a little cruise party
on a yacht owned by one of my Am partners, Mr Burton
'Burt' Hillcroft, who has made a ton of it in the carpet business. What I am referring to is that when I was trying to
write you on some stationery inside the cabin, these three
terrific babes dragged me away from the writing table and

hauled me out onto the deck, and I am not objecting to the idea at all because your boy is back to normal where he is noticing how good-looking good-looking babes can be. The only one I am having trouble with right now is Miss Marjorie Sundstrom who is sitting across from me in her steno office downtown, glaring over at me as if I had stepped on her line on the putting green or something. She is one of the prettiest gray-haired ladies you ever saw but she is making this dictation difficult by interrupting all the time and asking, 'Semicolon?' and 'Period?' and 'Paragraph?' and stuff like that instead of just picking the right club herself and playing the shot without bothering me. Now she is smiling finally.

As those three society girls who were hauling me around on the yacht was expressing it, this Seminole Pro-Am is what they call a fun tournament. At the same time, that is about the only word those girls use: the word fun. For a sample they say Mr Burt Hillcroft's yacht is a fun boat and so-and-so is throwing a fun party and your boy is fun company and so on like that. I guess when you have been to college like these girls and your family is loaded, you can toss the old vocabulary right out the window and use the same word over and over again.

During this tournament at Seminole I am staying as his guest at Mr Burt Hillcroft's house which he calls a villa, which is O.K. with me since there is nothing to give a guy a lift like living above your income for a couple of days. Mr Hillcroft has two daughters called Beedo and Kay Kay, which are their society nicknames, who are really put together, and I guess they are also good-looking; but you can't tell for sure since they both wear their sunglasses all day long and have never taken them off yet even when we ate last night with only the candles on. Incidentally Mr Burton Hillcroft and

I ought to finish right up at the top in the Pro-Am since he has got a very useful size handicap for a pretty good player being a member himself of the handicap committee, if you follow me in your window. He calls me 'Harry' or 'fella' and I call him 'Mister Burt' which is how if you are on the ball you address all your partners in a pro-am – the Mister and then the nickname – just like old Dutch Harrison does on that Sunday TV show. All in all, the only trouble I got to find with the set-up at Seminole is that they still have got those old wooden lockers. With all their dough you would have thought they would have smartened up long ago and changed over to some modern metal jobs.

Outside of me missing the money five straight weeks between Phoenix and Pensacola and making the cut only once, the sensation of the tour has been Arnold Palmer winning those four tournaments: the Desert Classical, the Texas Open, Baton Rouge and then Pensacola. I don't want to cut in on the act, and I know you'll keep this neutral between the two of us, but the turning point for Arnold this winter was the round we were paired together over Bermuda Dunes in the Desert Classical. Arnie, you know, hits the drive out of sight being a strong fellow with muscles like sinews, and when we played together he kept walking up to his ball after we drove and waiting for me to play it, not realizing I was out past him on the drive 10, 15 yards even when I caught it on the heel. What I am leading up to is that this is the best thing in the world that could have happened to Arnold. Suddenly he realizes he is not really a long hitter, he stops trying to hit the cover off the ball, he begins to put the emphatic on accuracy, and just like that he becomes a matured shot-maker and starts winning. Same thing five years ago, I hear. George Bayer joined the tour and Mike Souchak, no longer being the longest hitter, begins paying attention to his swing in general; just like that, Mike becomes a real golfer. I am thinking of maybe doing a story for the *Reader's Digest* called 'How I Straightened Out My Buddy, Arnold Palmer' by Harry L. Sprague, if they cough up enough.

The real reason Arnold Palmer is playing up a storm these past couple of weeks is he is not coming off the ball – meaning he is staying right down over it and hitting right through it without moving his left side out of the way too fast or moving the right side in too fast. Like I was telling Stan Leonard, this is a lot better than just releasing it, because if you come off the ball, what are you releasing? Nothing! This is the big thing all the boys are putting the emphatic on this winter: not coming off the ball. Lately I have been having my hands filled commuting between the practice tee checking their faults for the fellows and commuting to the practice green where I have been smoothing out the touches of some of the young kids like Dave Ragan and Mason Rudolph and Doug Sanders who I personally feel are promising material. Like I told the press here, they are good for the game of golf, which is an expression you always rope in when you can't think of no other reasons. Then I have been commuting back to the practice tee and helping the promising veterans how to avoid coming off the ball. For a sample, I was checking this for Dow Finsterwald and Freddy Hawkins, but here's a funny thing: Dow who has been a left-to-right player wants to hit the ball now from right-to-left and Freddy who is more of a natural right-to-left player keeps experimenting with left-to-right, which is very confusing when you are checking both of them to see if they are not coming off the ball. All of this is probably miles over your head, Mr Tabor, seeing as how you are lucky if you get the ball in the air at all, but I thought I'd tell you this since there are no flies on you when it comes to talking up a real storm even if you can't play up one. Am I right?

Yours from the back markers,
Harry Sprague
Playing Professional
Otter Lake C.C.

April 10, 1960

Mr Amos A. Tabor
c/o Curaçao Chamber of Commerce
Willemstad, Curaçao
Dutch West Indies

Dear Mr Tabor,
You sure get around, Mr Tabor. So you are so keyed up about how things are going with your new course on your French island of Martinique you are casing the rest of the Caribbean joint looking for a possible other new course to build! For an old guy, you certainly have a lot of catch-up and go and my hat is off to you seeing as how I won't always want to be traipsing all my life on the circuit and probably would not mind taking over as pro maybe later at one of your Caribbean developments. How are those Dutch women, by the way? The only ones I guess I ever saw was on those cans of kitchen cleanser. They were not my type at all but maybe those were old cans. Could be. Next time I see Dutch Harrison I'll ask him about his information about this subject. By the way, I am glad I brought that up. What you said in your letter I will do. What I mean is if you say you will fire me on the spot if I even begin calling you Mr Amos instead of Mr Tabor, I will make it a point not to dulge in calling you Mr Amos. Your boy understands.

Like they say, all human beings have got their peculiarities and you have got a right to be as peculiar as the next guy seeing as how you're my boss.

Vickary, Grissom and me are stalled here in Augusta like we were last year at the Joel Chandler Harris Motor Court. It was a lucky thing we made our reservations last year, because Augusta is really overrun this year with gallery people for the Masters, and there never was enough rooms to go around anyway. I have also managed to latch on to a steno by the name of Miss Ellie Louise Laneer. She has just finished educating me that her grandpa was a Confederate general named General Phineas Laneer who was sort of the assistant pro to a Confederate general named General Long-street at the second Battle of Bull Run. This is probably the truth since Miss Ellie Louise Laneer could have been at that battle in person and checked on things herself – get it? Her accent is almost as thick as Bob Jones' but she has got the same kind of typewriter as they have in all other parts of the country so the words will probably come out just as if she had no accent at all.

I am surprised myself I am in such fine fetters this morning which is the day of the fourth and final round of the Masters, being as how I didn't make the cut at the end of the first 36 and am just a well-dressed spectator for yesterday's and today's rounds. But it has been a real experience to have finally played in the Masters, which you remember I qualified for by finishing tied for sixth in the PGA Championship last summer. Each year there is a program for how things happen here at the Masters. On the Tuesday of each year you pick up your morning newspaper and then you know the tournament is going to start in two days, because there is always an interview with Gene Sarazen in which Gene is saying the players today don't have the finesse of the old players like Jones and Hagen and some guy by the name of Francis Ouimet who must be a relative of Sarazen's or something since he is always dragging him in. Then on Wednesday they either dedicate some bridge or water fountain to some half way old-timer like Hogan and Nelson or they hold a driving contest, or both. This year they put in a new renovation and instead of a driving contest we played nine holes on the par-3 course which Mr Cliff Roberts, who has something to do with the club, has added to the landscape maybe because his short game is better now than his golf game. I won't go into the details of the par-3 contest which I did not star in because I was wearing a pair of shoes with slippery spikes and hit three bug-cutters, which is not like my character.

The next day on the first round I was paired with a foreigner by the name of Bruce Crampton from Australia where all the cities are named apparently after people's first names – like Peter Thomson is from Melvin and Crampton says he is from Sidney. I had trouble on the greens and had to take a Sunset Strip. Because I was not in a contention after that 77 I was paired the next round with some amateur I never heard of called Jack Nicklaus. Jack has got a fair swing for a fellow who stays up north in the winter, but it is plain to see he is an amateur. By this I mean that when Jack Nicklaus hits a bad shot, he groans out loud at himself instead of knowing enough to cover up and look like he was wearing slippery spikes. Then when he hits an approach up stiff, he gets real excited about it and smiles all over the place instead of acting like the shot is sort of below average for him and he is practically bored by it. I holed a couple of snakes on the second round and hit the ball more like I am customed to, but I missed the cut anyway by two blows. Why I feel in such fine fetters I do not know, but I guess it is because when you play in the Masters you know you have arrived as a permanent feature of golf like Sarazen's uncle, that Francis Ouimet, and you just walk around the premises talking with everyone and looking for a good spot where after you win the Masters you can tell Bob Jones you want him to build you your bridge or your water bubbler, though personally I would prefer something like a pro shop seeing as how the galleries are tremendous here. Am I using the old squash?

This reminds me, Mr Tabor, that Bob Jones and I had a little conversation this afternoon. He was sitting in his golf car there on the 13th when we spotted each other. 'Harry,' Bob said to me, 'I saw you execute several superb shots yesterday. You will score this course better, I'm certain, once you get to know it better. It takes quite a bit of knowing.'

'Bob,' I said to Bob, 'I am not investing in any green blazer myself, since I am counting on you folks presenting me with one. But if you do not mind a construction suggestion, when you make your changes next in the holes here, you must do something about this here number 13.'

Bob is somewhat surprised by this because he says then, 'That somewhat surprises me, Harry. Most of us have always thought that this hole was perhaps the strongest on the course. There are not many par 5s to my knowledge which set up a finer strategic challenge for a golfer: whether or not to try to carry the creek before the green on the second shot.'

'Bob,' I said to him, 'now that is where you and I are horses of a different color. This hole is weak because a power-hitter has got no advantage. Take my case. I am getting home in two with a six iron or maybe a seven, but what good does that do me when the other guys can press a three-wood and also get home? Do you catch my drift?'

'Harry,' Bob says, 'who is making your equipment? Some company at Cape Canaveral?'

We both had a good laugh about that one. I was planning to tell Bob how he can also fix up the 10th hole into a real good 4, but I will save it for a rainy day now since before I could give Bob my ideas I was gulfed up by the big crowd that was following Palmer around.

Enough for now. Don't take any wooden shoes, Mr Tabor.

Yours from the back markers,
Harry Sprague
Playing Professional
Otter Lake C.C.

May 1

Mr Amos A. Tabor
Otter Lake Country Club
Otter Lake, Michigan

Dear Mr Tabor,

As you can piece out from the printing above saying Black Gold Motel we nomands on the tour are camping out this week in Houston. This motel is a good distance from the city and I am just going to sit down right here and write you in my own hand writing since I am too bushed to go looking downtown for a steno. What enerjy (spelling?) I have got left I am going to store up for tomorrow when we play the last round of the Houston Classical. Both Vickary and me are up there in the running in this one so after dinner tonite we will not spring into actiun in the Caddy and prowl around after the local talent but just watch 2 or 3 gun fights on TV and then hit the hay bright and early.

Like most of the nomands who have been consantly on root from turnament to turnament for 4 months without a let up from LA on your boy is growing a little stale from hitting the old gutter percheron every day. Grissom got so fed up with the grind that he picked up and left after Greensboro and headed up north to his club even if the greens are still covered up with branches and the fairways are still thoring out. 'I guarantee you boys one thing' Pete told us 'which is that I am golf blind now and even if the best dame I see up north has a face like an unplayaple lie I need the change.' How guys like Doug Ford and Jay Hebert can keep playing week after week and lite a fire under themselfs each turnament is something I dont understand. My own personnel plans are to stay on the tour thru the Sam Snead Festival for maybe I can break his record 59 on that easy Greenbrier track and pick myself up a shot in the arm of publisaty (spelling?). Then its up to Mich, for me. I see from your letter that you and Mrs Tabor are all ready back at the club getting things shaped up for the season, and I would be temted to chuck the whole shebang and join you this minute except that I just got a tellergram from that Lucy Ann Umpey in Fort Worth. She is counting on me she says to help her with her homework paper she is writing for Serra Lawns Colledge and I would hate to stand her up seeing as how she signed the tab for the tellergram.

When you get a look at my new swing you will see I was not being conseeded when I told you we had better exstend the practise fairway another 15 or 20 yards or else I will be hitting all those pine trees at the far end and you will think from the sound you are still back in the Carribbene listening to Carribbene music. I am getting known now for my big hitting and at the PGA Clinick we give before a turnament now demostrate the driver and George Bayer has been shifted down to demostrate the 1-iron which is a mongrel club nobody plays. Its been a mistery my coleague pros have been telling me all along how come I am not picking up

240

heavy checks since no one else is tagging the ball like me. Like I told Billy Casper when he asked me about this a couple of weeks back 'Its no mistery Billy. I am not scoring because I am wedging them up there like an old woman and I am not getting down in two from any place – period.' 'Harry' Billy says to me 'why is it then all we ever see you practising is the driver which you can hit and not practising the wedge which you yourself say needs work.' 'Billy,' I said after thinking it over, 'now I can see why you are the National Open tietlist. You have a sharp analidigal mind. Thats what I am going to do starting tomorrow – practise the wedge.' Thats probably the reason I snuck into the money at New Orleans Mr Tabor and then won the pro-am here at Houston the strictly between us I was getting my share of the 18 footers.

Incidently you would have been proud of the way your boy came thru here in the pro-am when the chips were down. I am standing on the last tee when I get the word from a press fellow with an armband that my team needs a 3 to win on a hole that is an average lenghth 4 par. I miss the drive cold like I am a cellebrity golfer or a ranked amachure (spelling?) and cut it way over into the heavy rough where it is practickly buried. 'Theres no way Harry can make 3 from here' I overhear one of the kids on the tour saying who has come out to shoo me in. 'Hes got to make 5 from there' I hear another recrute pro say. Well I closed the face of the 4-wood and hit down on the shot like it was an iron and I put it up there on the apern. From there I hole the chip and make 3. The morale of this story Mr Tabor is that only a pro who is turnament tough can pull off that kind of finish when the old pressure is on. I was thinking you might like to twist around in your mind raising my salary a nudge or two or cutting me into a slice of the electric golf carts consession. When you are twisting it around in your mind ask yourself 'How many pros in Northern Mich would have taken the old gaspipe where Harry made 3?' Fair enugh?

You ask me in your letter how come I went boge par boge boge the last 4 holes at New Orleans when I have a chance for some of the big money if I finish par birdie par birdie. The answer is the breaks of the game. Also New Orleans is a hard city to finish strong in if you are staying up all hours of the nite which is not too tough to do. First nite in town Vickary and I hit a spot called the Tout de Suite Club where we are trying out a drink called a sazarac which obviously somebody named after Gene Sarazen who couldent spell so hot. There is a girl at that club named Lupe Renaud who plays the piano there and sings those sofisticaterd cocktail songs all nite – you know songs like 'The Man in the Motel Wont Tell' and 'What Do You Think I'm Wearing Contack Lenzes For' which she writes herself. Between sets I went over and sat on the piano bench with her, and she just happened to turn out to be one of those women like I have often wrote you about who once they know you are a golf pro you cannot get rid of them with a fly swatter. Any how I went to the Tout de Suite Club each nite during the New Orleans Open and closed the joint up in the whee small hours with this Lupe Renaud till I am practickly part of the act. I dident tell you this before but your boy sings pretty good now. Sometimes I sound so mellow it can be imbarrassing like the time I was taking my shower after that pro-am event in Florida and dident know Perry Como was in the next stall listening to me warbling away. When I stepped out of the shower Perry is shaking like a leaf and his face is like ashes which you cant blame him for because he has his own career to worry about and he knows a comer when he hears one.

Well see you in a couple of weeks Mr Tabor.

Yours from the back markers,
Harry Sprague
Playing Professional
Otter Lake C.C.

P.S. Did the idea of setting up a Harry Sprague Festival Turnament ever twist into your mind? You might give it some thought. In his here world today you cant aford to stand still.

May 20, 1960

Mr Amos A. Tabor
Otter Lake Country Club
Otter Lake, Michigan

Dear Mr Tabor,
You have no idea, I'll bet, how good that last letter of yours made me feel, and in just a nick of time. I was handing the keys to the Caddy over to Vickary – he is going to stay on the circuit right through the Open and may stay on it after the Open if he continues to gobble up those putts and those heavy-size checks – when an official in one of those loud plaid jackets they wear as a guide that they are big wheels at Colonial brought me my mail which I hadn't called for at the desk. So Mercer Tolly is giving up the proship at Otter Lake and you are sticking him in charge of your new club in Martinique to push everything along so the place will be ready to open next November and he will be the manager! Very smooth going, Mr Tabor, cause Mercer has much more of a touch for operating than for playing the game of golf. I didn't open my mouth about this before since it would have

looked like I was trying to place a toboggan under him. I really appreciate your upping me to head pro to take over for Mercer, and I will follow your suggestion and really take my time about picking a good assistant pro to give me a hand with the lessons. The trouble here is that most of the guys I'd like already have pretty good jobs. Claude is all set at Wing Foot, for a sample, and Cary didn't seem real enthusiastic when I approached the idea to him. Sam would be okay but I don't think I can get him either because he has got all those tin cans filled with income buried all over the lawns here at White Sulphur, and it would be too much trouble to excavate them up and truck them all the way to Otter Lake and then bury them again. So I am thinking what I ought maybe to do is to hire a feminine sex pro as my assistant. She could give the lessons to the men while I concentrate like I have been doing on the women. I will contact you before I make a move, so there is no need to get jumpy.

You probably have figured out for yourself from the picture at the top of the stationery and the printing on it that I am here at the Greenbrier in White Sulphur this week where part of us pros are and the other part are at Hot Springs, like Albie Vickary. This place here is what they call a spa, meaning it's a resort which is hard to get to. They have a tremendous layout here at the hotel which my steno tells me has been in business for a long time. I saw for myself a plaque they put up to Robert E. Lee who used to come up here after the war was over for a breather now and then in the old days. My steno, who goes by the name of Sallie Flagler, tells me she did not know Robert E. Lee personally, but my guess is that she is just being modest. Or maybe he didn't go in for dictation and just played golf which most generals apparently go in for in a big way once they've got their discharge papers.

Since Sam Snead is the pro here at White Sulphur there is a lot of talk about how he will do in the National Open this year at Cherry Hills and will he finally snap out of his jinx and win it. What really would be good for the game of golf would be for Sam and me to tie for top place and then play off for the title over pay-TV. We swing almost incidental, and if Sam irons out that hitch he's got in his turn, the viewers would have a hard time telling which was Sam and which was me. This would be good for the game of golf. During yesterday's round I played right behind Sam and noticed he has picked up a couple of my mannerisms, like looking like I am sitting down at the top of the backswing and finishing with the hands up extra high. It is much easier for a copier to uncover the secrets of my action in my hotel room cause I swing much slower there than on the course, so maybe I have been negligee in leaving the curtains of my room wide open at night and should draw them shut when I am working on the old swing. I have got my eye on the Open too. My plans are to go out to Cherry Hills after I qualify locally and get oriental with the course early like Ben does, so that when the shooting starts I know every blade of grass like I grew up with it. I have already telephoned to Joe Dey who is in charge of routine for the USGA and filed my entry for the British Open. Here I was thinking ahead. If I won our Open and then didn't go over to St Andrews and try for a double, it would look kind of chicken, wouldn't it?

Well, not too much else has happened to fill you in about seeing as you will be looking at me in the flesh next week. In Fort Worth they have very good food when you know where to find it and your boy maybe is tipping the scales a little after all that steak and all that pie with ice cream which those Texans call pie Alamo after their famous fort, which is what you would expect in Texas, isn't it? I saw a little of Lucy Ann

Umpey at her old man's villa every night but she has gone on a serious kick this year. For a sample, the term paper she is doing for college has got the title of 'The American Athlete and His Effect on Temporary Mores.' This 'mores' she explained to me means practically the same as 'customs,' but you set yourself up for a much better shot at the professor if you go with 'mores.' Lucy Ann had a recording machine on which she was taking down my answers to her questions and she was strictly business all the way. The moment I would dawdle a little she would snap another question at me like, 'Is it your goal to be so well known you are recognized whenever you enter an air terminal?' Bing, bing, bing – one question after another like you were on a witness stand trying to remember what course you were taking apart on the night of February 16. This is what Lucy Ann calls research, which was not my plans of how to spend an evening with a terrific-looking redhead who wears those toreadora pants which have a bad effect on my own mores, but this is what education is doing to our country.

Now that you have upped me to head pro I am going to try to put on some extra dignity, but it is difficult to grow matured on the tour with all those knockout babes giving you the old reception at every tournament. It is like a fellow who is trying to give up reading so he goes and takes a room in the public library. But I will give it a real try, Mr Tabor, cause I know you want your customers to think of your pro as a fellow who is loaded with a little touch of class.

See you soon,
Yours truly,
Harrison L. Sprague
Head Professional
Otter Lake C.C.

P.S. That, I think, meaning the words under my signature, is how we should print my name on the sign outside the pro shop and also on the station wagon. Your boy is sort of counting on it for the evenings, so he can check on the condition of the course.

JOHN UPDIKE

FARRELL'S CADDIE

WHEN FARRELL SIGNED up, with seven other aging members of his local Long Island club, for a week of golf at the Royal Caledonian Links in Scotland, he didn't foresee the relationship with the caddies. Hunched little men in billed tweed caps and rubberized rain suits, they huddled in the misty gloom as the morning foursomes got organized, and reclustered after lunch, muttering as unintelligibly as sparrows, for the day's second eighteen.

Farrell would never have walked thirty-six holes a day in America, but here in Scotland golf was not an accessory to life, drawing upon one's marginal energy; it *was* life, played out of the center of one's being. At first, stepping forth on legs one of which had been broken in a college football game forty years before, and which damp weather or a night of twisted sleep still provoked to a reminiscent twinge, he missed the silky glide and swerve of the accustomed electric cart, its magic-carpet suspension above the whispering fairway; he missed the rattle of spare balls in the retaining shelf, and the round plastic holes to hold drinks, alcoholic or carbonated, and the friendly presence on the seat beside him of another gray-haired sportsman, another warty pickle blanching in the brine of time, exuding forbearance and the expectation of forbearance, and resigned, like Farrell, to a golfing mediocrity that would make its way down the sloping dogleg of decrepitude to the level green of death.

Here, however, on the heather-rimmed fairways, cut as

close as putting surfaces back home, yet with no trace of mower tracks, and cheerfully marred by the scratchings and burrows of the nocturnal rabbits that lived and bred beneath the impenetrably thorny, waist-high gorse, energy came up through the turf, as if Farrell's cleats were making contact with primal spirits beneath the soil, and he felt he could walk forever. The rolling treeless terrain, the proximity of the wind-whipped sea, the rain that came and went with the suddenness of thought – they composed the ancient matrix of the game, and the darkly muttering caddies were also part of this matrix.

That first morning in the drizzly shuffle around the golf bags, his bag was hoisted up by a hunched shadow who, as they walked together in pursuit of Farrell's first drive (good contact, but pulled to the left, toward some shaggy mounds), muttered half to himself, with those hiccups or glottal stops the Scots accent inserts, 'Sandy's wha' th' call me.'

Farrell hesitated, then confessed, 'I'm Gus.' His given name, Augustus, had always embarrassed him, but its shortened version seemed a little short on dignity, and at the office, as he had ascended in rank, his colleagues had settled on his initials, 'A. J.'

'Ye want now tae geh oover th' second boosh fra' th' laift,' Sandy said, handing Farrell a 7-iron. The green was out of sight behind the shaggy mounds, which were covered with a long tan grass that whitened in waves as gusts beat in from the sea.

'What's the distance?' Farrell was accustomed to yardage markers – yellow stakes, or sprinkler heads.

The caddie looked reflectively at a sand bunker not far off, and then at the winking red signal light on the train tracks beyond, and finally at a large bird, a gull or a crow, winging against the wind beneath the low, tattered, blue-black clouds. 'Ah hunnert thirhty-eight tae th' edge o' th' green, near a hunnert fifty tae th' pin, where they ha' 't.'

'I can't hit a seven-iron a hundred fifty. I can't hit it even one-forty, against this wind.'

Yet the caddie's fist, in a fingerless wool glove, did not withdraw the offered club. 'Siven's what ye need.'

As Farrell bent his face to the ball, the wet wind cut across his eyes and made him cry. His tears turned one ball into two; he supposed the brighter one was real. He concentrated on taking the clubhead away slowly and low to the turf, initiating his downswing with a twitch of the left hip, and suppressing his tendency to dip the right shoulder. The shot seemed sweet, soaring with a gentle draw precisely over the second bush. He looked toward the caddie, expecting con-gratulations or at least some small sign of shared pleasure. But the man, whose creased face was weathered the strangely even brown of a white actor playing Othello, followed the flight of the ball as he had that of the crow, reflectively. 'Yer right hand's a wee bit froward,' he observed, and the ball, they saw as they climbed to the green, was indeed pulled to the left, into a deep pot bunker. Furthermore, it was fifteen yards short. The caddie had underclubbed him, but showed no signs of remorse as he handed Farrell the sand wedge. In Sandy's dyed-looking face, pallid gray eyes showed the touches of morning light; it shocked Farrell to suspect that the other man, weathered though he was, and bent beneath the weight of a perpetual golf bag, was younger than him-self – a prematurely wizened Pict, a concentrate of Farrell's diluted, Yankeefied Celtic blood.

The side of the bunker toward the hole was as tall as Farrell and sheer, built up of bricks of sod in a way he had never seen before, not even at Shinnecock Hills. Rattled, irritated by having been unrepentantly underclubbed, Farrell swung five times into the damp, brown sand, darker and denser than any sand on Long Island; each time, the ball thudded short of the trap's lip and dribbled back at his feet. ''it at it well beheend,' the caddie advised, 'and dinna stop th' cloob.' Farrell's sixth swing brought the ball bobbling up onto the green, within six feet of the hole.

His fellow Americans lavished ironical praise on the tardily excellent shot but the caddie, with the same deadpan solemnity with which Farrell had repeatedly struck the ball, handed him his putter. 'Ae ball tae th' laift,' he advised, and Farrell was so interested in this quaint concept – the ball as a unit of measure – that his putt stopped short. 'Ye forgot tae 'it it, Goos,' Sandy told him.

Farrell tersely nodded. The caddie made him feel obliged to keep up a show of golfing virtues. Asked for his score, he said loudly in a stagey voice, 'That was an honest ten.'

'We'll call it a six,' said the player keeping score, in a forgiving, corrupting American way.

As the round progressed, through a rapid alternation of brisk showers and silvery sunshine, with rainbows springing up around them and tiny white daisies gleaming underfoot, Farrell and his caddie began to grow into one another, as a foot in damp weather grows into a shoe. Sandy consistently handed Farrell one club too short to make the green, but Farrell came to accept the failure as his own; his caddie was handing the club to the stronger golfer latent in Farrell, and it was Farrell's job to let this superior performer out, to release him from his stiff, soft, more than middle-aged body. On the twelfth hole, called 'Dunrobin' – a seemingly endless par 5 with a broad stretch of fairway, bleak and vaguely restless like the surface of the moon, receding over a distant edge marked by two small pot bunkers, with a pale-green arm of gorse extending from the rabbit-undermined thickets on the left –

his drive clicked. Something about the ghostly emptiness of this terrain, the featurelessness of it, had removed Farrell's physical inhibitions; he felt the steel shaft of the drive bend in a subtle curve at his back, and a corresponding springiness awaken in his knees, and he knew, as his weight elastically moved from the right foot to the left, that he would bring the clubface squarely into the ball, and indeed did, so that the ball – the last of his Titleists, the others having already been swallowed by gorse and heather and cliffside scree – was melting deep into the drizzle straight ahead almost before he looked up, with his head still held sideways as if pillowed on his right ear, just like the pros on television. He cocked an eye at Sandy. 'O.K.?' asked Farrell, mock-modest but also genuinely fearful of some hazard, some trick of the layout, that he had missed taking into account.

'Gowf shot, sirr,' the caddie said, and his face, as if touched by a magic wand, crumpled into a smile full of crooked gray teeth, his constantly relit cigarette adhering to one corner. Small matter that Farrell, striving for a repetition of his elastic sensations, topped the following 3-wood, hit a 5-iron fat and short, and skulled his wedge shot clear across the elevated green. He had for a second awakened the golf giant sleeping among his muscles, and imagined himself now cutting a more significant figure in the other man's not quite colorless, not quite indifferent eyes.

Dinner, for this week of foreign excursion, was a repeating male event, involving the same eight Long Island males, their hair growing curly and their faces ruddy away from the arid Manhattan canyons and air-conditioned offices where they had accumulated their small fortunes. They discussed their caddies as men, extremely unbuttoned, might discuss their mistresses. What does a caddie want? 'Come on, Freddie, '*it* it fer once!' the very distinguished banker Frederic M. Panoply boasted that his had cried out to him as, on the third day of displaying his cautious, successful, down-the-middle game, he painstakingly addressed his ball.

Another man's caddie, when asked what he thought of Mrs Thatcher, had responded with a twinkle, 'She'd be a good 'ump.'

Farrell, prim and reserved by nature, though not devoid of passion, had relatively little to offer concerning Sandy. He worried that the man's incessant smoking would kill him. He wondered if the tips he gave him were too far below what a Japanese golfer would have bestowed. He feared that Sandy was becoming tired of him. As the week went by, their relationship had become more intuitive. 'A six-iron?' Farrell would now say, and without word would be handed the club. Once he had dared decline an offered 6, asked for the 5, and sailed his unusually well-struck shot into the sedge beyond the green. On the greens, where he at first had been bothered by the caddie's explicit directives, so that he forgot to stroke the ball firmly, Farrell had come to depend upon Sandy's advice, and would expertly cock his ear close to the caddie's mouth, and try to envision the curve of the ball into the center of the hole from 'an inch an' a fingernail tae th' laift.' He began to sink putts. He began to get pars, as the white-caps flashed on one side of the links and on the other the wine-red electric commuter trains swiftly glided up to Glasgow and back. This was happiness, bracketed between sea and rail, and freedom, of a wild and windy sort. On the morning of his last day, having sliced his first drive into the edge of the rough, between a thistle and what appeared to be a child's weathered tombstone, Farrell bent his ear close to the caddie's mouth for advice, and heard, 'Ye'd be better leavin' 'er.'

'Beg pardon?' Farrell said, as he had all week, when the glottal, hiccupping accent had become opaque. Today the acoustics were especially bad; a near-gale off the sea made his rain pants rattle like machine guns and deformed his eyeballs with air pressure as he tried to squint down. When he could stop seeing double, his lie looked fair – semi-embedded. The name on the tombstone was worn away. Perhaps it was merely an ancient railroad right-of-way marker.

'Yer missus,' Sandy clarified, passing over the 8-iron. 'Ere it's tae late, mon. She was never yer type. Tae proper.'

'Shouldn't this be a wedge?' Farrell asked uncertainly.

'Nay, it's sittin' up guid enough,' the caddie said, pressing his foot into the heather behind the ball so it rose up like ooze out of mud. 'Ye kin reach with th' eight,' he said. 'Go fer yer par, mon. Yer fauts er a' in yer mind; ye tend t' play a hair defainsive.'

Farrell would have dismissed Sandy's previous remarks, as a verbal mirage amid the clicks and skips of wind-blown Scots, had they not seemed so uncannily true. 'Too proper' was exactly what his college friends had said of Sylvia, but he had imagined that her physical beauty had been the significant thing, and her propriety a pose she would out-grow, whereas thirty-five married years had revealed the pro-priety as enduring and the beauty as transient. As to leaving her, this thought would never have entered his head until recently; the mergers-and-acquisitions branch had recently taken on a certain Irma Finegold, who had heavy-lidded eyes, full lips painted vermilion, and a curious presumptuous way of teasing Farrell in the eddies of chitchat before and after conferences, or in the elevator up to the boardroom. She had been recently divorced, and when she talked to Far-rell she manipulated her lower lip with a pencil eraser and shimmied her shoulders beneath their pads. On nights when the office worked late – he liked occasionally to demonstrate that, well-along though he was, he could still pull an all-nighter with the young bucks – there had been between him and Irma shared Chinese meals in greasy take-out cartons, and a joint limo home in the dawn light, through the twin-ned arches and aspiring tracery of the Brooklyn Bridge. And on one undreamed-of occasion, there had been an invitation, which he did not refuse, to delay his return to Long Island with an interlude at her apartment in Park Slope. Though no young buck, he had not done badly, it seemed to him, even factoring in the flattery quotient from a subordinate.

The 8-iron pinched the ball clean, and the Atlantic gale brought the soaring shot left-to-right toward the pin. 'Laift edge, but dinna gi' th' hole away,' Sandy advised of the putt, and Farrell sank it, for the first birdie of his week of golf.

Now, suddenly, out of the silvery torn sky, sleet and sun-shine poured simultaneously. While the two men walked at the same tilt to the next tee, Sandy's voice came out of the wind, 'An' steer clear o' th' MiniCorp deal. They've laiveraged th' company tae daith.'

Farrell studied Sandy's face. Rain and sleet bounced off his brown skin as if from a waxy preservative coating. Metallic gleams showed as the man studied, through narrowed eye-lids, the watery horizon. Farrell pretended he hadn't heard. On the tee he was handed a 3-wood, with the advice, 'Ye want tae stay short o' th' wee burn. Th' wind's come around beheend, bringin' th' sun with it.'

As the round wore on, the sun did struggle through, and a thick rainbow planted itself over the profile of the drab town beyond the tracks, with its black steeples and distillery chim-neys. By the afternoon's eighteen, there was actually blue sky, and the pockets of lengthening shadow showed the old course to be everywhere curvaceous, crest and swale, like the body of a woman. Forty feet off the green on the fourteenth ('Whinny Brae'), Farrell docilely accepted the caddie's offer of a putter, and rolled it up and over the close-mown irregularities within a gimme of the hole. His old self would have skulled or fluffed a chip. 'Great advice,' he said, and in his flush of triumph challenged the caddie: 'But Irma *loves* the MiniCorp deal.'

'Aye, 't keeps th' twa o' ye taegither. She's fairful ye'll wander off, i' th' halls o' corporate power.'

'But what does she see in me?'

'Lookin' fer a father, th' case may be. Thet first husband o' hers was meikle immature, an' also far from yer own income bracket.'

Farrell felt his heart sink at the deflating shrewdness of the analysis. His mind elsewhere, absented by bittersweet sorrow, he hit one pure shot after another. Looking to the caddie for praise, however, he met the same impassive, dour, young-old visage, opaque beneath the billed tweed cap. Tomorrow, he would be caddying for someone else, and Farrell would be belted into a business-class seat within a 747. On the home stretch of holes – one after the other strung out beside the railroad right-of-way, as the Victorian brick clubhouse, with its turrets and neo-Gothic windows, enlarged in size – Farrell begged for the last scraps of advice. 'The five-wood, or the three-iron? The three keeps it down out of the wind, but I feel more confident with the wood, the way you've got me swinging.'

'Th' five'll be ower an' gone; ye're a' poomped up. Take th' four-iron. Smooth it on, laddie. Aim fer th' little broch.'

'Broch?'

'Wee stone fortress, frae th' days we had our own braw king.' He added, 'An' ye might be thinkin' aboot takin' early retirement. Th' severance deals won't be so sweet aye, with th' comin' resaission. Ye kin free yerself up, an' take on some consults, fer th' spare change.'

'Just what I was thinking, if Irma's a will-o'-the-wisp.'

'Will-o'-the-wisp, d' ye say? Ye're a speedy lairner, Goos.'

Farrell felt flattered and wind-scoured, here in this surging universe of green and gray. 'You really think so, Sandy?'

'I *ken* sae. Ye kin tell a' aboot a man, frae th' way he gowfs.'

IAN RANKIN

GRADUATION DAY

WE FLEW INTO Scotland on some carrier called Icelandair, which was a good and a very bad start to proceedings. Good, in that I hadn't booked the flights: our travel arrangements had been Mike's responsibility. During the drive to the airport, he'd kept telling us how he'd got this 'great deal': Boston to Glasgow via Reykjavik, business class, of course. Their idea of business-class food was raw fish – lots of raw fish.

'Where am I, Japan?' the Boss kept saying.

So the good news was, Mike had not endeared himself to our employer. The bad news was the fish.

There were four of us. Mike and the Boss, plus Pete and me. You better call me Mickey. Or if you prefer a little formality, Mr Dolenz, seeing how he was my favorite Monkee. I loved that show, still try to catch the reruns and have most episodes on tape. What follows is by way of a true story, with names and maybe one or two incidents changed to protect the guilty. So there's me – that's Mickey – plus Mike and Pete. Then there's the Boss, of course, but I can't bring myself to call him Davy. 'Davy' just isn't his style. So maybe he should stay 'the Boss.'

Mike thinks he's the suave one, Mr Sophistication. He does his job, but always with the air of thinking there could be something better for him out there someday. He thinks he's the brains of the outfit, too, The Boss's right-hand man.

Pete is just the opposite. He wears expensive clothes, but they don't sit right on him, and I swear, he buys a new pair of shoes? They're scuffed in the first hour. It was the same when we were kids: new pants, new shoes, Pete had worn them in big-time by sundown. Pete is not over-endowed in the intellectual department, but he is the approximate size of an abattoir door. Even the business-class seat proved a little troublesome for him, and when the steward turned up with the food, Pete was the usual soul of diplomacy.

'I can't eat that crap,' he said. Instead, he gorged on the snacks and some fresh fruit, the latter being maybe the first time I ever saw him eat something that didn't come in a wrapper or container of some kind.

'Careful, Pete,' I told him. 'That stuff's actually good for you.'

He had the headphones on and couldn't hear me.

Meantime, I tried the fish, but only when the Boss wasn't looking, and I have to tell you, it was fine, and not even all of it was raw. I read in the magazine that it was traditional, but kept the news to myself. Mike, meantime, who'd made sure he was sitting next to the Boss, kept staring down at his own plate, knowing if he ate any he'd start getting looks from his neighbor. Whenever Mike glanced over in my direction, I made sure I was chewing.

We landed in Scotland late afternoon, to discover that our final destination, the ancient city of St Andrews, wasn't any-where nearby. In fact, it was on the other side of the country and, studying the map we'd been given at the information desk, was actually in the middle of nowhere.

'We'll take a cab anyway,' the Boss said. But Mike had another suggestion.

'What if we rent a car? We need transportation while we're there, right?'

'We can take cabs.'

'What if there aren't any?'

'Jesus, Mike, it's got this huge university. It's the home of golf. We're not talking some hick town here.'

'Actually,' the woman at the information desk piped up in a heavy Scotch accent, 'St Andrews isn't all that big. I went there on holidays once when I was a child. Just a few thousand people . . .'

Well, that's what I think she said. We just stared at her, then at each other, shrugged eventually. As we moved off, searching for Avis or Hertz, the Boss mumbled:

'We're not still in Iceland, are we?'

'The signs are all in English,' I pointed out.

'Yeah? Then what language was she speaking back there?'

It was raining outside, not torrential but pretty good. We'd got through Customs and Passport Control, so should have been starting to relax, but we knew we couldn't do that till we were on the road. I was pushing one cart. It had my bags, plus Mike's and the Boss's. Pete had another cart to himself, two cases on it. Just clothes and stuff, unless someone got real nosy and happened to notice the weight. Then maybe they'd take their search a little more seriously and find the false sides and our personal firearms. Mike had taken care of the auto, and we were loading the cases into the back. Bit of a squeeze in the trunk.

'Biggest one they had,' Mike said, but the Boss's look said he had work to do before he got back on his good side.

'Got a great deal on it, too,' he added.

'Probably means it runs on raw fish,' the Boss grumbled.

Not that the Boss was tight with money or anything, but the business hadn't had its best year: lots of competition from new start-ups, established suppliers and clients a little rocky. Lean times made for financial constraints. The Boss had talked of traveling to Scotland alone. It took a lot of persuading that this was not a good idea. All those new competitors meant you never knew when someone might decide to take a try at whacking you. The further the Boss traveled from home turf, the greater the risk. This was the argument we used. Then he balked at the idea of four of us.

'Who you going to leave behind?' I'd told him. His look had given me my answer: Pete. My own look had asked a silent question: what if we need a fall guy? If there was trouble ahead, a patsy could always come in useful.

Back when Mike had been getting us transportation, I'd gone to the head, returning by way of a little book and newspaper concession where I'd spent the first of my British money on a guidebook. As we drove slowly out of the airport, I started to read it.

'They drive on the left here,' I reminded Mike.

'Contrary sons of bitches.'

The rental desk had provided another map, and the Boss was trying to make sense of it. He passed it back to me.

'Designated navigator,' he growled.

So it was me, Mickey Dolenz, who ensured the show went on, guiding Mike as he gripped the steering wheel like he was trying to choke a repayment out of someone.

We didn't do too badly in the end, though the roads left much to be desired. The last twenty, thirty miles, it was two-lane stuff, tractors and delivery trucks, and all these switchbacks. The Boss kept saying he should have brought the motion-sickness bag from the airplane. When I looked over toward Pete, who was sharing the backseat with me, he was gazing out of his window.

'Fields and trees,' he said quietly, as if he knew I was watching. 'That's all there is out there.'

And then suddenly we started seeing coastline. 'That's St Andrews, gentlemen,' I told them. Then I started reading from the guidebook. The Boss turned in his seat.

'It's not a city?'

'Just barely qualifies as a town,' I replied.

Mike was shaking his head. 'I don't like this.'

'You don't like what?'

'Middle of nowhere ... small town ... We're going to stand out.'

The Boss stabbed a fat finger into Mike's ribs. 'The travel was your responsibility. How come you couldn't do what Mickey did, buy yourself a guidebook? That way we'd've known what we were dealing with.'

'Forewarned is forearmed,' I agreed. When Mike looked at me in the rearview, I knew he wanted to give me a forearm of his own, right across my mouth.

Our hotel was the Old Course, and was easy to find, practically the first thing you saw as you drove into town. When we were shown to our rooms, Pete went to the window.

'Nice grounds,' he said.

'That's the golf course, sir,' the bellhop informed him.

And Jesus, I suppose it was beautiful – if you like that sort of thing. Me, I prefer the pool hall: cigar smoke and brightly lit tables, jokes and side bets. That's pretty much how I got started in the business. By the time I was seventeen, the Boss – then just approaching forty – said I'd spent so much time in pool halls, I could run one standing on my head. So he gave me one of his to manage, and Pete, who'd always hung around with me, hung around until he was part of the business, too.

'How could we have lived so long and not seen this, Mickey?' Pete asked as the bellhop left with some more of my British money. Something else I'd learned in my guidebook:

they didn't like it in Scotland if you called them English. 'British' was okay, mostly, though the book's author had hinted that things might change with the Scottish Parliament and everything.

'I don't know, Pete,' I said. 'Boston's not so bad.'

He looked at me. 'It's not the world, though.'

'Only world you and me are likely to know, pal,' I told him.

Just before dinner, I took a look in the hotel shop and came up with a couple of local books, one about golf and one about the town. This last had a good long section on the university, so I was able to tell the Boss a few things as we ate. There seemed to be a lot of our fellow countrymen in the dining room, and during the course of the meal, at one point or another, practically every one of them made the same gesture, gripping an invisible club and swinging it. They were illustrating some smart play they'd made, or maybe some unsmart one.

We were the odd ones out. I noticed there was almost a uniform: either loud sports shirts or woolen V-necks. We weren't dressed that way. We were dressed normally.

'That's interesting, Mickey,' the Boss kept saying. At first I thought he was being ironic, but he wasn't: he wanted to know what I knew about the place. Pete wasn't taking much of it in. He kept craning his neck, trying to see past the other diners, trying to spot more countryside through the darkening windows.

Mike arrived just as we were being served coffee. 'I don't like it,' he said. He was in full bodyguard mode now, and had forgone dinner to 'check out' the town. 'It's a security nightmare,' he added. 'Know how far the nearest hospital is?'

'For the love of God, Mike,' the Boss snarled. 'There's not going to be any hit!'

'Couldn't pick a better place for one,' Mike argued.

'This is a family thing, Mike,' the Boss went on. 'I appreciate your concern, but do us all a favor and *lighten up!*' The Boss made sure his words had hit home, then tossed his napkin onto the table. 'Now, you going to eat something or what?'

But Mike shook his head. Bodyguards didn't have time for thoughts of food. Instead, he concentrated on giving the other diners steely glances, which they, having drunk wine and port and whiskey, didn't even notice. Me, I had the inkling Mike would be placing an order with room service before the night was out.

It had been Mike's job also to book the accommodations, which was why I was sharing with Pete down the hall while the Boss and Mike had their own rooms next door to one another.

'Some mix-up in the reservations,' was Mike's explanation, and now that the hotel was full, we couldn't do much about it.

'Never mind, Mike,' I said, 'at least the room for two saves the business some money, right?'

'Right,' he said, unsure how serious I was being.

The hotel was full not just because St Andrews remained, as the book said, 'the Mecca of golf,' but because it was graduation time at the university, and this, I guessed, was where the richer parents, people like the Boss himself, stayed while they were in town for the festivities, festivities which were due to begin the following morning with some service in the chapel.

The Boss fully intended to be present at this service, since his daughter would be in the choir. Even though it meant us rising at what our body clocks would tell us was something like three in the morning.

Yes, we were in St Andrews because the Boss's only child

was graduating with honors or distinction or something in some subject or other.

'If only her mother could have been here,' the Boss said, enjoying a brandy after his coffee. Then he stared off into the distance, maybe thinking pleasant thoughts from the past, thoughts of the way his wife, Edie, had been . . . up until the time she'd run off with her tennis coach. We'd never been able to trace the pair of them, or the few hundred thou Edie had 'misappropriated' from the business in the form of cash and jewelry.

'We get lucky, maybe she'll turn up,' Mike said, patting his jacket. It was Hugo Boss, the styling described as 'un-structured'. Fashion was definitely on Mike's side, helping disguise the bulge of a shoulder holster.

'You not drinking, Mickey?' the Boss asked. I shook my head. Before setting off from Boston, I'd read a magazine article about surviving long hauls. Lay off the booze and take some melatonin before bed. The magazine had been left behind by someone in the pool hall. It's amazing the things I've learned down the years in places like that.

Next day Pete's jaw dropped further when he saw the medi-eval chapel, probably the oldest thing he'd ever seen in his life. I thought he was going to break his neck, staring up at the ceiling and the stained-glass windows. He'd already been out exploring before breakfast and told me about it afterward in our room. I'd offered him the guidebook, but he'd shaken his head. Never a great reader.

The service wasn't too long. A couple of hymns and two reverend gentlemen in charge. They both made speeches. You could tell the university professors: they were dressed in robes, and we all had to stand while they were led into the chapel. The rest of the congregation appeared to be students and parents. The choir was upstairs, positioned in front of the organ. Beautiful music; I couldn't make out Wilma's voice, but I could see her. She had a cape on, too; all the choristers did. She smiled down at her father, and he smiled back. There were actually tears in his eyes, and I handed him a fresh handkerchief. Mike didn't notice: too busy eying the crowd.

Afterward, we waited outside for Wilma. The day was clouding over, growing cool. Wilma came around the side of the chapel and broke into a sprint, nearly pushing her father over as she hugged him.

'Dad, I'm so sorry I couldn't come to the hotel last night.'

'Hey, you had to practice, I understand.' He pushed her back a little so that he could look at her. 'And you were fantastic. I was so proud of you, Wilma.'

There was one of the other choristers standing just behind her. He turned his head to Mike and offered a smile. Mike scowled back, perhaps hoping to persuade him to be on his way. Wilma suddenly remembered he was there.

'Oh, Dad, I want you to meet a friend of mine. This is Freddy.'

Freddy had thick dark hair and a pale, round face; looked a bit like he'd walked out of a sixties movie set in swinging London. But then he opened his mouth.

'A real pleasure to meet you, sir.'

'Fellow American, eh?' the Boss said, shaking Freddy's hand.

'Freddy's graduating, too,' Wilma explained.

'Well, congratulations, son.'

Only now did Wilma seem to notice the rest of us. We got our pecks on the cheek and a few words. I'd wondered about Wilma and Mike once or twice, but she didn't seem to treat him any different from me or Pete.

'We better go get changed,' Freddy told her. She looked down at her robe and smiled.

'See you for lunch, Dad,' she said, hugging the Boss again.

'Twelve-fifteen at the hotel,' her father reminded her. She nodded. Wilma's graduation ceremony was mid-afternoon, followed by a garden party and something called Beating the Retreat. Next day there was a graduates' luncheon, parents invited. We were booked on a flight out first thing the morning after that.

After Wilma and Freddy had gone, the Boss turned to us. 'I don't need you guys till later.' He looked at Mike. 'And I certainly don't want to be sharing a table and my daughter with you over lunch.'

Mike nodded. 'We'll take one of the other tables.'

But the Boss shook his head. 'You'll make yourselves scarce, understood?'

So that was us, dismissed. 'I don't like it,' Mike said as soon as he had me on my own. 'It's just the moment they'd choose for a hit.'

'Can we skip to the next track on the CD?' I asked.

'You mean you're going to go along with this?' Mike's eyes narrowed, as though he thought I might be cooking something up.

'Mike, we've flown halfway round the globe to be here. I'd like to see a bit of the place.'

'Sightseeing? What's to see?'

'Open your eyes, Mike.'

'My eyes are open, friend. It's you that's walking around blind.'

I just shook my head. 'I want something to tell the guys back home.'

'Such as?'

I shrugged. 'I don't know ... Such as playing a round of

272

golf at St Andrews.' Until then, the thought hadn't occurred to me, but Mike's disbelieving laughter sealed it for me. And when I suggested it to Pete, he was more than agreeable. Which left Mike out in the cold.

'Well,' he said, 'I wasn't too comfortable about that Freddy guy. Think I might do some background . . .' Like he was still in the neighborhood and only had to tap a few skulls to get some answers.

Meantime, Pete and I took a stroll down to the golf course. The hotel had already explained that St Andrews was a public course, and probably not expensive by American standards, but that its popularity was a problem. Too many people wanted to play, which translated as a raffle for the day's start times. However, if we wanted to risk it . . . In any event, a few showers seemed to have kept some people away and there were a couple of cancellations. We managed a slot late afternoon, which gave us time to visit the pro shop.

Pete was disappointed to find that 'pro' was short for 'golf professional' and that all they were going to sell him there were clubs, shoes and stuff. His second disappointment came when he discovered there were no plus fours. I think the cold and the rain were getting to him, because by the time we'd rented our clubs and shoes, and bought a tartan cap apiece along with some balls and tees, he was in one of his fouler moods.

'Ever played this game?' I asked him as he hauled our clubs – one set between us – toward the first tee.

'Watched it on TV,' he replied.

'Then you're practically an expert.'

Now, if you've ever been to a golf course, you'll know that the pockets are a good distance apart, and not with only flat green baize between them. The wind was whipping across us, and the little boxes on my scorecard didn't make any sense. As the gulls screeched overhead, I remembered that there was some ornithological aspect to the game: birdies and eagles and stuff. I also knew that the wooden clubs were for the initial tee drive, and that a putter was what you used in miniature golf.

'You don't know the game either, huh?' Pete said.

'Always meant to learn.'

'Well, I can't think of a better time or place.'

'You okay, Big Pete? You seem a bit down.'

He seemed about to say something, then just shook his head and mumbled something about jet lag. We were at the first tee now. Some players just ahead of us were marching up the fairway.

'They got wheels with their golf bags,' Pete complained.

'Wheels were extra. You tote them the first nine, I'll tote them back, okay?'

'You mean we're playing sixteen holes?'

'Eighteen, Pete,' I corrected him.

'We'll be here all day.'

'Fortunately that's exactly how long we've got.'

He bent down and pushed his tee into the turf. 'I wanted to see the harbor again.'

'Plenty of time for that,' I promised, following his example with the tee and the ball. Pete was selecting one of the two woods. 'Don't we wait for them to get out of range?' I asked, pointing to the golfers ahead of us. Pete shook his head and got ready to swing his club.

Now, some might put it down to beginner's luck, but me, I think it was a force much darker. Because Pete whacked that ball and it sailed up into the sky, perfectly straight and long. Very long.

I traced its trajectory with my eyes and watched it bounce off the head of one of the other players. As the man dropped like a stone, I watched Pete raise a hand, cupping it to his mouth and hollering, *'Fore!'* Then he turned to me and smiled. 'That's what you do.'

The player was being helped to his feet by his two playing partners. I couldn't make out their faces at this distance, but they were wearing loud sweaters. Also, they were looking at us. As I say, the pockets are pretty far apart, and we had to wait awhile for the men to reach us. The guy Pete had whacked, he'd had a lot of time to calm down during that walk. He didn't calm down, though; he just looked angrier and angrier. Even the sight of Big Pete didn't cause him to rethink any strategy he might have formed. There was a lump on the top of his head that looked like one of the gulls had laid an egg in the nest of his hair. He was swearing at us from about eighty yards out, his fellow players just a few steps behind.

'You stupid ... I swear I'm gonna ... of all the ...' But then he stopped. And if we'd been walking, we'd probably have stopped, too.

Because we knew him, same as he knew us.

'How you doing, Blue?' I asked.

'Unbelievable,' Blue said with a scowl. I didn't think he was answering my question.

They were Beating the Retreat when we caught up with the Boss. It was on the lawn in one of the college quadrangles and seemed to consist of some bagpipes and drums. Guests were huddled beneath umbrellas.

'Where the hell did you get those hats?' the Boss scowled.

'They were Mike's idea,' I lied, seeing his displeasure. 'He said we'd blend in more. Listen, Boss, we've got some bad news.'

'Bad news,' Pete agreed, drawing out the first word.

'What's wrong?'

I led the Boss a bit further away from the merry sound of cats being skinned alive. 'Guess who we just bumped into on the golf course?'

'Tell me.'

So I told him. Blue had been about to enjoy a round with his colleagues Buck and Manolito. Turned out that their boss, Big John, was in town, too.

'That's too big a coincidence,' the Boss said.

I had to agree with him; thing was, I didn't know what else to say. But then Mike came up, looking feverish. 'You'll never guess. I could give you a thousand years, and you'd still never guess.'

It seemed that his inquiries had borne fruit.

'You've discovered that Freddy is Big John's son?' I told him. He looked thunderstruck.

'Just as well you're not the betting type, Mikey,' Pete told him with a grin.

Okay, I need to explain a couple of things here. One is that the mob no longer exists. It was destroyed in a series of high-profile court cases. Everyone saw it happen on TV, so it must be true. The cops and journalists turned their attentions to other criminal gangs. I say this to make you aware that when my Boss and Big John met that evening, it was just two businessmen having a chat. Though Big John operated out of Miami, the two men (having so many interests in common, after all) knew one another, had met many times in the past.

This leads me to my second point, which is that while Big John and my Boss know one another, this is not to say that they are exactly on friendly terms.

The meeting took place on neutral territory: a disused

putting green down by the seashore. Pete knew the place, having passed it during one of his exploratory walks. There were the eight of us. Blue had his head bandaged. Mike asked which doctor he'd used, but didn't get a reply. Our two employers walked toward one another and exchanged a brief hug.

'Funny we have to come all this way to meet again,' Big John said.

'Yeah, some coincidence,' my boss replied. 'I didn't know Freddy was here.'

'Likewise myself with Wilma.'

'What's he studying?'

'Economics. And Wilma?'

'I don't know what it is exactly,' the Boss conceded. 'It's got the words "Moral" and "Philosophy" in it.'

'So what's she gonna do now? M.B.A.? Harvard?'

A shrug. 'She says she wants to teach.'

'Teach?' Big John frowned. 'Teach what?'

'Teach the thing she's been taught.'

Big John smiled. 'No disrespect to Wilma, but that sounds like some sweet scam.'

I could see the Boss bristle at this. 'So Freddy's going to Harvard?'

'That's the plan.'

'Not according to what Wilma told me,' the Boss said.

Big John opened his arms. 'That's why we had to meet, sort things out.'

'Wilma tells me they're in love. They're already living together.' Another shrug. 'The kids are happy, I say let them stay happy.'

Big John's eyes grew colder. 'And I say not.'

'I hope we're not going to have a problem here,' my boss said quietly. I could see Blue and Mike sizing one another

277

up. Same with Manolito and Pete. Buck . . . well, I've always sort of liked Buck, few times we've met. The pair of us were too busy listening to do any measuring. But it was Buck who made the outrageous suggestion.

'If you don't mind me interrupting,' he began, 'we've already got Blue here needing some sort of recompense, not so much for his injuries as for losing out on that round of golf.'

'What are you saying?' Big John asked.

'I'm saying it's not unknown for either of you two gentlemen to enjoy a bet. We could incorporate that bet into a game of golf. That's all.'

Big John looked at my boss. 'How about it? I know you can play.'

'You against me?'

Big John shook his head. 'All of us. Make it a bit more interesting.'

If the Boss had looked at me, he'd have seen me shaking my head. These guys lived the year round in *Florida*. Nothing for them to do all day but drive practice balls and Porsches. But my boss, he wasn't looking at anyone but Big John. Then he thrust out his hand.

'You got yourself a bet,' he said.

Mike spent the rest of the night on the phone, asking his contacts back home about the handicap Big John and his men might be expected to play off. Mike and the Boss could play, but as for Pete and me . . . well, you saw us in action, right? When Mike got off the phone, he had copious notes.

'Big John is a 7-, 8-handicapper, Blue's a 5.'

'Meaning what?' I asked.

Mike rolled his eyes. 'Meaning they'll expect to play only that many shots over par.'

'Each hole?' But Mike didn't even grace that one with a response.

The Boss was thoughtful. 'I'm a 4, you're a . . . what, Mike? An 8?'

'A 7,' Mike stressed. He studied his notes again. 'Manolito's played before, but never really got into the game. But Buck can play. So they've got three players against our two.'

'Hey,' I interrupted, 'you didn't see Pete's tee shot. We may have a natural here.'

'And how about you, Mickey?' the Boss said. 'You gonna let the team down or what? Get back to that practice room.'

The practice room was our hotel room. Both beds had been hauled out into the corridor, giving us space for a few swings. Some golf pro had been found, and money had changed hands. When I went back into the room, he was helping Pete with his grip. This had been going on for the best part of two hours. I shook my head and went back into the corridor. Wilma was standing there.

'This isn't the way things work anymore,' she said, her eyes sad.

'Your father knows that, Wilma.'

'They can't stop us from living together, loving one another, by playing a round of goddamned golf!'

'Your father knows that, too: didn't he tell you as much?' I knew he had. I'd been there at the time. 'But the thing is, it's like a gauntlet was laid down, you know? Your father had to pick it up.'

'Not for me, he didn't.'

'You're right, he's doing this for himself.' I put my hands out, palms upward. 'But maybe for all of us, too.'

'It won't change anything,' she said.

I nodded, telling her she was right. But I knew I was lying. If we lost tomorrow, Freddy would be spirited away somewhere, some university in the boondocks. He'd be where Wilma couldn't find him. Watching the tears form in her eyes, I knew we had to win. I walked back into the practice room and picked up one of the books on golfing rules and etiquette. If I'm being honest, I was looking for a loophole.

My last hope was, we wouldn't get a tee time. But we did: early morning, right after breakfast. The format was simple: each team member took a turn at hitting his team's ball. We also agreed to make it the best of nine holes rather than the full eighteen. Big John teed off for his side, the Boss for ours. As they walked down the fairway afterward, the Boss asked Big John where he was berthed.

'Rented a beautiful big house just outside town. All services provided. How about you?'

'The Old Course Hotel.'

'What's it like?'

'Pretty good.'

'I'm sure it is,' Big John said, his tone almost adding the words 'for a hotel.'

Pete took the second stroke and overhit it. That was when we decided he should maybe tee off at the second hole.

When my turn came, I had to chip onto the green, but rolled it right off again and into a bunker.

'Just as well we're playing hole by hole,' Mike hissed at me afterward as we walked to the second tee. 'We lost that one by three strokes.'

By dint of a massive tee shot from Pete, we managed to draw the next hole. Then at the third, Manolito, who was losing more interest in the game the further we moved from the town's female population, put the ball into some deep rough, from which it took Big John's players two more strokes to get it back onto the fairway. Although we took three putts, we still won by a single stroke, Big John's own massive saving putt stopping about an inch and a half from the hole.

It was all square as we walked to the fourth. 'Still shooting pool?' Buck asked me. I nodded. 'Then it's just as well it's golf we're playing.'

I smiled. 'How about you, Buck? Life treating you fair?'

'It's tough all over,' he said. But I knew it wasn't. Miami didn't have the same problems Boston did. Big John had made peace with the Cubans. This had allowed him certain avenues of diversification. First time my Boss and Big John had met, they'd done so in a state of parity, a state which could no longer be said to exist.

Blue played a spectacular 3-iron at the fourth. I knew the clubs now, thanks to a long night with the pro. I could even use them, in a rudimentary fashion. But if Pete's deficiency was his inability to hit the ball at anything short of full power, then mine was more a matter of accuracy deficiency. That ball . . . it seemed to have a mind of its own, I swear. A putt of fifteen feet ended up curving away from the hole until it came to rest nine or ten feet to the left of where I'd been aiming.

'It's called the run of the green,' Buck told me between holes. 'A local caddie, someone who's played the course all his life, they know it like they know the creases, slopes and hangs of their wife's body.'

That's when I knew Big John's team hadn't spent the previous night with a pro, but with a caddie . . .

We drew the fourth, lost the fifth and sixth. Buck had an elegant, easy swing, which I tried copying until Mike hissed that I looked like I was auditioning for Fred Astaire. Mike himself hadn't played a bad stroke yet, said something about teaching Tiger Woods everything he knew, then made the slightest adjustment to his leather driving glove.

When we won the seventh, it was in part because a cell phone went off just as Blue was taking his shot. The cell belonged to Big John, so they could hardly complain when Blue sliced his stroke and the ball got lost in more thick rough. The wind was growing stronger, and our tactic of having Pete tee off was beginning to lose efficacy. The problem was, he hit the ball too high, where the wind caught it and toyed with it, sending it literally off course. But at the eighth we were saved by another glorious shot from Mike, who took a 4-iron into the rough and brought the ball out and in a nice line with the pin. Manolito, meantime, had contrived to find a stream which, according to Mike, shouldn't have been a problem until the back nine. So they dropped a shot, and Buck had to play across the line of a foursome who were on their way home. They looked like locals to me, and just shook their heads. They'd probably seen lousier shots in their time, and maybe worse etiquette, too.

It ended up all square as we went to the ninth.

'Just the way I like my baseball,' I told Buck.

'Except when it's the Red Sox, right?'

I couldn't disagree with him there.

The Boss hit a sweet tee shot, then reached into the pocket of the golf bag and brought out a pakamac. The rain was coming down now. Someone had once told me they did most of their business on the golf course. Well, that's what we were doing out there, too. No place for small talk. My own short exchanges with Buck had earned frowns from both captains.

Pete, despite our encouragement, hit the ball another mighty swipe which sent it sailing past the green and off to the right. Somehow he missed two bunkers and left Mike a manageable chip, which he decided to take with an 8-iron. It landed sweetly about three feet from the hole, but the ball had arranged for some spin, and rolled back a further five or so feet. An eight-foot putt. Buck, meantime, had putted to within four feet of the hole, only to watch Big John's tap-in roll around the lip of the cup and pop back out again.

So instead of putting to save the match, suddenly I had a chance to win it. An eight-foot putt in the wind and rain, here on the Old Course at St Andrews. There was no pressure on me, no pressure at all. The pin was already out. I walked around the other side of the hole and crouched down, measured the line with my putter, the way I'd seen it done. Then back around to my ball again, crouching again, closing one eye to peer at the lie of the green, those curves and slopes . . . And something happened. The closer I got to the ground, the easier the putt looked. They started laughing at me as I angled my head, my hair getting wet as it touched the shorn grass.

'He going to knock it in with his nose or what?' Big John asked.

I got up again, brushed myself off and smiled back at him. 'It's regarded as good manners to keep silent during a player's stroke,' I recited.

'Why, you little punk . . .'

But the others could see that I had a point. Blue touched his boss on the arm, and Big John quieted, grinning a wider grin when he remembered that he was about to win. Me, I just looked at Buck and gave him a wink, then got down on my knees behind the ball, shimmying back until I could stretch out full length. I turned the putter around and imagined the golf ball was a straight black into the center pocket, the putter's rubberized grip a freshly chalked cue tip. I slid it back and forth a few times, until it felt right in my hands. Adjusted my elbow ever so slightly . . .

Big John was complaining now, his voice rising. I ignored

him, ignored everything but the pot. Hit the ball cleanly and watched it roll into the cup. As I got to my feet, there was laughter. Mike was patting me on the back. The Boss was clapping. Pete sent one of the clubs spinning dangerously through the air.

I walked across to where Big John was still scowling, still yelling that I was a goddamned cheat.

'Look at the rules,' I said. 'Or ask a good caddie.'

Then I went back to my team to celebrate.

Of course, by the time we'd finished that round, Wilma and Freddy, as I'd thought they might, had fled: just packed their things and gone. They'd turn up sooner or later, I didn't doubt, once the dust had settled.

We were due to leave before dawn next morning: the long drive back to the airport. But that didn't stop us partying into the wee sma' hours: champagne and malt whiskey, old stories and even a couple of songs. The Boss looked at me with new respect, and I got the feeling maybe I was about to graduate to something better . . . When I woke up, Pete was standing by the window, just staring out at the dark and silent world. No sodium glare, no sirens.

'You okay, old pal?' I asked him.

'Never better,' he assured me.

Next time I awoke, he was gone. We drove out of St Andrews without him. There was no question of us hanging around, looking for him. The Boss wanted to get back home and start spreading the word about the game. Besides, as I tried to explain, I didn't think Pete wanted to be found. There was a lot of world out there for him to explore. Me, I had a warm pool table waiting, and maybe a story of my own to tell.

DAN JENKINS

TEES AND TEENS

ASK ME IF I've ever read one of those advice columns for teens in the newspapers, and I'll say, yeah, sure, all the time, don't I look like I have an eating disorder? Don't I look like I need help trying to find the mall? And, hey – it's 2009 and I think after 50 years I've pretty much figured out how to deal with my parents, OK?

On the other hand, I wasn't about to pass up a chance to cover the Emily Turner Clambake. After all, it was the year's first major. Emily Turner, in case you don't know, is the woman who influences the lives of so many young girls in her syndicated column, Babbling with Emily, and on her popular daytime TV show by the same name.

Like if a teen babe wants to know where to buy a pair of cheap chandelier earrings, she asks Emily. Or if a teen babe wants to know where to find that new video game where she can rescue her platoon from the Taliban, she asks Emily.

Emily Turner knows all kinds of things about life, of course, and for the past five years she's been dipping into golf.

I'd never met Emily, but I introduced myself to her when I arrived at Rancho Trusto Fundo Country Club the day before the tournament started.

Rancho Trusto Fundo is carved out of the melted cheese, chili con carne and chopped taco salad of a California area only an hour and a half from La Jolla and San Diego.

It's the toughest course Pete Dye, Tom Fazio and Jack

Nicklaus ever collaborated on. Yeah, tougher, I think, than Piranha Nibbles, the course they designed on the banks of the Amazon in a part of the Brazilian jungle that can only be reached by paddle boat.

I might add that Rancho Trusto Fundo is woven through a residential area where the homes all look like two Merions and three Winged Foots have been added onto the Oakland Hills clubhouse.

The hills are alive with the sound of money, if you get my meaning, not to write a Broadway musical about it.

But it's sort of a fun place. When you're not playing the golf course, you can sit on the clubhouse terrace and watch the daily swarms of illegal immigrants go romping happily across the hills and valleys in their quaint regional costumes.

I found Emily Turner to be a trim, bouncy little thing. She's somewhere between the age of 55 and 82 – it depends on which side of her most recent facelift you're standing on. I wanted to ask if those were her own eyebrows creeping up her forehead, but thought better of it.

You've seen women whose facelifts have left them looking surprised. Emily looks permanently startled.

Right away, she invited me to join her for an adult beverage in the Teen Vogue hospitality tent.

We clinked highball glasses, and I informed her that I actually preferred watching teen babes play golf these days. I said, 'There's something about a young ponytail that can blow it out there 320 off the tee – uphill, into the wind.'

She looked pleased, although she seemed preoccupied with adjusting the hearing aid in her right ear.

I explained to her how it came about that grown-ups had driven me to covering teen golf. Forced me to resign from *Rampant Instruction*, the largest selling golf monthly, and take a job writing for *Divots and Shopping*, the successful golf weekly, the magazine that's devoted to curing your slice and presenting full-page ads for thong underwear.

I said I'd finally grown tired of having an IMG agent tell me to make an appointment if I wanted to talk to his billionaire client. Some college dropout who didn't know how to do anything but hit a golf ball and would have trouble finding a real job outside of lawn care.

The last time it happened to me was on the veranda at Augusta this past spring. I was standing there trying to have a conversation with this player, Sluggo Simpo, I'll call him, and his agent, Kaiser Wilhelm.

But no matter what I said, Sluggo and the agent only looked at me like I was supposed to be sacking their groceries.

Then Kaiser Wilhelm said if I wanted an interview with Sluggo I should call him, the agent, not the player, and make an appointment.

I said, 'Can I ask one question first?'

The agent frowned.

'Does the dummy talk?' I said.

Nothing. Blank faces. Both of them.

That's when I said to the agent, 'Tell you what. Rather than you, I think I'll call and make an appointment with a brain surgeon and see if I can have your client's name cut out.' And walked away. That was it for dealing with the guys.

As for the women, well, I confessed to Emily Turner I'd never even tried to cover an event on the LPGA Tour – they hadn't played in a town I'd ever heard of in 25 years. I spoke a little louder to Emily and asked how she happened to become interested in golf in the first place. I knew her tournament, the Clambake, was in its fifth year.

She said, 'I suppose you could say it started with Bing

Crosby. I loved his songs. Straight down the middle ... ba ba ba boo. And Dinah was an influence, naturally. My friend, Dinah Shore. Hidy, y'all.'

'I see.'

'All seven of my husbands played in the old Crosby every year. I would go with them, but only for the dinner parties and socializing with the movie stars at the Lodge. Jack Lemmon was such fun.'

'The Monterey Peninsula is terrific.'

'It's a quaint part of the state.'

'Did you say you've had seven husbands?'

'Seven. Yes.'

'And they all played golf?'

'Every waking moment, darling.'

'But you didn't play?'

'No.'

'It sounds like you didn't have much in common with any of your husbands, if you don't mind me saying so.'

'Oh, we did,' she said, smiling. 'We liked being rich.'

Emily's seventh and last husband, Elbert F. (Flash) Pembroke, was a former president of the American Junior Golf Association. He had been the person who encouraged her to sponsor a tournament for young girls.

The tournament ran smoothly for two years, she said, but the third one broke up her marriage. Two years ago, as it happened, Flash Pembroke fell hopelessly in love and ran away with the 16-year-old winner, Annika Danica Koonce.

Flash Pembroke and Annika Danica spent a romantic year together, but then Flash died suddenly this past February. His heart exploded as he was thumbing through an issue of *Golf for Women*.

Emily finished her highball and said she had a column to write about eating disorders, but she was delighted I was covering the Clambake, and she expected us to be seeing a lot of each other.

Other pressing matters in journalism kept me from covering last year's majors. I hated to miss the Clambake. I'd liked to have seen Harriet Scroggs shoot that 64 in the last round and win it by five.

Harriet Scroggs was a powerful, wide-body 17-year-old everyone thought was a cinch to be a star on the LPGA Tour. Unfortunately, she let her temper get the best of her after only six months with the pros.

I was sorry to hear it when she gave up golf completely, but I've read where she's doing quite well on the European track and field circuit. The javelin is her best event, and they say she's throwing it almost as far as she could throw her Ping putter.

Lurkers won the other three majors last year. Li Lang Lo took the iPod Invitational, Lang Lo Li captured the Nordstrom Mall Rat Classic, and Sing Sang Sung grabbed the Whataburger-USGA National Girls' Junior.

Research told me lurkers never do well in the Clambake. You can always count on a headliner to come through. That's because the par-72 Rancho Trusto Fundo course plays to 7,800 yards from the tips, or what the members call 'the portfolio tees.'

The Clambake drew its strongest field in history this time. The 60 invited contestants, who would battle it out over two rounds of stroke play, came from 32 states, six different countries, and ranged in age from 12 to 17. Between them, they had won 1,569 amateur tournaments.

Another statistical breakdown revealed that 16 of them were named Paula, 16 were named Michelle, six were named Lolita. The other 22 were South Koreans.

I was surprised by the press coverage. I didn't expect anybody to be on hand but myself and maybe a local reporter, but there were men and women writers from *Teen Vogue*, *Cosmo Chick*, *Parent Zap*, *Hottie*, *Navels Galore*, *Back Talk*, *Me!*, *Greed*, *Where's Mine?*, and the AP guy in his beard, khaki shorts, sombrero, BlackBerry and backpack of fresh fruit and natural spring water.

Emily furnished me with a cart so I could drive around and watch the ponytails challenge Rancho Trusto Fundo in the first round.

I stuck with the feature twosome. I went the full 18 and watched the charismatic Paula Jean Wagner fire a four-under-par 68 to take a three-stroke lead over the charismatic Michelle Janine Taylor. Paula Jean Wagner was the fetching 14-year-old whose fame since age 6 had turned her mother into a terrified mute and transformed her father into a hunchback invalid from holding down five jobs at once in his effort to pay for his daughter's instruction and schooling at the golf academy in Florida.

Michelle Janine Taylor was the 14-year-old dynamo who'd won 233 tournaments since the age of 7, and had been found innocent of beating her mother to death with the 120-pound scrapbook the mother had kept of her daughter's golf accomplishments. A bushy-haired stranger, arranged by IMG, was later charged with the crime.

Michelle Janine came to the press room interview area first. Emily Turner took it upon herself to conduct the interview. She sat beside Michelle Janine at the table. They shared a microphone as they faced the press.

Emily said, 'Michelle, would you like to make a general comment about your round before going through your card?'

'No,' Michelle Janine said.

She looked very unhappy.

'No? No, what?' Emily said.

'I hate my round.'

Michelle Janine stared off, tight-lipped.

'But you shot a wonderful 71,' Emily said.

'I took a dirt nap.'

Her eyes flashed with anger.

'You took a dirt nap? What's that?'

Emily smiled sweetly at the child, then glanced at the audience and shrugged, as if to say she was doing her best.

'It's a dirt nap, what do you think it is?' Michelle Janine said.

'You're saying dirt nap? Like someone would lie down in the dirt and go to sleep?'

'I played like I was dead, dumbo!'

After her press conference Michelle Janine went to the game room in the clubhouse to relax. She climbed into a seat in a large plastic bubble and began squeezing the trigger on a toy AK-47 that was pointed at a video screen on which swarms of Osama bin Ladens were rushing toward her.

I was pouring myself a Coke in a cup of ice as I waited for the tournament leader, Paula Jean Wagner, to come into the interview area. Suddenly, I felt a tap on the shoulder. I turned around to find Paula Jean Wagner.

'Hi, sailor,' she said with a grin. 'Buy a lady a root-beer float?'

To say she won me over in that instant would be an understatement.

Studying her for a moment, I sized up a more mature person than I'd watched on the golf course. Even cuter, up close and personal. Shapely. Tan. Blond. Far beyond her 14 years. She could have been, oh, 16 or 17.

I told her I enjoyed watching her play today. Frankly, I was amazed at their length, she and Michelle Janine both.

She said, 'We were laying metal on it.'

'Michelle Janine is rather impressive herself.'

'M. Diddy struck it, but she cratered on the greens.'

'M. Diddy?'

'That's what we call her out here. M. Diddy.'

'Which means . . . ?'

'I gotta go.'

Up at the table with the microphone when Emily asked her to comment on her 68, Paula Jean said, 'I lit it up, man.'

She was bombarded with a variety of questions. Among them, the leader was asked if she considered it a two-player competition now, just she and Michelle Janine.

'No way,' Paula Jean said. 'There are a bunch of SoKos right behind us. They're pretty killer.'

It was generally decided among the press that by SoKos she meant South Koreans.

Somebody asked Paula Jean which part of the golf game the South Koreans were best at.

'Chipping and bunkers,' she said. 'They can download it, man.'

Another question. What was the favorite club in her bag?

'My 3-comp,' she said.

'Your what?' said Emily.

'We don't call it a 3-wood or a 3-metal,' Paula Jean said. 'M. Diddy started calling it a 3-comp, and we picked it up. You know, like, the clubs are all composite material? Titanium, carbon, uranium . . .'

'Three comp!' Emily said, looking as if she'd just scored big on a 'Jeopardy' question.

'You got it,' Paula Jean said.

When the press conference ended, Paula Jean went to

the game room and started cutting down her own share of Osamas.

That evening I accepted Emily's kind invitation to attend a dinner party at her home, which bordered the golf course. Home might not be the right word. It resembled four Rivieras with a Medinah soaring off of each end.

The best view was from the south veranda. You could look down on No. 7, one of the course's six island greens, the hole that inspires the most conversation because of the small replica of Mount Rushmore on a cliff behind the green.

I say Mount Rushmore. The faces carved into the rock of the cliff were actually those of Bobby Jones, Ben Hogan, Jack Nicklaus and Jimmy Jack Foster.

I didn't know who Jimmy Jack Foster was either, but I learned that he was the man who originally developed the property and had the golf course built.

There were 16 for dinner. I was Emily's companion, seated on her right. All of the deeply tanned guests were dressed in various shades of pink, green and yellow. Each guest had a waiter standing directly behind him or her, and each waiter held a bottle of red and a bottle of white.

Emily asked that we all hold hands while she said a prayer before we dined. The thin lady on the other side of me removed all her jewelry before she gave me her hand. Emily then asked the Lord to continue to bless golf and wineries and fashion designers, and please tell the terrorists to show a greater respect for rich people.

Emily gave me a tour of her home after the guests either left or passed out. She said she believed she was developing a crush on me, and if I were to become her eighth husband, I could have an entire Medinah to myself.

* * *

The last round of the Clambake was full of surprises. Paula Jean and Michelle Janine each came out dressed for action – they wore short skirts that showed a lot of leg and breast-hugging, navel-exposing T-shirts. Ponytails dangled out of the back of their visors.

They both drove the first green, a downhill 345-yard par 4, and two-putted for birdies. Michelle Janine drew gasps from the gallery when she reached the 610-yard par-5 sixth hole in two with a driver and a 5-iron. She made the 20-foot eagle putt to pick up two strokes on Paula Jean.

Paula Jean pouted and bit her lip.

Michelle Janine picked up another shot on Paula Jean when she reached the 485-yard par-4 ninth with a 3-comp and wedge and made the six-footer for birdie.

Michelle Janine played with her earring as she walked down the fairway.

Paula Jean fought back at the 10th, a 490-yard par 4 that required a 280-yard carry off the tee over pure wasteland. She smashed a drive 320 yards and almost holed a 9-iron. She made the tap-in birdie and her lead was back to two strokes.

Paula Jean played with her own earring as she walked away.

Then it was Michelle Janine's turn. The 16th hole was the last of the island greens, a 287-yard par 3. They reached the green safely, but after Paula Jean three-putted for a bogey, Michelle sank a 25-foot birdie and now they were tied with two holes to play.

It was while they stood on the 17th tee that they heard the roar and found out what Hee Hon (The Hog) Ding, one of the SoKos, had done.

Hee Hon (The Hog) Ding had been five strokes back starting the last nine holes, but she had quietly birdied four holes in a row, the 10th through the 13th, two of them with chip-ins, and then (what the roar was all about) she had holed out a 2-iron at the 16th for an ace.

The SoKo was now the leader by one.

I might have kicked a tree trunk. I know I kicked the front wheel of my golf cart.

All Paula Jean and Michelle Janine could do was smote their foreheads at the news and try to par the last two holes. Which they did. The only thing they could do then was wait after the scoreboard confirmed that Hee Hon (The Hog) Ding had parred the 17th hole and needed a par on 18 to win the Clambake.

I waited by the 18th green with Paula Jean and Michelle Janine, and watched their eyes tear up when word reached us that Hee Hon had parred the 17th by holing out a 40-yard bunker shot.

The way Hee Hon (The Hog) Ding played the last hole, a par 5, was what I think almost any golfer would describe as unforgivable.

She topped her tee shot. She shanked her second. She topped her third. She put her fourth in the pond just short of the green, but she could see the ball only an inch or two below the surface, and decided to try to play it out with a sand wedge.

She took a mighty swing at the ball, made a horrendous splash and out came the ball along with about a half-pound of mud.

The ball and the mud all went into the cup together for Hee Hon's par 5 on the hole – and her victory in the Clambake.

A second after the ball landed in the cup I was driving the cart back to the press room to write the game story on my trusty laptop.

I finished in a little under an hour and went to find Emily Turner and say goodbye. She was in the Teen Vogue hospitality tent having a glass of vodka and pretending to be happy for Hee Hon (The Hog) Ding.

I explained to Emily about the mysterious skin disease I'd been fighting for the past nine months, but I said doctors had given me some reasons to be optimistic. She said she certainly hoped it could be cured before I came back for next year's tournament.

I left for the airport in a taxi and sat back to read a printout of the story I'd filed. I was satisfied that I'd pretty much summed up the event and how I felt about teen golf in general. My lead read: 'I don't want to live in a world where the cutest girls don't win golf tournaments.'

RICK REILLY

HOMER

AT PONKAPOGUE GOLF CLUB, once described by *Golf Illustrated* as 'the single-worst golf facility in America,' the locals were basically a lot of guys who were out-of-round and should've been taken out of play years ago. Case in point: Homer. We called him Homer the Human Screwmanoid, because he'd swing so hard that he'd literally screw himself into the ground. Homer just felt the golf ball – his sworn enemy in life – deserved as much punishment as a person could deal out. The golf ball, for its part, usually mocked Homer in some cruel way, either hooking madly out of bounds, slicing crazily over the fence into Manelli's dry cleaners, or rolling lazily off the tee and stopping six inches from where it had started. Sometimes it stopped rolling before Homer was done screwing himself into the tee box.

But no matter which way the ball chose to humiliate Homer, one thing remained constant: Homer would lose his mind. He had all the patience of a Rome cabbie with a toothache. And the way he most often lost it was by throwing the offending club. Homer threw more clubs than Tommy Bolt ever *dreamed* of throwing. Homer threw more clubs than a professional bridge player. It would be a draw, in my mind: Homer and clubs or Stevie Williams and cameras.

In fact, Homer threw so many clubs so often and in so many directions that one day before a big match, we decided to hold an intervention. We wanted him to come down to the range and start throwing his clubs. We wanted this for two reasons: One, safety. We wanted to know exactly what was Death Range when Homer lost it, which was only on two-syllable days. The day before, Homer gagged on an 18-inch putt, picked up his ball, flipped it into the air and took a mighty swipe at it with his putter, only he missed and the putter went flinging out of his hands, helicoptered over the green, headed for the 14th tee box and smacked into Cementhead, who was knocked out colder than a popsicle and carried a Fred Flintstone lump on his head for a month. Remarkably, it actually improved his IQ four points.

The second reason we needed a club-throwing chart on Homer was a bet Hosel Harry and Two Down got into, which was whether Homer could throw a golf club 50 yards. Harry's President Hamilton said he could. Two Down's said he couldn't.

We stationed Cementhead out about 50 yards to measure the throws.

'All right, Homer. Start with the putter,' Two Down said.

'Why?' he said.

'Because we need to get some yardages on you,' Hosel Harry said. 'You're a movable hazard.'

'Triple screw you guys,' Homer said.

Two Down said, 'look, we've talked about it and we've all agreed to never play with you again unless you do it.'

'Up yours, diagonally.'

'OK,' I said, 'how's this? Wally promises to go the entire front nine without ever coming near you today and he just came back from a golf trip to Alabama. He's going to be absolutely brutal today with his golf-trip stories.'

Homer heaved the putter. It went a measly 20 yards.

'No good,' said Hosel Harry.

'Very no good,' I said. 'You aren't mad enough. You've got to be $20,000-a-month-alimony mad. Only then can we get an accurate reading.'

'That's bull,' said Homer. 'I don't want to be mad. It's not good for my chakras.'

'Have him hit a few balls,' said Chunkin' Charlie. 'That'll get him pissed.'

'Get bent,' said Homer.

'Tell you what,' said Two Down. 'Five zops says you can't hit a 5-iron shot past Cementhead on the fly.'

Homer looked at him for a moment and then looked around at the semi-circle of all of us watching him and said, 'Bank.'

So Homer hunkered down over his 5-iron, studied his grip, checked his alignment, regripped his Hogan cap, waggled back and forth, drew it back with his skinny-ass arms and chunked it 15 feet.

'Do it, Homer,' urged Dominic.

'Let it rip,' said Parking Lot.

Homer set his jaw even tighter, gripped the breath out of the club, and said, 'Double it.'

'Bank,' said Two Down.

This one he shanked about 40 yards to the right, where it hit the ugly yellow netting that keeps balls from killing the guys on the first tee.

'Let one fly,' begged Chunkin' Charlie.

'Let it out of your system,' I said.

The vein over Homer's right eyebrow was growing purple.

'Triple it,' said Homer.

'Bank,' said Two Down.

'Dribble,' said the Titleist 8, sporting a fresh new smile.

'$#*@$%!!!' screamed Homer and, in classic Olympic shot-put form, let the 5-iron set sail. Everybody ducked, and it went *backward* over his head, over the putting green, and onto the patio, where it flew into the chicken salads of the two old geezers who play gin every day together.

'Now we're talking,' said Hosel, and he began stepping off yardage toward the chicken salads. Chunkin' Charlie ran over and wiped off the old geezers. Then Harry said, 'Sweet. Thirty-eight yards, backwards, slight fade on it.' Wally wrote it dutifully down on a yellow legal pad.

Meanwhile, back on the range, Homer wasn't anywhere near done. He was so hacked off that everybody was laughing and ducking and mocking him that he tapped new levels of tormented chakras. These were perfect clinical conditions, so I kept handing Homer more clubs and he kept flinging them this way and that in a blind rage, with everybody stepping off yardages as quickly as they could and Wally writing down the figures as fast as he could write: 'Driver, 23 yards, a little draw.'

Finally, Homer stopped, laid flat on his back, and flung off his Hogan cap. 'Rats get fat,' he muttered. 'Good men die.'

From that day on, we were prepared. *What's Homer hitting?* somebody would say. *8-iron. Let's see, 8-iron is what, about 27 yards? OK, we're safe here. Fire away, Homer.*

'Iraqi slobs,' he'd say.

CHARLES McGRATH

SNEAKING ON

HENRY BIGELOW HADN'T sneaked on to a golf course in decades, but the moment he slipped through the bushes bordering the fifth hole at Valhalla Country Club he felt the old illicit thrill, that simultaneous stab of fear and exhilaration that punches up the rpm's in the trespasser's heart. He looked in both directions, then quickly dropped a ball, and struck it with a nicely judged 5-iron. The shot was so pretty – soaring up, drawing into the green, bouncing once, and rolling to within 10 feet of the flag – that for an instant he almost wished there were someone around to see it. One o'clock on a cloudless Sunday afternoon in mid-summer – didn't the members at this place ever play?

As he walked toward his ball, Henry couldn't fail to notice the lushness of the fairway, the manicured edging of the bunkers, the velvety texture of the green. If it was true what they said – that Valhalla cost an arm and a leg and people were nevertheless dying to get in – then he could see why. There had been a huge fuss when the bulldozers first began creeping over what used to be the Prentice Farm. The ecology crowd objected, and so did the affordable housing people, and then the two groups objected to each other's objections, though everyone agreed that there was no shortage of golf courses in the area. 'Why, with just a sand wedge, you could play from one side of town to the other,' Jack Lewis said at the town meeting, and a couple of his cronies stamped their feet in agreement.

Actually, Henry was pretty sure you'd need more than a sand wedge. The carry from Valhalla across Route 22 and onto Weasel Run, for example, had to be at least a 7-iron – or maybe a punched 6, because you'd need to keep the shot under the phone wires. You could probably bounce a chip shot all the way across the Weasel Run parking lot, and from the grassy strip at the side of the road have a 9-iron onto the 13th fairway at Laughing Hollow, but it might be smarter to hit a 5-wood and stay clear of the whole mess – the cars, the sign out in front, anybody who might be driving past – leaving yourself with just a pitch to the green. How you got through Hopper's Woods, next to the public course down by the highway, Henry wasn't sure yet. You might have to roll it along with a putter.

But he was off to a good start here with a birdie at Valhalla's No. 5 – well, half a birdie, considering he hadn't actually hit a tee shot – and on the sixth he cracked his drive so far he lost sight of it. He sucked in a lungful of air and strode happily off the tee. Was it grand to be alive, or what!

Oops. No. 6 at Valhalla turned out to be a dogleg, and after searching around a bit (Henry's eyes, he had been noticing, weren't quite as sharp as they used to be) he found that he had rolled through the fairway and onto the lawn of a bordering condo, a big gabled place with a wraparound deck. He was just lining up his shot when he heard someone say, 'Henry?'

He turned and saw a woman he recognized almost immediately as his wife, Polly. Ex-wife, rather. She had left him a decade ago, after some uncharitable and not entirely accurate reports drifted north from a Myrtle Beach trip about Henry and a mother-daughter pair of cart girls. 'Pol!' he said. 'You live here now?'

She smiled and said, 'Been here since it opened.'

'Well, you look great,' he said, thinking to himself that they really did do wonders with Botox these days. There wasn't a wrinkle on her face.

She smiled again (her teeth gleamed like a new Titleist, Henry noticed) and put her hand on his arm. 'Henry, I was really sorry to hear about . . . you know?'

'You know?' Henry said.

'You know,' she said. 'That thing that . . . happened.'

Henry had no idea what she was talking about, but he felt a surge of affection for sweet old Polly nonetheless, and he reached over and pinched her on the butt.

Henry saved par at six, and again at seven, a pretty little par 3, with a nice sandy coming out of a right-hand bunker. And his shot over Route 22 and onto Weasel Run was a little work of art. It didn't go under the phone wires but between them, and for an instant was framed there, between the two dark lines, like a note on a musical staff. His drive deserted him at Weasel Run, however, and he kept leaking right, where a couple of times he had trouble finding his ball amid the fallen leaves. He didn't think much of the Weasel Run maintenance crew, he decided, if they couldn't keep up with leaves in the middle of summer.

His irritation affected his swing, moreover, and he chunked a couple of easy approaches.

All in all he was not sorry to leave this course, and when he took out his 5-wood to negotiate the parking-lot flyover and landing onto Laughing Hollow, his haste brought on disaster. He hit a low screamer that ricocheted off a Saab, rattled a BMW, and left a dimpled ding in the fender of a Caddie Escalade, before rolling to a stop beneath a black Mercedes. One of the valet parkers came running over, yelling, 'What are you doing! What's wrong with you, man?'

Henry held up his hand in apology. 'I'm sorry, I'm sorry,' he said.

The parker looked at him sharply. 'You a member here?'

'It's OK,' Henry said. 'I know Warren Smith – he's an old friend of mine.'

'Warren Smith?' the parker said.

'Warren Smith,' Henry said. 'He's the president here.'

The parker looked at him again. 'Ain't no Warren Smith here anymore, pal. You'd better get out of here before I call the cops.'

Henry thought for a moment about trying to retrieve his ball from under the Benz – his hope had been to play from one end of town to the other using just a single ball – but thought better of it and instead shouldered his bag and scooted down the drive and onto the road, where he was nearly run down by some teenagers in a white convertible. 'Watch where you're going!' one of them shouted. 'Old idiot!'

Safely on the 13th at Laughing Hollow, Henry had to wait for his heart to stop pounding and his nerves to unjangle. He bent over, took a few deep breaths, and then found he had trouble straightening back up. His bag, when he picked it up, felt heavier than he remembered, and somehow he had lost the elasticity in his swing, and found himself punching the ball, the way the retired guys did. Laughing Hollow was where he needed distance – four long par 4s and a par 5, all heading westward, in the direction Henry needed to go – and just popping it along now, he realized that he was falling behind schedule. The sun was much lower in the sky than it should have been and was casting late-afternoon shadows. His shoulder was sore, there was a stabbing twinge in his right elbow, and for the first time Henry began to wonder if this was such a good idea after all. When he finally holed out on 18, he thought about stopping in for a drink – a little something to jump-start his swing – but when he scanned the patio for a familiar face, someone who could sign for him, he didn't see a soul he knew.

Nor did he recognize anyone at the muny, which really was just a sand wedge away, and the muny itself had altered since whenever it was Henry had been there last. Not that long ago, surely. There were now cross bunkers on the fourth, deep enough so that Henry took two shots coming out of the right-hand one, and the pond at No. 8, once so thick with scum that you could practically roll your ball across, now was aerated by a fountain. So this was where Henry's tax dollars were going! He made a mental note to make a little call to the First Selectman, until he realized with annoyance that he didn't remember anymore who the First Selectman was.

At the back of the tee on 11, the downhill par 3, there was a teak bench that Henry didn't remember either, and a plaque on the back said that it was there in memory of Roger Grant, who last thing Henry knew was still alive. They had played gin together just – well, whenever it was. Even though the shadows were creeping even further across the fairway, Henry sat gratefully down on Roger's bench, and thought that if only he had a cigar he'd light it up.

He didn't know how long he'd been there when a boy of about 10 or 11 came past, playing by himself and pushing a motorized trolley, for which Henry felt a lurch of envy.

'Hey, mister – you all right?' the boy said. 'I've been watching you, and you've been sitting there like forever.'

'I'm fine,' Henry said. 'Just catching my breath. I'm playing my way across town,' he added, 'and I'm almost there. Through Hopper's Woods and then onto Whispering Valley, the home-stretch.'

'You're playing golf all the way across town?' the boy said. Henry nodded and said yes.

The boy looked at him and said, 'Why would you want to do something like that?'

In the middle of Hopper's Woods, Henry Bigelow became lost. The leaves, bright red and orange, were so thick on the ground that he couldn't roll the ball through, and the trees were so close together that many of his punch shots resulted in ricochets and bounce-backs. Meanwhile, the wind had come up and was stripping even more leaves off the treetops, and the sun had plunged beneath a dark purple cloud. Henry ferreted through his bag and found a mothy old sweater and a faded windshirt. He put them both on and still felt a chill in his bones, which, unless he was imagining things, were now discernibly closer to the surface of his skin. Playing across town was apparently more of an ordeal than he imagined. In the course of a single afternoon, he reckoned, he had lost about 20 pounds. There was a stirring overhead, and first a flock of swallows and then a gang of noisy, shadow-casting crows settled in the trees. From over by Hopper's Pond there came the honking of Canada geese.

To make things worse, Henry had now caromed off so many trees that he was spun around and no longer knew in what direction he was headed. And he couldn't find his ball. He stirred up the leaves, poked through the brush, peered behind tree trunks, and foraged, for how long he didn't know, deeper into the thickets. At one point he was startled to hear a hoarse-sounding voice and, looking around (his eyes didn't seem to be what they used to), he spotted a shadowy, crouching figure about 50 yards away.

'Pinnacle 3,' the voice said. 'You see a Pinnacle 3?'

'No,' Henry called back. 'I'm looking for a Titleist 2.'

'Good luck,' the voice said. 'I've been looking for – I don't know, must be three days now. Starting to get a little dehydrated.'

'Jeez,' Henry said. 'Anything I can do?'

'Nah,' the voice said. 'If I have to, I'll head over to where I met these guys yesterday. Must be 20 or 30 of them camped out over there to the east a little, and they go out every morning marching in a row and looking for their balls. They're drinking from the pond, though. Terrible diarrhea.'

The east! Henry turned in the opposite direction from the voice and saw the sun, now a huge red ball, sinking behind the black, bare treetops. Seeking its warmth, he crashed through the underbrush, yanking himself away from grasping thorns, leg-grappling vines, and finally, blessedly, burst through some honeysuckle onto the 17th at Whispering Valley, his home course, the place where everyone knew who he was – the caddies, the locker-room attendants, the lovely, patient barmaids who had so sympathetically poured for him night after night following the Polly debacle. He dropped a ball – well, placed a ball; he knew every inch of this course, where he had been a member all his life, and understood that you didn't want to be left of the little knoll here – and hit a sweet 7-iron, which he almost converted into birdie. Half a birdie, that is – considering that he didn't hit a tee shot.

It was nearly dark by the time Henry reached the 18th, a long par 5, uphill to the clubhouse. He teed up, waggled, and smacked a beauty so long that he couldn't see the ball in the shadows, but it didn't matter. He could tell where it was going just from the sound and the concussive feel in his fingers – even if those fingers were getting a little stiff in the cool and the damp, Henry made a mental note to pop a couple of ibuprofen next time.

His second was pretty good, too – a 3-wood with what turned out to be a half swing, though Henry had it in mind to crank it. As he came up the hill, he had to pause a couple of times to catch his breath; his knees were achy; and his right shoulder now throbbed so much that he had to stop and shift his bag to the left. He bent over to snag an extra breath. What was with this air? It was so dense and fragrant it practically knocked you over.

Limping a little, all his joints having turned a little sludgy, Henry came, panting, over the rise and groaned a little to see that the white speck in front meant he had a downhill lie. But then he lifted his eyes and saw the clubhouse glowing in the twilight. There were lights shining in the upstairs dining room, Chinese lanterns were flickering on the outside rafter, and a golden glow had pooled around the putting green. It had to be one of the club's live-music Sundays, because snatches of Dixieland music came wafting down, along with snatches of laughter carried away by the wind. There were sherbet-colored dresses and white dinner jackets swirling on the porch.

Henry zoned his third – or was pretty sure he did. (Squinting after the ball, he decided he really needed to get a new eyeglass prescription.) And as he came nearer, the clubhouse, looming up now like an ocean liner in the purple twilight, seemed so inviting it brought tears to Henry's eyes. Was there anything sweeter than to be playing up the 18th at your home course? At the end of a perfect summer day. When the greens are like doeskin, the fairways like a bolt of shot silk. When the setting sun casts a purple halo over the clubhouse roof. Is there any place you'd rather be?

There was a rattle of wind and Henry shivered and thought longingly of a hot shower and a drink. No, two drinks – single malt. And maybe there'd be a fire in the Trophy Room.

As he walked up toward the green, a golden retriever came bounding out to greet him, so large and so friendly it could have been sweet old Bailey, Henry's companion on so many early morning rounds – except, of course, that Bailey was now buried underneath the rosebush in Henry's yard. While the dog waited, Henry sank his putt, enjoying once more that satisfying kerchink as the ball rattled in the cup, and then headed for the clubhouse.

The party was in full swing now, with the band playing ragtime and some couples dancing on the lawn. Waiters were shouldering trays of champagne, a guy in a tuxedo was handing out cigars. It seemed to be some sort of costume affair. There was a guy who looked just like Ronald Reagan, and another who was a ringer for Dwight Eisenhower. There was a Jerry Garcia lookalike – who let him in? – and a woman dressed to look like Audrey Hepburn. Talking to her was a man who resembled a jacket photo of the writer John Cheever, and when this man saw Henry he scowled and beckoned with his index finger. Over in a corner was a guy in Einstein disguise, black glasses and big white wig, and talking to him were – how amazing! – a couple who could easily pass for Henry's mother and father.

Confused but excited, almost light-headed, Henry walked toward the porch steps, but was stopped by a stout, bearded guy in a double-breasted blazer and a tweed cap with some kind of badge attached. He held out his hand and Henry dropped his ball into it. In a thick Scots accent the man gently explained that before he could join the party Henry had to go to the locker room, put away his clubs and turn in his scorecard. 'Aye, and I hope it's accurate,' he said.

JAMES KAPLAN

THE MOWER

SHE RAN EVERY morning at six-twenty. At first I hardly noticed, but then it got so I'd look for her, and worry a little if she was late. She'd come out of the trees along the sixteenth fairway, run through the rough down the side, cut across the street, go down the seventeenth, then over the creek – there's a little wooden bridge – onto the third tee, and out of sight. I would never see her after that. If she finished where she started, though, she must have run four or five miles. Jesus. I couldn't run a mile if you paid me a million bucks. I never saw where she finished, because even though I was almost always on the fifteenth or sixteenth when she started – you cut them alternate days, usually – as soon as she got out of sight I had to go down the hill and do the eleventh or the tenth, and then back into the garage before the foursomes started showing up at seven. Benito, the greenskeeper, had his own special little system; he completely flew off the handle if you did it any other way, and he was always around, in that yellow cart with the flag on it, to make sure you did it right. Benito was *everywhere*.

Practically as soon as I began seeing her I hoped two things: one, that Benito wouldn't catch her – he'd love that – and two, that she got off the course before the foursomes came on. There's something about four guys together that I don't especially like. There's something about *golf* I don't like, as a matter of fact. But the course – that was different. Have you ever been on a golf course at six in the morning?

It's very misty, kind of spooky; all the hills and bumps look like giant animals or something. Then the sun comes up – if you're lucky and it's clear out. I saw the sun rise every clear morning for six years. Not many people can say that. I'll take a sunrise over a sunset every time. But even if it's raining, it's beautiful out there. Ask most people what color a rainy day is, and what do they say? Gray. Not on a golf course. Everything is green – but not the same green. There are about eighty-two different kinds of green out there. Blue green, gray green, yellow green, orange green, brown green, purple green, green green. You name it.

I'd show up at five-thirty, try and steer clear of Benito, and get on one of the machines. Usually I'd do roughs first – not much fun. Then I did around the greens – kind of finicky work; the edges are the worst. But my favorite was the fairways. The big eighteen-foot mower – you feel like a king, going right down the middle. You have to use a different machine for each length of grass. They don't adjust like your little Lawn-Boy. There were three of us; we did nine holes every morning, three apiece. Benito had this whole complicated system worked out so you could trade machines with another guy when you were through. It was all done by the clock. Six-ten was when I started the sixteenth fairway, and six-twenty was when she came out of the trees.

It was nice watching her. Most people look terrible running. Most women, especially, don't look very good running. They don't seem to be built for it, usually. The only people I've ever seen that look any good running are these really skinny guys who run cross-country for the Catholic school across the mountain. They practice every afternoon; I see them when I drive home. They always look like they're about to die, extremely thin guys with sweaty undershirts and bony chests, their mouths open and their eyes staring. And their eyes kind of go dead every time one of their feet hits the ground. But there they are, running, mile after mile – you can't imagine them doing anything else. And then you see one of these fat guys huffing along in sweat pants and fluorescent shoes. Or one of these housewives. (I should talk. I could stand to lose twenty myself. Beer.) But you should have seen *her*. Once, when I was in high school – it seems like about thirty years ago – my music-appreciation class went to the ballet, and all of my friends and I were getting off on how faggoty it was, which is the kind of thing you get off on in high school. Most of the time I was pretty bored, I have to admit, but there were a couple of things I really liked, like when the guys jumped. Those guys can *jump*. And when they picked the girls up. You can't be that much of a fag if you can pick up somebody who weighs about a hundred pounds and make it look easy. I also liked it when the girls ran off the stage. I loved watching the way their behinds moved when they ran off the stage. That's just the way she ran. Exactly the same. Down the sixteenth fairway and out of sight.

She waved to me three or four mornings after the first time I saw her. I almost fell off my mower. Came out of the trees and waved at me, and did I wave back? Schmuck. I was too startled. But the next morning she waved again anyway. This will sound dumb, I know, but she had the nicest wave I ever saw. Most people just put up their hand and shake it back and forth, but she did something different – how can I describe it? It was sort of a periscope wave, or maybe like a little sea monster. Her arm was up, but her hand was at right angles to it, the back of her hand was arched, and she fluttered her fingers, like a pianist or something. When I got home, I did that wave at myself in the mirror. I felt like my hand didn't belong to me.

At the end of the month, it rained, hard, for a solid week almost. Sometimes when it's raining just a little bit, a lot of these guys who are nuts about golf will put on their funny hats or bring out their cute umbrellas and play anyway, but this was *rain*. I mean, there were swimming pools on the greens. Nobody was playing golf, running, anything. Or maybe she did run. I don't know. I wasn't out there to see her. When it was like that out, all you could really do was sit around the garage, pretending to repair stuff. The club paid you anyway. Big deal. I'd rather be outside. The guys I really felt sorry for were the caddies. What the hell could they do? But the four of us, mostly we'd just sit around, smoking, shooting the breeze, even playing poker. The funny thing was, when the weather got like that Benito was the first one to break out the cards. He'd make the amazing change, from a little rat into a sweetheart. Then he'd always worry about the manager, Mr Mahaffy. He'd talk real quiet while he dealt the cards, and look over his shoulder a lot. I loved it. I loved the way it smelled in the garage when it was raining out – sort of a combination of wet grass and gasoline and cigarette smoke. You could almost go into a trance with the rain coming down on the roof. It was like being high. Over on the wall, next to the fire extinguisher, somebody wrote in pencil: 'JULY 2, 1961. RAIN.' I used to stare at it and wonder what the hell it was like on July 2, 1961. It seems like at least four hundred years ago. What day of the week was it? Who was cutting grass? What did they look like? Were they playing cards? Was the course still full of creeps then? Who was greenskeeper? (Benito's only been there since '67.) Kennedy was President. Probably everyone had crewcuts. Then I wondered where *she* was then. Probably not born yet. No, probably like three, four years old.

I wondered if I ever saw her someplace – a supermarket, maybe.

The rain finally stopped after five days. One afternoon it just stopped, and the sun came out, and all of a sudden it was real hot, and we had to go out and cut. Benito made us stay late. There were still big puddles on the greens. Clouds of mosquitoes everywhere. Clumps of wet grass stuck to the blades. Usually we didn't cut in the afternoon, but Benito was panicking. Mahaffy was on his ass. So the next morning the regular schedule was all screwed up. I was way the hell on the other side of the course, and suddenly it hit me: I wasn't going to get to see her come out of the trees. And it was killing me. That's when I knew I was in trouble. I was cutting the seventh green, going around and around in circles, cursing and punching the steering wheel. Around and around. Christ, I hated greens. And then, bang, I see her, running down along the trees. And she waves, kind of nonchalant, like we're old friends, like it hasn't been raining for the past week, like we always meet this way on the seventh hole. But what could I do? Bawl her out? I waved back – not a big wave, just a little one. I was pretty mad. Then on an impulse, I cut the engine and yelled to her. 'Hey!' I said. She was on her way to the eighth tee. 'Hey!' I yelled. But she just sort of half turned around and gave that wave of hers. Then she was gone. I got *really* wrecked that night.

You know how it is when you drink too much. It's pretty hard to sleep. Maybe I got four hours that night, I don't know, but I dreamed I was awake the whole time, and the room felt like I was riding that Goddamned mower around and around the seventh green. I dreamed about her. When I woke up, in the dark, I made up my mind that I would *definitely* talk to her at six-twenty. Definitely.

* * *

The sun came up through the trees like a giant orange golf ball sitting in the rough, the birds were making a racket, and I was riding down the sixteenth fairway at six-fifteen, with a head that felt like a piano or something, not a head. I was just riding, not cutting. I was really supposed to be on the fifteenth – Johnny D. had already done the sixteenth the day before. So I had the blades up, and I was just riding along, watching the trees. Benito would've murdered me. Out she came, right on schedule, and she waved. I was not feeling too sharp. I couldn't have looked too sharp, either, but I just cruised up next to her, about as close as I could get with the blade arm sticking out, and I said, 'Hi!' She waved again. I don't think she heard me. The engine was pretty loud. We went along together for a little bit, just smiling at each other. Then I got up my courage. 'What's your name!' I yelled. She smiled and put her hand up to her ear. I forgot to say she had really nice ears. She wore her hair up, and there were those little wisps of blond hair coming down. 'Your name!' I shouted. 'What's your name?' Then she said something, but I couldn't hear. I cut the engine. Now she was out ahead of me. I asked again. She called something back over her shoulder. Juliana?

I really think that's what she said. Juliana. What the hell kind of name is that? Practically all the girls I ever meet are named Cathy. Sometimes I think half the girls I've ever *known* have been named Cathy. Their favorite song is always 'Cherish.'

There was no rain at all the next month. Zero. Plus, it was about a hundred out every day. The course almost fried. We were allowed to water the greens but not the fairways. Town ordinance. Benito would just stand there and stare at his precious grass shriveling up and look like he was about to pop a blood vessel. The weird thing was, every afternoon there were all these big black clouds, sometimes even some thunder and lightning – but no rain. There was always a lot of static on the radio. I wanted to say something to her about running on the fairways – Benito was at the point where he would've shot someone for taking a divot – but I was scared to talk to her. Can you believe it? The funny thing is, usually I'm never that way. Usually I'm just the opposite.

Then Benito put us back to just doing greens. My favorite. That's all that was growing. And he said if the weather didn't break he was going to have to let one of us go. He said we could draw straws. I should've told him what he could do with his straws. He assigned me to the first six, way the hell on the other side of the course from where she ran. I asked him if I could switch with somebody else, but he just gave me this look.

Then, next morning – it was *hot*; by six-thirty my shirt was soaked – I was coming over the hill to the fourth green when suddenly I just got goose bumps. I knew what was happening even before I knew, if you know what I mean. Way down the fairway, about 350 yards out, I could see this yellow dot and this red dot. That was all. I knew right away what was going on. I don't know why, but it reminded me of November of seventh grade. We were playing football one Friday afternoon, and Mr Finelli, my gym teacher, came running across the field with his hands in his pockets. I knew it was bad news. I just knew. Everybody else on my team kept running, and I stopped in my tracks and watched him coming across the field. It was the same way now. I should've started on the green, but I headed down the fairway. We were only supposed to drive on the service roads, because the course was so dried out, but I just went right on down the middle. She was standing there with her hands on her hips, sweating like crazy, and Benito was shaking his finger in her face. I could've killed the little bastard. But I couldn't *get* there. It was like a bad dream: the stupid mower would only go about ten miles an hour. I should've just hopped out and run, but I probably would've dropped dead, my heart was beating so hard. Then Benito heard the engine noise and turned around. He started jumping up and down – I swear it, jumping up and down. You should have seen it. I must have been trailing a dust cloud half a mile wide. And then she just took off. Vanished into the trees. I couldn't really blame her. I still can't. What was she supposed to do – wait around till Benito got finished with me?

So now I'm looking for work. My brother-in-law has this Arco station out on Route 17. Maybe I'll go there. Anything but cutting grass. I mean, in a way this whole thing might have been kind of lucky. Can you see me sitting on a mower when I'm forty? Every once in a while I miss the course a little bit. Not the job – the course. I liked the way the sky looked over it, all the different kinds of clouds. The way the grass smelled. The wind in the trees. You don't get that on Route 17. But I won't miss Benito. I won't miss the golfers.

For a while I kept thinking I was seeing her places – in the mall, walking down the street – but it was always someone else. Once, this white 280-z pulled up next to me at a light and my heart almost stopped. She was at the wheel. I honked, but when she turned around I saw it was another girl. She gave me the finger. I gave it to her back.

ACKNOWLEDGMENTS

E. CLERIHEW BENTLEY: 'The Sweet Shot'. Reproduced with permission of Curtis Brown Group Limited, London on behalf of the Estate of E. Clerihew Bentley. Copyright © E. Clerihew Bentley, 1937.

BERNARD DARWIN: 'The Wooden Putter' by Bernard Darwin taken from *The Strand* (1924). Reprinted with permission from A. P. Watt Ltd. on behalf of Paul Ashton, Ursula Mommens and Philip Trevelyan.

IAN FLEMING: Chapter 4 of *Goldfinger* by Ian Fleming. Published by Penguin Group USA.

DAN JENKINS: 'Tees and Teens' taken from *Golf World* magazine, Sept. 2, 2005, special issue guest-edited by Charles McGrath. Reprinted with the kind permission of the author.

JAMES KAPLAN: 'The Mower' by James Kaplan. Reprinted by permission; copyright © 1981 by James Kaplan. Originally in *The New Yorker*. All rights reserved.

REX LARDNER: 'Triumph at Crestwood'. Reprinted with permission of Scribner, a division of Simon & Schuster, Inc., from *Out of the Bunker and Into the Trees*, by Rex Lardner. Copyright © 1980, 1988 by Rex Lardner. All rights reserved. 'Triumph at Crestwood' taken from *Out of the Bunker and Into the Trees*. Reprinted with permission from the Lardner family and the Scott Meredith Agency.

RING LARDNER: 'Mr Frisbie' reprinted with the permission of Scribner, a division of Simon & Schuster, Inc., from *The Ring Lardner Reader* by Ring Lardner Jr.; edited by Maxwell Geismar. Copyright © 1928 by Charles Scribner's Sons.

Everyman's Pocket Classics are
typeset in the classic typeface Garamond and
printed on acid-free, cream-wove paper
with a sewn, full-cloth binding.